Light on Water

A Visionary Young Adult Novel

MARIAN MILLER

BALBOA
PRESS

A DIVISION OF HAY HOUSE

Balboa Press books may be ordered through booksellers or by contacting:

Balboa Press
A Division of Hay House
1663 Liberty Drive
Bloomington, IN 47403
www.balboapress.com
1 (877) 407-4847

Because of the dynamic nature of the Internet, any web addresses or
links contained in this book may have changed since publication and
may no longer be valid. The views expressed in this work are solely those
of the author and do not necessarily reflect the views of the publisher,
and the publisher hereby disclaims any responsibility for them.

The author of this book does not dispense medical advice or prescribe the use
of any technique as a form of treatment for physical, emotional, or medical
problems without the advice of a physician, either directly or indirectly. The
intent of the author is only to offer information of a general nature to help
you in your quest for emotional and spiritual well-being. In the event you use
any of the information in this book for yourself, which is your constitutional
right, the author and the publisher assume no responsibility for your actions.

Any people depicted in stock imagery provided by Thinkstock are models,
and such images are being used for illustrative purposes only.
Certain stock imagery © Thinkstock.

Print information available on the last page.

ISBN: 978-1-5043-3296-5 (sc)
ISBN: 978-1-5043-3298-9 (hc)
ISBN: 978-1-5043-3297-2 (e)

Library of Congress Control Number: 2015907736

Balboa Press rev. date: 07/27/2015

Dedication

This book is dedicated to the strong women in my family who have gone before me. Thank you for your legacy of faith, hope, and love.

Acknowledgments

*A*lthough this story has been in my heart for years, it would never have been published if it weren't for the love and patience of my family—James, Lynette, Cameron, and Vanessa.

In addition, I extend my deepest gratitude to my editors, Susan Buckley and Marlene Dalziel, to my teenage content readers, Daisy and Bailey, to Reverend Noel McInnis and all the members of the writer's group at the Center for Spiritual Living for graciously sharing their insight, expertise, and encouragement.

And during those moments when we forget, I thank Spirit for reminding us that we are loved. Always.

Light on Water

A Visionary Young Adult Novel

Prologue

The moonless night is filled with sinuously moving shadows. The agonized panting of the couple running through the wooded undergrowth reverberates through the stillness. In the distance, the agitated sound of barking hounds. Exhausted, she slows. He knows she is near the limit of her endurance.

"Please," she gasps, struggling for breath. "Go on without me. I'm only slowing you down."

Ignoring her pleas, he half drags, half carries her, hoping he has enough strength left for both of them. They can't stop now—to do so would mean capture and, if not physical death, it would mean death of life as they know it. They are so very close to freedom.

He drops the pack from his shoulders, rifles through it for money and passports, which he stuffs into his jacket pockets. He reaches deep into the bottom of the pack searching for the key. The cool metal slips through his fingers into the thick undergrowth. Swearing, he drops to his knees, frantically searching. Unhampered by darkness, she spots it easily, hands it to him.

The barking of the hounds is much louder now. The trackers are closer. Despite the darkness, through the periphery of the trees she can see the lake clearly. "We're almost there," she murmurs.

Soon they hear the low, rhythmic sound of lapping water. In the darkness the lake spread across to an unseen shore like an endless expanse of black ink. The barking fades, as do the other night sounds. He steps to the edge of the water, feels it flow over his feet, beckoning, calming, welcoming. He knew this moment would come.

Everything he has learned, believed and hoped for is riding on this inevitable moment. She turns toward him, hesitantly, an unspoken question on her lips. Although he can't see the expression in her eyes, he knows they are filled with fear. She can't swim.

He lifts her into his arms, feels her relax. He presses his lips to her forehead. If his life should end with hers, so be it. After all, the best things in his life began with her.

Inhaling deeply, he feels the familiar energy surge through him. Carefully edging forward, he steps up and onto the surface of the water.

Chapter 1

*L*arger and better equipped than most parks found throughout the Midwest suburbs, the locals speculated one of the county's most prominent citizens created Oak Park as a philanthropic gesture.

Majestic Bur oaks surrounded the park's borders. Thick trunks almost fifty feet tall stretched heavenward. Broad branches provided a shady respite during sweltering Midwestern summers. Beneath the oaks, scattered throughout the park, heavy wood and wrought iron benches offered spots for rest and contemplation. In the very center of the park stood a circle of maple trees.

On this oppressively hot July afternoon in the park, the molten sun vied for attention with the cloudless, cerulean blue sky.

Fenced tennis courts and a baseball diamond with two sets of bleachers were on the east side of the park. In spite of the heat, a man and a teenager played catch. To the west was an Olympic-sized swimming pool where most of the park's occupants gathered in an attempt to keep cool.

Families assembled around shaded picnic tables, grilling hot dogs and burgers on iron barbecues. The smoky, pungent aroma blended with the smell of the recently mowed park lawn, and the faint scent of chlorine.

Amidst the laughter and snatches of conversation, the sweet sound of a Meadowlark's flute-like call graced the air.

Maddy, an attractive woman with rich mahogany-colored skin and expressive ebony eyes, sat at a wooden picnic table shaded by one of the large oak trees. She wore a simple white cotton dress; her wide-brimmed straw hat lay on the table next to a wicker picnic basket.

She sat with her chin in her hand watching her daughter, Evalyn, build sandcastles with the brightly colored plastic bucket and shovel purchased the day before. She sighed, thinking of the ten dollars impulsively spent on toys when every dollar needed to be stretched to its limit just to take care of necessities.

Although it was warm, Maddy and Evalyn had walked to the park. It was only a couple of blocks away and they came here often. Taking the car wouldn't have made much difference anyway since the car's air conditioner was broken.

She watched her daughter play for a few more moments, then turned to remove food and drinks from the basket. She neatly arranged sandwiches and potato chips on paper plates and squeezed a dollop of ketchup onto her daughter's dish. It seemed gross to her, but Evalyn liked dipping the chips in ketchup. Evalyn liked ketchup on almost everything. Maddy smiled, shook her head, and poured lemonade into two flowered paper cups.

Eating outside on such a lovely day made the ordinary lunch seem special. A picnic in the park and the plastic toys were the best she could do now and they seemed to make her young daughter happy.

Not that Evalyn was *unhappy*. Unless she was having one of her rare, stubborn spells, most of the time she seemed content and even-tempered,

Even so, Maddy wished she would laugh more—giggle in the way little girls do. Instead, Evalyn lived in a dreamy, imaginative world of her own, with dolls and stuffed animals as playmates. She was creative and curious to a fault but interwoven throughout it all ran a solemn thread—for which Maddy often blamed herself.

Perhaps there was an element of truth to the old wives' tale that the thoughts and emotions of expectant mothers affect the child in the womb. She brushed her thoughts away. *Don't all mothers feel guilty about something?* She opened her library book and began to read.

A middle-class family of six, all of the Boldsens were tall, blonde, and blue eyed—a legacy from their Scandinavian ancestry. They lived a block away from Oak Park in a dove gray two-story house trimmed in white. A meticulously mowed yard surrounded by neatly trimmed boxwood hedges featured a curving stone walkway leading to wide steps, which then led to a broad, white front door.

The three youngest members of the family often played in the park. Their parents, Bob and Emily, didn't mind the children's frequent excursions to the park as they felt the neighborhood was relatively safe. Last winter someone called the police to remove an old drunk who had fallen asleep on one of the park benches. Rather than reporting a crime, the anonymous caller had been worried the man might freeze to death.

The only rule the Boldsen parents enforced regarding the park was that an older sibling had to accompany their youngest child, six-year-old, towheaded Christopher. This responsibility usually fell to either his sister Becca who was ten, or his nine-year-old brother Ace. Matt was the oldest, but at fourteen he professed he was "way too cool for playgrounds."

Christopher loved playing in the park. The back yard of their home was small and compared to Oak Park, seriously lacking. He would be there every day if he could, especially if it meant he could go swimming, but his brother and sister would often sneak off to the park without him to meet their friends. They called him a "tag along" or a "pest." Ace regularly told him to "find a shovel and dig up your own friends!" As long as Becca wasn't doing anything else, she usually agreed to take him if asked.

On this warm summer day, Christopher, clad in swim shorts, was in the spacious kitchen filling his glass with pure, filtered drinking water from the spigot built into the refrigerator door. Unlike many children, he preferred water to other beverages. Nothing pleased him more than a drink of icy cold water on a hot day.

He held the glass up to catch the sunlight streaming in from the window. Sometimes, when he held the glass just so, he could see a rainbow of colors shine through the water and onto the white kitchen wall. A rainbow, even a small one indoors, delighted him. Something told him his glass held a mystery he was meant to solve.

Water always fascinated Christopher. For instance, he noticed that, although it looked clear in a glass, water had a faint hint of blue when poured into a pitcher (he remembered the family vacation to the Caribbean where the sky's reflection made the sea appear truly blue).

As he took a sip, he heard the front door close quietly. *Too quietly.* He sat the glass down on the granite countertop and ran to the door, opening it. He peered out and saw Ace making a beeline for the park. He'd wanted to sneak away and see if any of his buddies were hanging out at the pool.

"Hey Ace!" Christopher yelled, running down the front steps. "Wait for me!" Shoulders dropping with resignation, Ace realized he had not gotten away fast enough and it was just too hot to run.

"Ok, you can come, but no whining!" Ace commanded sourly, brushing sandy blonde hair out of his eyes. He badly needed a haircut.

"And if any of my friends show up, I'm telling you now, Christopher—the answer is 'No, you can't hang out with us!' So, just go over to the other side of the pool and stay out of my hair!"

He glared at Christopher to make sure he got the point. Christopher nodded his head quickly in agreement and Ace turned, walking toward the park, swearing under his breath, even though his parents had strict rules against such language. *He's a damn nuisance! Don't know why he won't play with somebody his own age!*

Ace's eyes scanned the park to see if any of his friends were hanging out. Christopher followed him, keeping a respectful two paces behind. Ace had been known to swing at random, especially when he was irritated.

In this heat, a dip in the pool would be refreshing. Evidently, most of the neighborhood thought so too. According to the sign posted outside the fence, beside the closed entry gate, the pool had reached maximum capacity. The attendant let people enter only when someone else left.

"Damn!" Ace exclaimed, "By the length of this line, we won't get in the pool today."

Christopher was disappointed. He enjoyed the water immensely and although he was only six, he could swim well.

Not seeing any of his friends around anyway, Ace headed for the iron bars in the sand pit, Christopher at his heels.

Christopher watched wistfully, as his nine-year-old brother swung agilely on the monkey bars, a skill Christopher had yet to master. He did not have enough strength in his arms and hands to bear his own weight while moving along the thick iron bars.

A few weeks ago, he'd asked Ace for help. Appearing to comply, Ace lifted Christopher until he could reach the highest bar. His brother laughed and let him hang there until his hands hurt. Ace laughed even harder when Christopher fell and landed in a heap in the sand.

Ace's unrelenting teasing and bullying didn't make Christopher cower or intimidate him in the least. To the contrary, it fueled his resolve.

His oldest brother, Matt, was nearly as tall as their father, and Ace was several inches shorter than Matt. Christopher knew he wouldn't be little forever. Until then he would bide his time.

Today he was determined to try the bars himself, without asking for help. He crouched under the lowest rung and sprang up, straining to grasp it. He tried until he was breathless and panting before finally giving up.

Frustrated, he wandered over to a set of slides. The smaller slide, about six feet tall, was made of dull gray metal. Next to it, glistening in the sunlight was a silver slide about eighteen feet high. The local kids called this one the "Silver Bullet."

Out of the corner of his eye, Christopher could see Ace smirking. He squared his small shoulders with determination and marched toward the daunting "Silver Bullet." He climbed the tall ladder and sat for a moment feeling the warm metal against his bare legs, contemplating how far down the bottom appeared. He noticed his older brother had paused to watch him. He pushed off quickly when Ace turned away. Christopher felt a rush of adrenaline as he gained speed. The air swooshed past, hot and dusty.

Three quarters of the way down, his shorts caught on a razor-sharp rivet protruding from the edge of the slide, cutting him deeply from knee to thigh. Gasping in pain, he landed in the sand at the bottom. He held his hand over the long gash, trying hard not to cry. Beyond the throbbing pain in his leg, he couldn't bear the humiliation of having his brother call him a "cry baby." With unusual self-control, he pressed his eyes shut to hold back the tears.

Playing in the sand nearby was a little girl with skin the color of caramel. She wore a pale green flowered sundress. Multicolored barrettes held a myriad of corkscrews curls neatly in place. Although smaller than Christopher, she appeared to be around the same age. She heard his quick intake of breath and paused, her dusky green eyes regarding him solemnly.

Immediately, she grasped his predicament, saw the pain etched across his face. She put down the plastic shovel and nimbly crossed the sandbox to where he sat, his left hand covering his bloody wound, his face contorted in pain.

Hearing her approach, his tear-filled eyes saw her standing over him. She knelt down and tenderly placed her small, warm hand on top of his. Christopher's blue eyes widened in amazement as a gentle tingling flowed into his body, growing stronger, centering directly on the pain in his knee and thigh.

The tingling intensified, a sensation that made him feel warm, safe, and cared for. It felt great! Suddenly, she removed her hand and the pain disappeared. Christopher wiped away the wet blood and stared at the place where the cut had been. There was no wound—not any indication he had ever been hurt. Speechless, he stared at the girl. It seemed she shimmered--the way heat on hot asphalt tricks the eye into seeing water. He squinted against the sunlight, his young mind scrambling to understand what had just occurred.

Maddy glanced up from her book, looking toward the area where she last saw her daughter playing. She wasn't there! The bucket and shovel lay abandoned in the sand. Maddy put the book on the table, her eyes quickly scanning the grounds nearby. With relief, she spotted Evalyn standing next to a blonde boy sitting at the bottom of the slide. She guessed he was about six, the same age as Evalyn.

As she watched, Evalyn slowly took the boy's hand. Maddy observed his startled reaction as his expression changed from pain to pleasant surprise. Maddy stood hastily, lips pressed together, her eyebrows furrowed. *Oh no! Not here! Not now!*

Concern shadowed across her face. "Evalyn!" she called, beckoning to her daughter, "Lunch!" Promptly, Evalyn dropped the boy's hand. Running gracefully toward her mother, she glanced over her shoulder at the boy, his mouth still agape. With a quick wave goodbye, she tossed him a jewel of a smile—tiny pearl-like teeth flashing in her pretty, dark face.

Evalyn scrambled into her seat at the picnic table. Happily dipping a chip in ketchup, she popped it into her mouth. She picked up half of the sandwich and began to eat, taking small dainty bites.

Maddy picked up her drink, her hand trembling slightly. She cleared her throat. "Were you playing with the boy?" she asked hopefully, dreading the answer.

Evalyn shook her head. "No," she mumbled, her mouth full. "Not playing… he cut his knee, there was blood."

Sensing her mother's apprehension, she swallowed the morsel in her mouth and laid the rest of her sandwich on her plate, her eyes set on her mother's face.

"I fixed it for him," she whispered.

The trembling in Maddy's hand increased. Lemonade sloshed over the rim of the paper cup. She put it down and hid her shaking hand in her lap.

This was the first time Evalyn had displayed her unusual ability outside of the house. "Did I do something wrong, Mama?" she asked worriedly, seeing the concern reflected in her mother's dark eyes.

"I just fixed him … you know…" her voice lowered. "You know … the way I fixed your headache."

Maddy knew *exactly* what Evalyn had done for the boy. Not long ago, her daughter had done a similar thing for her.

Ten years earlier, Maddy met the man who would become her husband and the father of their child. Both born and raised in Texas, they married six months after meeting.

A member of the air force, Evan was stationed at Offutt Air Force Base in Bellevue, Nebraska shortly after their marriage. They bought a charming, three-bedroom brick house in Omaha. Their first real home, it suited them perfectly.

Soon after Maddy discovered she was pregnant, Evan was killed while on assignment in Bosnia. She was told his death was an accident, that he'd been killed under "friendly fire," a term she found ironic. *Friendly fire*, as though they were describing a campfire or a hot dog roast.

She had been a schoolteacher, but had been unable to continue working. She became ill, totally incapacitated by pregnancy complications brought on by extreme grief. She developed migraine headaches, which she'd never had previously.

Overpowered by this grief, she wandered through the empty, memory-filled house. The third bedroom would never hold the second child they had planned to have.

In spite of her poor health, Maddy didn't want to return to Texas. Although she loved her family dearly, they held many rigid beliefs that had never really suited her, particularly religious ideas about an inflexible, vengeful God hurling fire and brimstone if you didn't follow His instructions to the letter—vague instructions with stringent standards that could never be reached.

Until she met her husband, she had been terrified of God. But, instead of a punitive deity, her husband introduced her to a caring, divine being that had her best interest at heart. This was the Being she wanted her daughter to know.

Later on, when Evalyn's unusual gifts were apparent to Maddy, she knew her family would never accept her. They would find her repugnant or worse. If she lived in such close proximity, Maddy knew she wouldn't be able to hide from them forever.

Besides, Omaha and the surrounding small country towns were beautiful—not flat like most of the Midwestern plains, but liberally interspersed with gently rolling hills. Bluffs could be seen from across the lazy Missouri river. Yes, they would stay in the Midwest, where most people minded their own business and life was steady and comfortable.

Although overjoyed to be carrying her beloved husband's child, Maddy's joy was interspersed with sadness. Her despondency continued well into Evalyn's first year.

She knew there would never be another man for her other than Evan Williamson. This was something she could live with. She counted herself among the blessed to have been loved by such a man. His smile could light up a room and make anyone within its radius feel good.

Evalyn inherited her father's caramel coloring and her eyes were like his—a deep, smoky green that could change to smoky topaz depending on what color she was wearing—or her mood. She also had her father's smile—a smile which Maddy never tired of seeing.

While her grief lessened over the years, it never totally disappeared. She channeled the fierce love she had for her husband into her love for her daughter.

Maddy had known Evalyn was special from the moment she was born, from the second she held her in her arms—although she couldn't have explained exactly *how* she knew at the time. She named their daughter Evalyn, a melding of their names. She felt their daughter was a combination of the best of both of them.

Evalyn walked when she was ten months old and learned many things earlier than other children her age. Maddy attributed her daughter's quick progress to being exceptionally bright and also because Maddy began her education so very early. Even before this, however, there had been other things—unusual things that Maddy never taught her and couldn't explain.

Such as Evalyn's ability to see in the dark like a cat, and the way she glowed. This was the only way Maddy could describe it. *Glowing.* She had first seen Evalyn display this phenomenon when she was about three months old. Evalyn had been asleep in her crib for several hours when Maddy noticed a soft radiance that seemed to be coming from somewhere nearby.

Puzzled, she walked over to the crib, searching for the source of the illumination. She had been astounded to see that the light appeared to surround the slumbering Evalyn, extending about an inch or two from her tiny pink pajama-clad body. Startled, Maddy realized the light was coming *from* her daughter. It seemed as though she was lit up from inside. When Evalyn stirred, the light shifted with her movement. Alarmed, Maddy picked up her baby. Evalyn awakened for a moment before falling promptly back to sleep in her mother's arms.

Maddy thought she was losing her mind—that her grief was taking over and consuming her. She sat in the nearby rocker and held her child, crying, and praying. She talked to God regularly and this occasion was no exception. Earnestly she prayed for sanity.

She rocked her sleeping baby for a few hours. After a while, the soft radiance shimmered once again. Except this time, while holding her child, Maddy felt no panic. Serene, loving warmth permeated the room. Maddy relaxed and breathed deeply. After a few minutes, she fell peacefully asleep in her chair, her daughter secure in her arms.

As the weeks and months, progressed, Maddy began to grow calmer and Evalyn grew larger. The glowing occurred periodically, but it ceased to alarm Maddy. She told no one. She no longer thought herself to be insane—or if she was—it was a harmless type of insanity. In addition to the unexplained phenomenon, her baby seemed to require more sleep than most infants. Evalyn never awakened during the night and she regularly took one or two naps every day.

Maddy noticed the shimmering radiance didn't occur when Evalyn took a short nap. It only seemed to occur when she had been sound asleep for more than a few hours. She strongly suspected it happened more frequently, during times when she must have been unaware, or perhaps asleep herself. She also noticed it was almost impossible to see the glowing in daylight or in a well-lit room, which made sense—for only in darkness is light fully appreciated for what it is.

If indeed Maddy *was* sane and the occasional radiance surrounding her daughter was not a figment of her imagination, she wanted to make sure her daughter was not being adversely affected by whatever this *glowing* was. She took her to her pediatrician where Evalyn was given a clean bill of health. In fact, her daughter was never sick, or injured. Not even a sniffle.

One afternoon when Evalyn was about two, she and Maddy had been lying quietly in the bed she once shared with her husband. She was suffering from severe migraine headaches, which she attributed to worry, to fear, and to the many other things plaguing the harried life of single mothers. The headaches had begun to occur more frequently and to gain in intensity. The heavy bedroom curtains were drawn to darken the room. Even the slightest bit of light made her headaches worse.

Maddy thought Evalyn was napping until she felt her daughter stir. Painfully, she opened her eyes to see the soft glow and Evalyn's green eyes staring into hers. Maddy remembered Evalyn's eyes held such deep empathy it had surprised her at the time.

"Mama," she whispered, in her musical toddler's voice. "I'm sorry your head hurts."

Before Maddy could respond, Evalyn reached over and gently placed her tiny palm on her mother's forehead. Maddy felt a slight tingling sensation flow from her daughter's hand. At first, the tingling was strongest in the area around her head and face, and then it extended throughout her entire body, like a mild electric current.

Initially, the feeling stunned her—it was unexpected but it didn't hurt or frighten her. It felt comforting, soothing. It flowed with happiness and reminded her of the sound of her husband's laugher. Gradually the soft glow surrounding her daughter subsided. Evalyn removed her hand, smiled sweetly at her mother.

Maddy's headache stopped immediately and never returned. An unexpected side effect was her vision also improved. She had worn glasses since adolescence and now no longer needed them. That had been almost four years ago.

"Did I do something wrong, Mama?" Evalyn repeated, jolting Maddy back to the present, worriedly peering into her mother's eyes. Abruptly, Maddy pulled her thoughts back and centered on the child sitting across from her.

Maddy smiled, leaned over and patted her daughter's soft cheek.

"It's Ok, honey," she murmured. "You're my special girl."

Evalyn smiled as the worry left her mother's face. She picked up her sandwich and quickly devoured it, then started eating her chips, crunching happily. With her chin in her hand, Maddy watched her.

Evalyn had a particular soft spot for wounded animals. Last month she found a bird with a broken wing in the shady corner of their backyard and gently lifted it from where it fluttered helplessly on the ground.

Maddy watched though the window as her daughter crooned gently in her childlike voice while cupping the bird in her small, brown hands. A soft light surrounded her. After a few minutes, Evalyn raised her hands high above her head and commanded, "Fly away, birdie!" The bird circled around Evalyn a few times, as if to thank her before winging skyward.

"Evalyn," she murmured quietly. "You do know the way you fix animals and people is something that other people can't do?"

Evalyn nodded solemnly, eyes wide. Although she never been alone with anyone else, she sensed she was different. On the rare occasions in which she'd been around others, it was always under Maddy's watchful eye.

"You'll be starting first grade when summer's over and you'll be around a lot of children then. Maybe some of them might get hurt, like the boy you helped today."

She gave Evalyn a direct look. "Even if they get hurt, Evalyn, you can't fix them."

"Even if they're bleeding?" she asked softly, her little face pained. "Even if they cry?"

Maddy shook her head. "No, Evalyn, not even if they cry!" she exclaimed emphatically. "You can't help them, no matter what. No one can know about this. Just us."

"Can I fix animals, then?" Evalyn whispered, her deep green eyes brimming with tears. Unbeknownst to her mother, she had healed several animals—dogs and kittens mostly. Instinctively the sick animals had crept near to her. After they were healed, they seemed reluctant to leave her side.

"They can't talk, they won't tell anybody."

"But someone might see you."

Averting her eyes, Evalyn's shoulder sagged. Maddy reached over, taking Evalyn's chin in her hand and lifted her face up. It was necessary for Evalyn to obey. Her future might depend on it.

"Other people won't understand, honey. And most people are afraid of things they don't understand."

Maddy felt truly fearful for Evalyn—afraid of what others might do if they found out about her abilities, afraid of those who might want to exploit her, to use her for their own gains. Her Texas relatives would probably try to perform an exorcism, she thought wryly. Maddy shook her head to clear it, to lighten the mood and to change the direction her fears were taking her. The sunny day was much too beautiful to waste on worry.

"So… what do you think school is going to be like?" Maddy asked, changing the subject.

"Easy." Evalyn scoffed. She remembered walking to the school with her mother and registering for the fall. "They're just going to do baby stuff!"

14

"Well, you'd just better do exactly what they do." Maddy laughed and added, "No showing off!" Evalyn gave her mother an impish grin.

After six years of not working, with her savings account depleted and living exclusively on Evan's military life insurance benefit, Maddy realized she needed to go back to work. She discovered an opening for a teaching position working with homebound students. She applied and was offered the job.

Maddy refused to send Evalyn to a babysitter and return to work any earlier, preferring to educate and care for her daughter herself while simultaneously protecting her and monitoring her gift until she got old enough to understand.

She believed now was a good time for Evalyn to attend school, sensing she was old enough to understand the depth of her abilities. However, she felt the results could be disastrous if she underestimated her daughter's capacity for self-control and her ability to comprehend what she saw as danger if Evalyn's special talent was discovered.

After being homeschooled since age three, Maddy knew her daughter would probably be more advanced than most of the other children in the class. In fact, after taking standardized tests, the principal suggested Evalyn skip first grade and go directly to second grade. Maddy vetoed the idea. Her daughter was smaller than most six-year-olds, and Maddy was afraid the second graders would overpower her.

Although agile, graceful, and extremely bright intellectually, emotionally she was six and Maddy did not want to rush Evalyn's normal development. She wanted her to progress at her own pace. Until the other students caught up with *her,* she would continue to tutor her at home in the evenings. Maddy believed school should not be about grades, but about cultivating a love of learning. As a high school teacher, she had seen many students with excellent grade point averages—but uninformed parents—lead imbalanced lives. Above all, she wanted her daughter to be happy.

Together they packed up their lunch things, retrieved the bucket and shovel from the sand. Evalyn paused, her gaze distant. Placing her hat firmly on her head, Maddy looked to see what distracted her daughter. Across the grassy field, Maddy spotted the little boy Evalyn had helped. He was playing with another boy a few years older. When he spotted Evalyn, he stopped. He nudged the older boy, and pointed. The boys started in their direction. Before they could reach them, Maddy quickly tossed their things in the picnic basket, grabbed her daughter's hand, and hurriedly left the park.

Christopher's eyes followed the girl and her mother as they left, watching intently as they crossed the wide expanse of grass. Instead of heading for one of the cars in the parking lot, he was pleasantly surprised to see them walk to the street that ran along the east side of the park.

Ignoring his brother's protests, he dashed across the grass. He watched them walk down the shady, tree-lined street and make a right turn at the corner. He realized they couldn't live far.

Somehow, Christopher felt connected to the girl, as though she filled a place in his young heart he hadn't realized was empty. As soon as he got the opportunity, he planned to search for her. Besides, his mother had told him whenever someone does something nice for you, you're supposed to say, "Thank you," and he had been too astonished at the time to do so. He'd find her and thank her properly.

Friday morning Christopher awakened to the sweet smell of rain and the persistent sound of tapping against his bedroom window. Throwing the covers off, he leaped out of bed, opened the curtains and peered out, hopefully.

He was in luck—it was raining! The only thing he liked more than rain was snow, but since it was summer, he knew he had a while to wait before snowflakes made their appearance. He raced downstairs in his boxers, through the empty kitchen, and dashed out the back door. The summer rain was warm and fell in huge drops. Gleefully, he splashed in every puddle he could find, ran through the wet grass in his bare feet.

Emily and Becca entered the kitchen; the rest of the family would be stirring shortly. Emily started filling the coffee pot with water.

"Have you seen Christopher this morning?" Emily asked her daughter, "He's not in his room. I thought I heard him come downstairs."

Becca looked through the kitchen window into the back yard. She could see her little brother twirling and whirling, stomping and splashing.

"He's out back doing some sort of weird dance," Becca announced, her tone irritated. "I don't know what's with him—I sure hope none of the neighbors are watching."

She opened the back door. "Christopher! Get in here!" she hissed.

He paused for a second. Seeing it was only his sister, he decided to ignore her.

"Mom, make Christopher come inside!" Becca wailed.

Emily came to the back door. She smiled, watching her son's antics.

"What's everyone looking at?" Bob asked, walking into the kitchen. He kissed his wife, and peered over her shoulder at his son.

"Oh, Christopher's out playing in the rain again," he remarked calmly, sitting down with a cup of coffee. He picked up the newspaper and turned to the sports page.

"I'd better get him in here before someone sees him and calls Child Protective Services about a half-naked child left out in the rain," Emily laughed.

"And wouldn't that be ironic, since you're a social worker— they'd be calling you," her husband chuckled.

"Mom," Becca wailed, "Please get him, it's embarrassing!"

"Grab a towel from the dryer, Becca." Emily held the door open wide. "OK, Christopher, your rain dance is over!"

Christopher held his face up toward the sky. He opened his mouth to catch a few last drops of rain before skipping to the door where his mother dried him with a towel. She kissed him on top of his wet head.

"Guess you've had your shower for the day, huh?" she joked.

Christopher grinned. He was missing his two front teeth. She loved all of her children dearly, but her youngest held a special place.

"Go get dressed, then come and eat breakfast," his mother ordered.

Christopher scampered out of the room, obeying his mother. By the time he dressed and returned to the kitchen table, the sun had come out. Christopher was only slightly disappointed. Since the day proved to be sunny, he would be able to continue his search.

On several previous occasions, whenever Christopher could escape alone, he rode his bike along the street bordering Oak Park. He would turn right, as he'd seen the girl and her mother do, and ride up and down, searching. He had never been on these streets before. In fact, he'd never ridden his bike on any street other than the one on which he lived, but Christopher considered himself daring, and viewed these excursions as adventures.

The houses were very similar to the ones on his street— two storied, conservatively colored, with neatly trimmed lawns. However, despite his best efforts, his searches were unsuccessful.

Later that afternoon his parents were at work. Matt and Ace had gone to the movies. Christopher stayed at home with Becca who was talking on the telephone with a friend about what they were going to wear when school started on Monday. Because she was talkative, it would be quite a while before the conversation ended.

He filled a water bottle and attached it to his bike. With school starting Monday, he wouldn't have a lot of free, unmonitored time. For good measure, he grabbed an apple and a granola bar out of the snack bowl his mother kept on the kitchen counter. Today he would search longer than usual, so he wanted to be prepared in case he got hungry.

He rode to the now familiar street at the east of the park and turned right. He circled the block several times, before stopping in the shade to take a drink of water. He hadn't found her, but he knew he had to be close. He paused at the corner and inspected the street to his left. Until now, he had not searched in that direction. He squinted. He thought he spotted a brightly colored bucket in the front yard of the second house from the corner. *That was it! The pail he'd seen the girl playing with in the park. He'd found her house!*

He pedaled quickly and pulled up short in front of a cheerful brick house trimmed in white. There were shutters at the windows and window boxes overflowed with brightly colored blossoms. White picket fencing covered by rambling rose bushes encircled the front and sides of the house. The gates were open, inviting. A brick walkway led to a white door with a small beveled glass window at the top. He sat on his bike in the empty driveway, wondering if he should go up to the door and knock.

He'd never gone to someone's house before without his parents or older sister and brothers. After a moment's hesitation, Christopher laid his bike on the driveway, bravely walked to the door and knocked loudly. He spotted a doorbell on the right, and rang it several times for good measure. He waited a few moments and began the knocking, ringing routine again. No one answered. Disappointed, he walked to his bike.

A white haired woman, wearing a wide brimmed hat and carrying garden clippers, came out of the house next door. She spotted Christopher, climbing on his bike.

19

"Looking for Evalyn?" She asked cheerfully, pulling the brim of her hat down to shade her eyes. *Evalyn! So that's her name!* Christopher nodded. And now he knew where she lived.

"They said something about going down to the river today."

"Thank you!" Christopher shouted to the woman as he pedaled down the driveway. Taking no more notice of Christopher, she began clipping her hedges.

He turned the corner, heading back to his house. He planned to return to her house as soon as he could. He wondered nervously, *what if she doesn't remember me?* He certainly would never forget *her.* His life had changed forever the moment she touched him.

Chapter 2

Standing at the door to her classroom, Miss Smith nervously straightened her skirt and ran her hand over her dark brown hair, checking to make sure no rebellious strands had escaped from the neat twist at the nape of her neck.

So many firsts today! Her first teaching assignment after completing her internship and the first day of school for these twenty-five first-graders.

Miss Smith smiled and shook the hands of parents dropping off their precious cargo. Ushering the children into the classroom, she showed them where to put their things. The cubbies at the rear of the classroom were labeled with each child's name—a few of them blank in case an unexpected student was assigned to her room. She led the children to their assigned seats. The bell rang. She took a deep breath, and shut the door.

As Miss Smith called the roll, she noticed a tow-headed boy had moved from the seat she had assigned to him and now sat next to a pretty, petite girl with caramel-colored complexion and dusky green eyes. Checking her clipboard, she saw the little girl's name was Evalyn. Miss Smith walked down the aisle toward the boy

"What is your name?" She asked, bending over him.

He raised his eyes to look up at her. Miss Smith was startled, although she managed not to show it. The child's eyes were the most incredible blue she had ever seen—deep indigo flecked with silver, reminding her of sunlight on water.

"Christopher," he responded with a slight lisp. He was missing two of his front teeth.

"Well, Christopher," she admonished gently. "You're in the wrong seat."

Christopher leaned around the teacher toward the girl. Miss Smith saw the little girl's full bottom lip tremble and her eyes fill with tears.

Flustered, Miss Smith's eyes darted back and forth between the two children.

"I want to sit here," the boy announced to Miss Smith. "Evie'll be sad if you make me move." Stubbornly, he crossed his arms in front of him.

Evalyn started sniffling loudly, confirming Christopher's words.

"It's okay, It's okay," she patted the girl on her shoulder to comfort her. "He's your friend?" The girl nodded. "Fine then, he can sit next to you if you both promise to be good."

The little girl dried her eyes and rewarded her teacher with a smile that seemed to light up the entire classroom. Startled once again, Miss Smith managed not to show it. *What a smile!* She thought.

The crisis averted, Miss Smith walked to the front of the class. These two children, the blonde boy and the little black girl were undoubtedly buddies. They were also two of the most beautiful children she had ever seen.

Evalyn arrived home from her first day of school, bubbling with excitement.

"Mama!" she exclaimed, "Guess who's in my class!"

Until now, Evalyn had spent virtually all of her childhood at her mother's side. Maddy deliberately isolated her daughter to keep her away from prying eyes. Maddy shook her head, puzzled. As far as she knew, Evalyn didn't know any other children.

"It's the boy...you know...the one I helped." She handed her mother a drawing that she had done in school. "I made you a present! See?"

The drawing depicted two children standing side-by-side. One was a brown girl in a green dress, with braids and large green eyes; the other child was a yellow-haired boy wearing a red T-shirt and jeans, a cowlick sticking up in the middle of his head. Both children wore big, bright smiles. The boy's smile showed a gap where two front teeth were missing.

Frowning, Maddy regarded her daughter solemnly, thinking of the close call in the park. *Maybe I should have kept her home for another year.*

Evalyn gave her mother a reassuring smile. "Don't worry, Mama," she said cheerfully, hugging her mother around the waist. "He promised he wouldn't tell. Not *ever*." Evalyn's bright smile lit her face. "He's my best friend. His name is Christopher."

Oh, just great! Maddy thought. *Why couldn't the boy have gone to some other school? Why did Evalyn have to see him get hurt? Why did I take her to the park anyway?* The questions flew through her mind like a flock of noisy crows.

As she studied the drawing, Maddy took a deep, steadying breath. She had protected Evalyn the best she knew how. She couldn't keep her daughter in isolation her entire life. Eventually she'd grow up and have to learn to live a safe life on her own. In the meantime, she would teach her all she could.

"Are you going to save it, Mama? You could put it in the book where you keep my other pictures!" Evalyn urged. She looked at her child's happy face. Intuitively Maddy knew this boy was going to become a part of their lives, like it or not. "Yes, it's a very nice picture. I'll save it with the others," her mother murmured softly. "I have a present for you, too," she added.

"A present? For me?" Evalyn looked around, her green eyes bright.

"Later, after dinner." Maddy stooped down to her daughter's level and lifted her chin gently. "Do you remember the promise you made, Evalyn?" she asked softly, searching deeply into her child's dark green eyes.

"Yes, Mama." She nodded. "Not to heal anyone at school—no matter what."

"And not to talk about it to strangers?"

"And *never* to talk about it."

She hugged her daughter again, and kissed her cheek. Hand in hand, they walked into the kitchen. Evalyn climbed into her regular seat at the table, and told her mother about her first day in first grade.

"The best thing about my day was seeing Christopher," she chimed.

"What was the worst thing?" Her mother asked. Maddy handed her a crisp, fresh apple for a snack. Dinner wouldn't be ready for another hour and she knew Evalyn was hungry.

Pensive, Evalyn's eyes lifted to the ceiling. "There was no worst thing," she answered cheerily. "But there *was* a second best thing—my teacher, Miss Smith. She's really nice. I like her."

Evalyn took a bite of the apple, and then stopped abruptly. She held the apple in front of her face, studying it closely. A tiny white tooth was embedded firmly in the apple. Her front tooth *had* been rather wiggly lately. Delighted, she showed her mother. Most of the six-year-olds in her class were missing front teeth. Now she could join that club, too. She would be sure to show it to Christopher tomorrow.

"Evalyn, let me put it under your pillow. The tooth fairy will come and get it tonight." Evalyn studied the tooth for a moment, then handed it to her mother.

"What will the tooth fairy do with it?" Evalyn asked, her bright, innocent eyes peering up at her mother.

Maddy, like most mothers faced with such questions, had to think quickly. "She...ah...will give it to a newborn baby who doesn't have any teeth yet," Maddy responded.

Evalyn's eyes grew wide. "So that's how they get them," she whispered, her voice filled with wonder. Maddy ducked her head to hide the smile playing at the corners of her mouth.

She sent Evalyn out to play in the backyard while she finished preparing their meal. Evalyn had a good appetite—she'd eat just about anything as long as it came with ketchup.

Preoccupied making dinner, Maddy didn't hear the side gate open, nor did she see anyone enter. At the bubbly sound of children's laughter, her eyes flew to the kitchen window. Evalyn and the little blonde boy she called "Christopher," were chasing a ball in the yard. For an instant Maddy felt uneasy—then she relaxed. Her daughter looked so *happy!*

Madelyn had guarded Evalyn all of her life. Perhaps it was time to allow her to grow up, while she was still close enough to catch if she should fall. Besides, Maddy had a contingency plan in case Evalyn was discovered. She and her daughter would move away to some place new. She prayed that would never happen. She liked living in Omaha, and this house held many wonderful memories of her husband.

She called through the window and told Evalyn it was dinnertime. "See you tomorrow, Evie!" Christopher shouted, as he scurried out the side gate. Through the large kitchen window, Maddy could see him barreling down the street on his bicycle.

After dinner, Evalyn picked one of her favorite books to read aloud to her mother. Maddy listened patiently, helping her with the words she stumbled over. After they had read for a while, Maddy retrieved a small wrapped package from the mantle and handed it to her daughter.

Evalyn felt the package. She and her mother enjoyed playing guessing games with gifts. "Can you guess what it is?" Maddy queried.

"It feels like a book," she responded eagerly. She loved books and enjoyed reading. She quickly unwrapped it. The book was covered in a light and airy floral pattern. She flipped it open. The pages were blank. Puzzled, she looked at her mother. "There's nothing written in it."

"That's because it's a diary. You get to write in it and it becomes your story."

"What sort of things should I write about?"

"Oh, whatever you want, your feelings, what you think about, that sort of thing. As much or as little as you want, whenever you like."

Evalyn threw her arms around her mother's neck. "Oh, thank you! My own story!" she said, excitedly. She ran to her room to make her first entry:

Deer Diaree. Today I sat nex to Kristofer at school. He is my best friend.

During bath time, Evalyn was talkative, especially excited about the pending visit from the tooth fairy. After her prayers, Evalyn placed the tooth into a clean white sock and put the sock under her pillow. Maddy tucked her in and kissed her goodnight.

Later, after Evalyn was fast asleep, her mother crept back into her bedroom, holding a bottle of glitter and a sock (matching the one under Evalyn's pillow) containing several coins. As she opened the door, she could see the soft glow surrounding her child. Although she had seen it so many times, the beauty of the light continued to amaze her.

Quietly, Maddy spread glitter on the floor, leaving a "fairy trail" from the bed to the window. She switched the socks, taking the one containing the tooth with her. Kissing her daughter once again, she left the room, quietly closing the door.

The next morning, as soon as she opened her eyes, Evalyn spotted the glittery trail leading from the window to her pillow. "The fairies came!"

Delighted, she lifted her pillow and found the fairy's gift. When she peered into the mirror above her dresser, she saw that a new tooth had already grown in. Evalyn was disappointed. She thought it would have taken longer.

Mrs. Potts had been Benson's nanny since birth. He spent more time with Mrs. Potts than he did with his own mother, a beautiful jet-haired socialite who whiled away more of her days in London with friends, than with her husband and son.

Since Benson Cunningworth II was often absent on business, young Benson was placed in the care of Mrs. Potts. This wasn't unusual for the Cunningworth family. Nannies and governesses raised generations of Cunningworth offspring (although Benson recently discovered the family's butler had reared his great-grandfather because none of his nannies would remain with him for more than a month).

Today Benson was being driven to the same elite, private boarding academy where generations of Cunningworth males attended.

His straight black hair was neatly combed. He was wearing dark trousers and a navy blazer with the academy's red emblem on the left top pocket. Sitting in the huge back seat of the sleek, dark sedan, he looked very small and pale. Behind horn-rimmed glasses, his pewter gray eyes stared blankly out of the window at the passing scenery.

Even though the large, impressive house where he had lived his entire life had held little warmth, it had been familiar. Today, he felt frightened.

When he arrived at the academy, Benson was shown to his dormitory room. His belongings had been sent weeks ago. He entered the large room, which contained two beds, two desks. A boy sat at the desk on the far side of the room, gazing out of the window. He appeared bored.

Benson greeted his new roommate. "Hi," he said shyly.

27

The boy glanced in Benson's direction and scowled. "Oh, great," he responded sullenly, "I wanted this room to *myself.*" He turned back to the window, annoyed.

Benson had not had the opportunity to be around many other children. Occasionally he would spend holidays in London with cousins. They were several years older and they teased him mercilessly. He never enjoyed the visits.

Trembling, Benson walked slowly over to the vacant desk in the corner and sat on the wooden chair. With raspy, shallow breaths, he took all of the new pencils and pens from the desk drawer and lined them up very carefully according to length, making sure the imprints faced up and that none of the pens touched pencils. If one touched accidently, he began this painstaking process all over again. It took him almost an hour to get all of them perfectly in place. By the time he finished, the trembling had stopped.

Evalyn and Christopher were standing together near the chain link fence in a corner of the schoolyard. "Evie, we need to make a spit pact."

"A pack of what?"

"No, pact." Christopher emphasized the 't.' "It's like a promise."

This sounded interesting. Eyes wide, Evalyn asked, "Ok, what's the promise?"

"To be best friends forever."

"And to never keep secrets from one another." Evalyn added. Christopher nodded in agreement and spit into his palm. Evalyn looked appalled.

"Go on, spit into your hand," he urged. "It means the promise can never be broken"

Reluctantly Evalyn spit the tiniest drop into her palm.

"Now we shake on it." The two children solemnly shook hands.

As the year progressed, Christopher and Evalyn became inseparable. In the autumn, they ran laughing through piles of dry leaves in Oak Park, crunching them underfoot. They built a snowman in Evalyn's front yard in winter, and in spring, they picked the daffodils growing along the school fence.

At school, they played together and ate lunch together. Bethune Elementary was one of the few schools in town that allowed a short nap for first graders. Evalyn and Christopher placed their mats side by side each afternoon. When Miss Smith monitored the classroom while the children were resting, she often heard them giggling together. On a few occasions, the arm of one of them draped over the other in slumber.

She felt a pang of regret when June came and Christopher and Evalyn passed on to the next grade.

Because Bethune Elementary was a very small neighborhood school, there was usually only one classroom per grade. Since Christopher and Evalyn were the same age, they were always in the same class. Every year when school started, Christopher would insist on sitting next to Evalyn, and every year their teachers allowed them to do so.

Now and then, a teacher would try to make them sit apart. On these rare occasions, Evalyn would put her head on her desk and cry until her shoulders shook. Christopher would glower—arms folded defiantly across his chest—and refuse to relinquish his seat. Their combination of tears and stubbornness worked every time.

On wings, the years flew by. Christopher and Evalyn grew quickly. Their cheeks lost the roundness of young children, their remarkable faces accentuated by striking planes.

Christopher's Scandinavian heritage allowed him to tan quickly and easily. This, and his tendency to wear shorts and sleeveless shirts, even in winter, when he could get away with it, kept his skin bronzed and his nose freckled. His hair had darkened to burnished gold; a stubborn cowlick defied hair gel.

Evalyn, often wearing her favorite color, green, resembled an ethereal forest sprite, with long braids, lovingly arranged by her mother, brushing her shoulders. Her exquisite features hinted at the delicate beauty to come.

Christopher and Evalyn chose to spend most of their school day together. It wasn't that they didn't enjoy playing with their classmates; they simply preferred each other's company to anyone else's. Christopher would make Evalyn laugh, and she always cheered and applauded enthusiastically when he'd win at games and races, as he often did. He was taller and stronger than most of his classmates.

The other children liked them both, but they were particularly fond of Evalyn. She was cheerful and affectionate. Christopher, on the other hand, was rather possessive regarding Evalyn. He had been known to stand between her and classmates who wanted to play with her, telling them she was *his* best friend. However, unlike Christopher, Evalyn was an only child, and liked playing with other children. She particularly enjoyed playing dolls with the girls—which was fine with him. Christopher drew the line at playing with dolls. Gradually, the other children grew to understand that Christopher and Evalyn were members of a private club—all others excluded.

Maddy heard of an affordable ballet class in downtown Omaha. The school, La Bella Ballerina, had an excellent reputation and was owned and directed by an Italian ballerina who had studied at the Accademia dell'Arte in Tuscany.

The director's first name was Antonia, but everyone called her Panzella, her maiden surname. The local gossip was that she had fallen in love with an American, married him and settled in the Midwest, leaving behind a flourishing career. She often said the decision to leave Italy and follow the man she loved was the easiest decision she ever made.

When Maddy called to inquire about dance instruction for her daughter, Panzella grilled Maddy over the telephone. She was mainly concerned about commitment and whether or not Evalyn was the type of child who finished what she started. Maddy had heard good things about the studio so, in spite of the director's curt manner, she obligingly answered all of her questions. She knew the director interviewed all the students initially and if the interview was successful, they were assigned to one of the dance instructors. The instructors worked with each child individually and the children were placed in a class according to their ability.

Maddy pushed open the wide glass door to the studio and Evalyn followed closely behind. It was early and the large studio was empty. They entered a minimally furnished lobby, with a high counter and six chrome and leather chairs. Several pair of doors led off the lobby into what appeared to be smaller practice rooms. A staircase to the left of the entrance led to a second level.

Not seeing anyone, Maddy took Evalyn's hand and walked through two large, open double doors. They entered into what she assumed was the main dance studio. The walls were mirrored and bars were placed along two of the walls.

A small, willowy woman in black, leaning against a bar on the farthest wall, watched them enter. She smiled as she watched Evalyn walk toward her.

What an enchanting, graceful child, thought Panzella. She had seen many beautiful people during her lifetime—had seen even fewer beauties who danced enchantingly.

The director glided toward them in a few quick steps. Cordially, she shook Maddy's hand and greeted them. Her voice had a slight accent. She smiled warmly at Evalyn. Evalyn returned her smile, intuitively sensing Panzella's kind heart.

Panzella offered Maddy a nearby chair and asked Evalyn to take off her shoes. All of the students regularly wore some type of dance footwear in the studio; she didn't want street shoes marring her carefully polished floor. Evalyn quickly obeyed and stood in pink, short socks, wiggling her toes. Evalyn liked going without shoes—she could tell she was going to like this.

Panzella stooped down, so they were eye to eye. The child's beautiful dusky green eyes stunned her. In the Italian village of her birth, green was known as the color of healing.

"You want to dance, yes?" the instructor asked.

Evalyn nodded. "Yes," she replied, shyly.

"Dancing is easy, anyone can do it. Dancing *well* is very hard work." Panzella regarded Evalyn sternly, though a smile played along the corners of her full lips.

"I can do it!" Evalyn said emphatically, her shyness falling away.

Still stooping low, Panzella ordered, "Walk across the floor and then I want you to turn and run back to me."

Evalyn did as instructed. Lithely she walked to the far wall, her arms and hands held quietly at her side. Giggling, she turned and ran as fast as she could, her hands floating gracefully behind her, straight into Panzella's outstretched arms. Hugging her, with typical Italian warmth, Panzella met Evalyn's laugh with a throaty one of her own.

Yes! The dance instructor thought, *this pretty little one has a dancer's balance, grace, and agility—such potential!*

Rising, Panzella took Evalyn's hand in hers and together they walked to where Maddy was sitting.

Maddy smiled watching them. They both looked so happy. Panzella wasn't the only one doing the interviewing. In spite of all the fine things she heard about the studio, Maddy wanted to make sure she was leaving her daughter in the hands of a good, caring person.

"Yes, I think I will instruct your daughter myself," Panzella offered, "I teach a very special class of children and I think Evalyn will fit in perfectly."

Of course Maddy was delighted Panzella admitted Evalyn into her dance studio, although she wasn't surprised by her offer to teach Evalyn personally. Since her first nimble step, Maddy sensed her daughter had been born to dance.

Most of the rumors about Panzella were true—she was a tough taskmaster and demanded perfection from her students. Only those closest to her realized she also demanded perfection from herself and that she was a deeply loving and caring woman.

Even though it was a school night, instead of going to sleep after her mother had kissed her goodnight, Evalyn removed her diary from under her mattress and scribbled in it for over an hour.

The streetlight, about a hundred feet from the house, cast enough light for her to read without turning on her lamp. Lamplight filtering under her bedroom door would have been a dead giveaway. She turned on lamps at night out of habit— because her mother did. In truth, Evalyn's night vision was better than most cats.

It had been a couple of weeks since she'd made an entry and a lot had happened that she wanted to write about. She wrote about school, about learning to dance. There was a lot about her best friend, Christopher.

The next morning, when her mother awakened her, it was hard for Evalyn to get out of bed. She required more sleep than most children her age, usually twelve to fourteen hours a night and occasionally needed to take a long nap right after school, particularly if she hadn't gotten her quota the night before.

This morning, she dawdled getting dressed and almost missed the school bus. Evalyn barely had time to chug a glass of milk and grab the lunch her mother had packed the night before in her cherished Pocahontas lunch box.

Her lunches were wholesome and nutritious of course, but Maddy often managed to indulge her daughter by slipping in one of her favorites, either a red velvet cupcake, or a double chunk chocolate chip cookie. Always homemade. Her mother didn't know it, but Evalyn always ate her dessert first.

By late morning, because of her late night and light breakfast, Evalyn was hungry and feeling quite tired. The droning of her teacher's voice only made her sleepier. She couldn't help herself— she nodded off.

She felt a nudge on her shoulder.

"Wake up," Christopher warned softly. "Or she'll catch you."

Evalyn sat up straight in her chair and rubbed her eyes, drowsily. She'd been caught napping before and had found it embarrassing. Her mother warned her that sleeping for an hour or more in the wrong place could be dangerous.

She yawned and her stomach growled at the same moment. Christopher heard Evalyn's rumblings and sent a sympathetic glance her way. "It's almost lunch time."

The lunch bell rang moments later. All of the children retrieved their lunches and noisily exited the classroom. Christopher and Evalyn went to sit at their favorite table in the center of the cafeteria. She spread her lunch in front of her and reached for her cookie, one her mother had baked with special large chunks of chocolate. Before she could grasp it, Randy, a chubby redhead with beady, close-set eyes, shot his hand out and snatched it from in front of her nose.

"Hey, this is good!" he exclaimed, greedily biting into it.

Evalyn was momentarily stunned. Then her temper flared. For the last hour, her stomach had been growling as she waited patiently for lunchtime to arrive. She had anticipated the moment when she would taste the sweet chocolate and feel it melting in her mouth.

Without thinking, she picked up her sandwich and threw it at him. Peanut butter and jelly slid down the front of Randy's shirt. Fuming, he turned bright red. He stood and pushed Evalyn so hard she fell on the floor in a heap. She heard her dress rip as she went down.

Quickly Christopher came to Evalyn's defense. No one was going to push his best friend and get away with it! He balled up his fist and swung it hard (his brother Ace had given him plenty of practice in dealing with bullies). He hit Randy in the face, bloodying his nose.

Simultaneously and with great enthusiasm, other children joined the flying food frenzy. Soup, sandwiches, and chocolate milk flew through the air, meeting unsuspecting targets. Hearing the uproar in the center of the cafeteria, teachers monitoring the lunchroom rushed to stop the melee.

Evalyn and Christopher sat on the bench in front of the principal's office. Several of Evalyn's braids had come undone; her dress was torn and rumpled. Christopher's hair was smeared with peanut butter (or maybe it was mustard) and multi-colored stains decorated the front of his shirt.

Randy was in with the nurse. "I should help him," Evalyn whispered sadly, her small hands covering her cheeks. She felt bad for Randy.

"What? Help that creep?" Christopher whispered back angrily. "No way!"

"But he's hurting..."

"So?" Christopher retorted. "Let him hurt."

Determined, Evalyn stood up. She couldn't stand to see anyone suffer, not even Randy. *I should have let him have the dumb cookie,* she thought. *Then Christopher wouldn't have punched him and ...* Christopher grabbed her hand, pulling her back.

"Evie!" Christopher whispered loudly. "You can't help him! He'd blab all over—besides, it would probably scare him to death."

"Were you scared when I fixed you?"

Christopher snorted. "I'm not a chicken liver, like Randy."

Evalyn sat back down on the bench with her chin in her hands. "Maybe if you had knocked him out or something... then I could have fixed him without him knowing."

"I should have knocked his head off!"

Evalyn smiled. "I don't know if I could fix that!"

Her expression grew serious. "Mama made me promise not to fix people… not even if they're bleeding. She says if people found out, they might take me away someplace."

Christopher hadn't thought of this. He had simply thought if the other kids knew what Evalyn could do, they'd either be afraid of her or worse—they might think she was cool and want to hang out with her all the time and that option was *out*. After all, she was *his* best friend and he wasn't sharing her with the entire fourth grade.

Since their children had been in the same class for the past few years, Madelyn and Emily were well acquainted, although their relationship was primarily based on the friendship of their children. Years ago, they exchanged telephone numbers and at least once a week Christopher rode his bicycle to Evalyn's house.

Every now and then one of his parents would call and ask Maddy to send him home. Occasionally the Boldsen's would invite Evalyn over for dinner and play dates.

After the first dinner invitation however, Evalyn would only accept the play dates, and politely refused all offers to join Christopher for meals. When her mother asked her about it, Evalyn's only reply was to put her finger down her throat and make gagging noises.

Over the years, no mention had ever been made of the incident in Oak Park. Maddy guessed correctly. The boy kept the promise he'd made to Evalyn. Her secret was safe.

Maddy and Emily arrived at the door of the school at the same time. Both mothers spotted their dejected children, benched in front of the principal's office.

"Evalyn, what happened?" Maddy asked, surveying the disheveled culprits.

Evalyn looked exhausted. Her mother found this puzzling, but attributed the fatigue to today's mishap. Last night she put her daughter to bed at seven—her regularly scheduled bedtime. She should have gotten plenty of sleep.

When she received the call at work, she found it puzzling as well as disturbing. The principal informed her that her usually well-mannered daughter had been involved in an altercation—specifically, a food fight.

Emily stood in front of Christopher with her hands on her hips. She had three rambunctious sons and a loudmouthed daughter with a mind of her own. This was not the first telephone call from the school principal ordering the Boldsen's to come collect one of their errant offspring. Either Bob or Emily made the trek to Mr. Randolph's office at least once a semester. This was the first call they'd received regarding Christopher.

Emily took in his disheveled appearance. Each morning she sent him to school in clean clothing. Each afternoon he returned home with grass stains or ripped jeans. Today, he looked worse than usual.

"Christopher Boldsen," she barked, "tell me you did *not* punch a boy in the nose!"

Stubbornly, Christopher pressed his lips together. Emily's eyes narrowed. She had years of practice dealing with her Boldsen brood and knew how to handle the children. When pushed, she could be more stubborn than the lot of them combined.

"Christopher! Talk. Now!" Emily demanded.

"He pushed Evalyn on the floor," Christopher announced, heatedly. "*After* he stole her lunch!"

Maddy and Emily exchanged glances.

"Wait here," Maddy ordered Evalyn, before marching into the principal's office.

Emily was half a step behind her. They closed the door firmly behind them.

The children sat on the bench, waiting. They could hear loud voices coming from inside the office, mostly those of their mothers. Abruptly the door opened and both mothers stormed out.

Each one took her child by the hand and walked quickly out the door, down the school steps to the sidewalk. They paused at the bottom of the steps to catch their breaths and calm themselves. As they did so, a sleek, dark sedan pulled up to the curb. A portly man, resembling Randy, climbed out and rushed up the stairs into the school building.

The women stared at his retreating back, then turned to one another. Emily gave Maddy a quick look and a slight nod.

"Hmm... I wonder who that could be." Emily muttered cynically. Maddy raised an eyebrow.

"I'm hungry!" Christopher wailed, tugging at his mother's hand. Irritated, Emily looked down at her wayward son.

"Well, after all, they did miss lunch," Maddy sighed sympathetically. "Christopher seems to be wearing his," she observed. Emily grinned. "So it seems. I could use a bite too... worked up an appetite in there."

Maddy laughed. "Meet you over at the Golden Burger by Oak Park?"

The children gave a whoop of excitement, thrilled by the prospect of eating their favorite hamburgers and perhaps even more thrilled because the restaurant's play area held a huge enclosure filled with brightly colored balls.

Emily and Maddy eyed one another over the children's heads. They sighed in unison, thinking the same thing, *It's not good to reward children for bad behavior.*

"Let's try to see it Christopher's way," said Maddy, her voice low. "He was a hero, really. He did what he thought was right." Emily gave a wry grin, and agreed.

Evalyn scrambled into the back seat of her mother's car and buckled her seat belt. Christopher peered up at this mother questioningly and nodded his head toward the vacant seat next to Evalyn.

"Can I ride with them?" He asked.

"If it's okay with Mrs. Williamson," his mother replied.

"Of course."

He slid into the seat next to Evalyn, grinning and buckling his seat belt. He gave her a high five.

"So I guess he's riding with you then. I'll follow, just lead the way."

Over lunch, while the children enjoyed themselves in the play area, the women joked about the incident. They realized the main fault lay with the other boy and sided with their children. Yes, Randy ate Evalyn's cookie, but he got his true "just desserts" by the bloody nose ungraciously bestowed upon him by Christopher.

"This behavior is out of the ordinary for Evalyn. I'm really surprised by it," Maddy admitted, watching her daughter and Christopher as they played with the colorful balls.

"I wish it was the exception at my house. Unfortunately, it's more of the rule. While Christopher doesn't start trouble, he has been known to finish it. Had it been Becca, Chris's sister, she would have punched that boy and more." Emily sighed. "Since she turned thirteen she's become quite a handful."

Maddy patted her arm sympathetically, grateful that she still had a few years left before Evalyn became a teenager. Despite a few differences, their families were like families everywhere.

When they got home, Evalyn headed upstairs to take a much-needed nap. She hung up her sweater while her mother fluffed her pillow. With a clatter, her diary and pen fell to the floor.

"So that's what happened," Maddy scolded, lips pursed, "You stayed up late last night writing."

Shamefaced, but exhausted, Evalyn slinked past her mother and crawled into bed. She fell asleep before her head hit the pillow.

Maddy placed the diary on the nightstand and tucked the comforter around her sleeping child before quietly going downstairs to start dinner.

In the weeks and months that followed, Madelyn and Emily discovered they had quite a few things in common besides having children in the same class and homes bordering Oak Park.

The Boldsen's lived on the west side and the Williamson's on the east, closest to the river. Both women had occupations involving children, and they both had relatives near the Dallas-Fort Worth area. Occasionally a rare opportunity arose when they were free from one obligation or another. At these times, they could meet at the park without the children to share laughter and good conversation.

On this warm Saturday at the beginning of June, children were counting the days until school let out for the summer. The majority of the parents were dreading it.

The pool at Oak Park had been open for a month and most of the kids in the neighborhood were taking advantage of it as often as possible.

In the winter, the swimming pool was emptied except for about a foot of water. When the temperature dropped below freezing, the park's swimming pool became a skating rink. Of course, the Boldsen children were there.

The Boldsen's believed in keeping their children active, so having Oak Park nearby was a godsend. Depending on the season, they signed their children up for team sports such as baseball, soccer, and basketball. All of them had taken lessons at the park at one time or another.

Christopher enjoyed sports and was good at all of them. However, he excelled at swimming. He felt more comfortable in water than out of it.

Once, as a toddler, he ran away from his parents and jumped feet first into the deep end of the pool. He was still too young to be enrolled in swim class and couldn't swim, or so his parents thought. Immediately, Bob dove in after him. Emily knelt by the pool, scared stiff.

Under the water, he swam away from his father and broke the surface, giggling and dog paddling. Playfully, he took a deep breath and dove down again, out of his father's reach. When he resurfaced, Emily grabbed him and pulled him out of the pool, simultaneously frightened and amazed. Christopher struggled against his mother, trying to get back into the water.

Shortly after this incident, Bob and Emily asked the park's swim instructor if he would accept him into the youngest swimming class, the Guppies. After watching two-year-old Christopher paddle around in the shallow end of the pool, the instructor agreed.

On this Saturday morning, Christopher was at the pool and so were several neighborhood kids, a few of whom were in his class at school. Although it was early June he was already tan, his hair shot through with gold streaks from the hours spent in the sun. He swam almost every day and as a result, his chest and arms were unusually wiry and strong for a ten-year-old.

The only thing that could have made swimming more enjoyable for Christopher was if Evalyn could swim with him. The rare occasions when she entered the pool were usually precipitated by a heat wave. Even then, she stayed in the shallow end, under the spray.

Christopher noticed Evalyn peering through the fence at the swimmers. Spotting him, she smiled and waved. He climbed out of the water to speak with her.

"Hi," she said brightly, "I was looking for you. Figured you'd be here."

"Evalyn, they're starting a swim class for beginners" Christopher implored, "why don't you sign up?"

"You know that I don't like to put my head under the water," Evalyn pouted, stubbornly. "I can't breathe and my eyes burn when I open them."

"I'll help you," Christopher persisted.

Evalyn shook her head stubbornly.

Christopher tried again. "But it will be easy, I promise."

Evalyn shook her head again. "No."

"Pleeeeese?" His appeals were growing louder. A few children paused to listen. "No!" Evalyn scowled. "Stop talking about it." She put her hands over her ears.

Christopher felt his irritation mounting. "You're just scared," he voiced, at full volume, "You're a chicken liver!"

Evalyn felt her face grow hot with temper and embarrassment. Several more kids from school stopped what they were doing to listen. None of them had ever heard the friends argue before—at least not seriously.

How dare he embarrass her in front of them!

Ignoring her, Christopher did a back flip into the water, quickly resurfacing

"You're just a show-off, Christopher Boldsen!" Evalyn shouted. "And you are *not* my friend. I don't ever want to talk to you again!" Evalyn turned on one heel and stomped away, her beaded braids swinging angrily.

The impact of her words hit Christopher hard. He felt as though the air had been let out of him. He had always known Evalyn was afraid to swim. Teasing her about it only made him feel small.

A few of the kids were still watching, so he dove under water and swam a few unenthusiastic strokes, just to show them he didn't care. *But he did!* Evie said he wasn't her friend anymore. Dejectedly, he climbed out of the pool, dried himself haphazardly, and walked slowly home.

Chapter 3

Benson was lonely, although he didn't recognize it as such. He had known nothing else. But he did sense a frozen, empty place deep inside of him that ached sometimes and filled him with a longing he couldn't explain.

Science was undoubtedly one of his favorite courses in school. He enjoyed the preciseness of it all—the careful scrutiny, incongruently balanced by the unpredictability of experimentation. The only class he found more enjoyable was music, particularly piano lessons. He would lose himself in his music and for a short time could forget his monotonous and rather empty life.

On this day, after completing a science experiment, he was the last one out of the classroom. The rest of the class finished almost thirty minutes earlier, and had already gone to the dining hall.

Benson had little interest in food. He disliked eating alone, which happened often, so he frequently skipped meals. As a result, he was much too thin.

He hurried through the halls, his eyes down. He found not making eye contact with anyone was the easiest way to avoid trouble, but Benson had a way of observing everything around him, while appearing to be unaware.

Before going on to his next class, he slipped into the boy's restroom to wash his hands. They smelled funny. The odor came from the chemicals he had used in science. Usually he wore gloves, but he had been so eager to get to the experiment that he had forgotten to bring them. When he didn't wear gloves, he washed his hands. A lot.

A boy about two years older than Benson entered the restroom with three other boys. Recognizing them, his heart sank. They were the school's troublemakers.

"Told you I saw the four-eyed geek come in here!" A tall boy blurted out.

They gathered around Benson, pushing him against the sink.

"Smells like he could use a good flushing."

"Yeah, let's dump his head in the john try flushing away some of those brains," the tall boy snickered, "Might make him less nerdy."

Laughing loudly, the boys grabbed Benson's arms and legs and dragged him towards one of the stalls. His glasses fell to the floor. Benson struggled against the boys, but they were bigger and stronger and they held him tightly.

They opened the stall door and tried to force him inside. Just then, the first class bell rang.

"Hey, it's the first bell. We'd better get going or we're gonna get another Saturday detention," one of the boys warned. The second bell rang. They dropped Benson unceremoniously on the hard tile floor, grabbed their books and rushed out. One of the boys turned, sneering over his shoulder at Benson, "Until next time, Nerd."

When he was sure the boys had gone down the hall, Benson retrieved his eyeglasses, slipped out of the restroom, and entered the room of his next class.

The teacher had just started a video and barely noticed Benson as he slid into his seat moments before the tardy bell rang.

Ignoring his shaking hands, Benson took out a dozen sheets of plain white paper. He cut the paper into perfectly precise squares. While the video played, he folded the squares into flawless origami cranes and lined them straight across his desk. He took a deep breath, relieved. The shaking had stopped.

After class, Benson made it to his room without further incident. He leaned against the door, his eyes shut tightly. At least his room was safe, peaceful. Luckily, or rather due to the large donation his father had made to the academy a few years ago, he had been moved to a private corner room with windows. He had filled it with books, video games and other pastimes he enjoyed.

He took off his jacket and draped it carefully on the back of the chair in front of his desk. He noticed two sealed envelopes lying on the desk. He sat down, looking at the return addresses. One was from his father, postmarked Tokyo. The other, from his mother in London. It had been months since he'd heard from either of them.

Carefully, so as not to tear the paper, he opened the envelopes. The one from his father contained a check for one thousand dollars. The other contained a birthday card from his mother, a hastily scribbled note at the bottom.

Happy 9th Birthday, Love Mother.

He stared at the card for a few moments, stroking the words with his fingers. After a while, he carefully placed the envelopes in a wooden box in his closet. It held other cards from past birthdays and Christmases. He took off his shoes, placing them neatly beside his other pairs. He lay on his bed and stared at the ceiling until he fell asleep.

Maddy realized she hadn't seen Christopher around for several days. Evalyn hadn't asked to go over to his house either, which was odd. Also, her daughter seemed rather out of sorts lately.

"Where's Christopher?" Maddy asked, while sweeping the kitchen floor. "I haven't seen him around lately."

Evalyn's eyebrows knit together, her lower lip trembled slightly. She brushed past her mother without answering and ran up the stairs to her room.

Could something be wrong with the boy? Maddy wondered, leaning the broom against the wall. She had grown quite fond of Christopher over the years. It was nice having him around, despite some of the 'boy noises.'

Reaching for the telephone, she dialed the Boldsen's number. Emily answered on the first ring.

"Hi Emily, it's Maddy. Is Christopher not feeling well?" she asked,

Emily laughed shortly. "Other than moping around here like a lost puppy, he's fine."

"Do you know what's going on? Evalyn's moping too."

"Well, Christopher told me they aren't friends anymore."

"Oh. That explains why she's eating lunch with the girls at school. She also asked her teacher to move her seat."

"Hmmm." Emily was quiet for a moment, mulling this over. "I think it will pass. You know, kids will be kids."

Maddy was not so certain it would blow over quickly. Evalyn could be stubbornly dramatic on occasion, magnifying things out of proportion.

The women talked for a few minutes more.

Several days passed. Evalyn still brooded. Maddy didn't pry, and Evalyn didn't talk about it. Occasionally friends have disagreements. Even she and her beloved Evan had argued. Maddy saw it as one of life's more unpleasant, but occasionally necessary evils allowing folks to clear the air. Given enough time, she had no doubt the children would 'kiss and make up.'

Saturday morning dawned bright and sunny. Evalyn dressed in a cool green and white short set and ate breakfast quietly at the kitchen table. After breakfast, she walked to the front gate, her eyes searching the street as though looking for someone.

The air was filled with the fragrant smell of the blooming rose bushes trailing along the fence. Evalyn barely noticed them. Dejected, she went inside to find her mother.

"May I go over to Christopher's house?" she asked resignedly.

"Of course," Maddy replied, studying her daughter.

Evalyn slipped her feet into white sandals, opened the gate, and walked slowly down the street.

Through the bay window in the living room, Maddy watched her leave. Her daughter looked sad, yet determined, as if she were facing a thoroughly unpleasant task.

The phone rang. Maddy quickly hurried to the kitchen to answer it. It was Emily.

"Just wanted to give you a head's up." She advised. "Christopher is on his way to your house. You might have to act as referee," she joked.

"Evalyn just left here on her way to see Chris," Maddy volunteered. "I guess they'll be Ok."

"I sure hope so!" Emily exclaimed, exasperated. "We're sick and tired of Chris's sour mood. He's arguing and bickering with his sister and brothers and is being a regular pain in the neck. I'll be glad to see things get back to normal."

Maddy hung up, and went outside. She took a basket and gardening shears so she could cut a few blooms to place on the kitchen table. Besides, it gave her something to do while she waited for her daughter. She clipped several long-stemmed beauties, enveloped in their heady fragrance. She had a sense that as the children grew and matured, so would their friendship. Of course, as to how this future friendship would develop, she could only speculate.

Evalyn walked toward Christopher's house. Before she got to the end of the street, closest to the park, she spotted him marching toward her, his shoulders squared. They stopped for a second before running pell-mell toward the other. Evie threw her arms around him, laughing. *It was so good to see him!* He returned her hug tightly. *How he had he missed her!*

"Race you to the park," he shouted, sprinting ahead.

Evie took off after him, running as fast as she could. Chris slowed, until they ran side by side. He slowed even more, letting her win. In the manner of children, all arguments were forgotten. No apologies necessary.

The Boldsens avidly encouraged their children to try any sport they found interesting. As a result, all of them enjoyed sports and each of them excelled in at least one. When Christopher mentioned that he'd like to try climbing, he had their full support.

The entire family agreed their favorite college football team was the Cornhuskers. However, during football and basketball season, their home filled with excitement and rivalry since each family member rooted for a different NBA and NFL favorite.

They truly went mad when the Super Bowl came around. They celebrated Super Bowl Sunday even more than designated national holidays. Evalyn and Maddy often joined the fun, although one family member or another needed to explain the plays.

Being around the active Boldsen's was beginning to rub off on Evalyn. The weather was great and she thought it might be fun to try something different, something that wasn't a water sport.

Every now and then she had stopped to watch the tennis players in Oak Park. It seemed fairly simple—just hitting a little ball back and forth with a racket that looked like a waffle. How hard could it be?

She phoned Christopher, asked to him to meet her at the tennis courts and to bring an extra racket. He had been practicing at the courts regularly for a couple of years, and at eleven, he was already fairly good at it.

"I want to be like Serena Williams. If she can do it, I can do it," Evalyn affirmed enthusiastically. Christopher looked dubious.

Evie was about a foot shorter than the lanky tennis champ and there were spatulas in his mother's kitchen that had longer reaches.

"Come on, Christopher, help me practice." Evalyn hopped from foot to foot imitating what she thought were tennis moves. Her ponytail bounced on top of her head.

Christopher showed her how to hold the racket and began to give her an elaborate explanation of the game. Evalyn looked at him blankly.

"Never mind, I'll explain the rules later," he offered. "For now, just hold the racket and hit the ball."

He served a ball in her direction. Evalyn missed it. He sent one after the other, Evalyn missed them all. He sent another and this time she wacked it into the next court interrupting the occupant's game. Scowling, they returned Evalyn's ball. For another hour, she tried her best.

"Evalyn," Christopher insisted. "Give it up. You'd have to grow another foot to play like Serena anyway. Maybe you should try jacks—it's a game with a little ball and you won't be able to hurt anyone."

Evalyn stuck out her tongue at him.

Christopher mopped the sweat off his damp forehead with his shirtsleeve. "C'mon. Let's go to your house ... it's the closest ... and get something cold to drink."

Discouraged by her overall lack of progress, Evalyn stomped off the court. Agilely, she jumped on top of a picnic table, doing a graceful pirouette before leaping lightly to the grass.

"Ballet is more fun, anyway."

"And a whole lot safer for the rest of us," Christopher agreed.

They continued on to Evalyn's house, idly swinging their rackets.

The sweet smell of baking floated down the driveway through the open window, welcoming them. Christopher sniffed the aroma expectantly. He thought Mrs. Williamson was undoubtedly the best cookie baker in the state.

Maddy smiled, greeting the children as they entered the kitchen.

She set two filled glasses on the table, milk for Evalyn and iced water for Christopher, since was what he usually preferred to drink. She placed a plate of cookies in front of them.

"So, how was tennis?" Maddy inquired.

Christopher laughed, almost choking on a cookie. He reached for the glass of water and took a big gulp. "Well ... ah ... the only way Evalyn will be a good server is if she decides to become a waitress."

Maddy laughed. "That bad, huh?"

Christopher shook his head. "Worse. She hit the couple playing in the other court with her ball. Twice."

Evalyn made a face, chewed a bit of her cookie. "Just a little accident, really," she mumbled. "I had so hoped to learn to play well." She waved the half-eaten cookie in the air. "I've had this dream of wearing a tennis outfit in mint green while competing for the championship at Wimbledon."

Maddy gave a short laugh, "Guess you'd better let that dream die."

Christopher tucked the tennis rackets under his arm and walked home munching on a freshly baked chocolate chip cookie from a tin Evalyn's mother had sent home with him. In the tin were oatmeal raisin, peanut butter, a melt-in-your-mouth buttery shortbread, and Evalyn's favorite—chunky chocolate chip.

He stuffed a second cookie into his mouth before opening the broad white door to his house. Immediately his ears were assaulted by shrill sounds coming from the kitchen. His mother and sister were in another argument. They seemed to argue a lot lately—about curfews, clothing, and about Becca monopolizing the family's one telephone line.

"I'm tired of wearing Matt's hand-me-downs!" Becca shouted. They're *boy's* clothes!"

"They're cut off jeans and T-shirts! Who can tell?" Their mother shouted back.

"I'm not wearing them!"

"Go naked, then!"

Christopher couldn't understand what all the fuss was about. As the youngest boy, practically everything he wore had belonged to one of his brothers or the other. What was the big deal?

Hoping to make peace, Christopher interrupted them by placing the tin containing the cookies loudly on the table.

"Mrs. Williamson sent over a dozen of her freshly baked cookies," adding what he hoped was a cheerful smile.

"At least *somebody* cares enough about kids..." Becca insinuated, reaching for a cookie, "... to *bake* for them!" She glared at her mother, known more for her culinary *disasters* than her culinary *skills*.

Emily opened the refrigerator door and took out a pre-packaged roll of cookie dough. "You want cookies," she snapped, slamming the plastic roll on the table in front of Becca. "Then bake 'em yourself!"

Walking out of the kitchen, Becca mumbled something unintelligible under her breath. "Watch your mouth, young lady!" Emily yelled after her.

Christopher took another cookie before going upstairs to his room. His mother sister were strong-willed and quick tempered and although it kept things interesting, it sure was a lot quieter at Evalyn's house.

Above the main floor of La Bella Ballerina, where Evie had been dancing for several years now, was a suite of rooms which reflected the studio owners comfortable, yet practical European flavor.

Panzella had made the smaller room into her personal office. It was simply furnished, with an antique desk and matching chair she brought with her from Italy that had belonged to her grandmother. On the other side of her study was a small comfortable sofa that fit perfectly into the corner.

Across the hall, there was a large breakroom for the instructors and an occasional student. It contained a dinette set, a well-stocked refrigerator and microwave, and a large, comfortable couch.

During her career Panzella had seen too many young female dancers who had health problems commonly found only in old women. She believed that, in addition to having excellent dance skills, a good instructor must have adequate rest and eat well.

Panzella thought most Americans seemed overly tired, actually sleep-deprived. She strongly encouraged her instructors to rest between classes whenever possible.

The only student she had seen utilizing the napping sofa was Evalyn. Once during a private lesson, Panzella noticed Evalyn stifling a yawn. She led her to the employee lounge, telling her to resume practice after resting awhile. The child seemed to know when she was tired and took catnaps when she had been practicing for a couple of hours on a particularly challenging routine.

For four years Panzella had instructed Evalyn in a group with several other gifted dancers, in addition to an hour a week for her private lesson. Occasionally when Panzella left the building during the early afternoon, while other classes were still in progress below, she would see Evalyn catching a catnap on the sofa or working out in one of the practice rooms, wearing her leotard, or in cooler weather, a pair of sweats.

The instructors who held late evening classes told Panzella that Evalyn would often be in the practice rooms three or four days each week, until the studio closed for the night. During the summer when it was still light outside, she would ride her bicycle home. On dim, cold winter evenings her mother would drop her off after school and pick her up at dinnertime. Now at age eleven, Evalyn displayed a level of talent that many of the older students had yet to achieve.

Today was one of Panzella's early days and she was eager to get home. Her husband was returning this afternoon after spending several weeks abroad on business. As she was leaving the studio, she glanced in one of the practice rooms and stopped short. Evalyn was practicing without ballet slippers. She was dancing in her bare feet! Panzella sharply reprimanded her.

"But I have always practiced this way. I only put on my shoes when class is about to start." Astonished, Panzella wondered why hadn't the instructors mentioned this to her.

"No!" Panzella was genuinely alarmed. "You will ruin your feet, dancing in pain."

Evalyn looked puzzled. "But... my feet don't hurt at all. They never have."

"Let me see your feet," Panzella demanded, carelessly dropping her expensive handbag on the dance room floor and squatting down. Evalyn sat on the floor and put her tiny brown feet in Panzella's lap. Panzella had seen the spectrum of foot injuries as well as other wounds endured by dancers, having had experienced most of them herself. Even now, her right hip was painful due to an injury which had happened more than twenty years ago. Dancers paid dearly for their art.

Frowning, she examined the child's feet carefully, turning them gently in her hands.

"How often do you dance barefoot," she asked, amazed.

"Most of the time, here and at home. I only put on shoes when I have lessons. I like the way my shoes *look*—I just don't like wearing them all the time."

Panzella tried to make sense of this. She had never seen anything else like it in her entire career. Evalyn started ballet lessons with her at age seven. And in spite of dancing in bare feet, Evalyn's feet were perfect, soft. The toenails were thin and clear. And even more startling—there were no bruises, blisters or calluses (the bane of ballerinas everywhere).

A barefoot ballerina, she mused. Because Evalyn was proud of her shoes, she wore them for lessons and of course, recitals. So this explained why Evalyn's shoes always looked new, Panzella thought ruefully. The shoes were never fully broken in. She had mistakenly assumed Maddy was indulging her only child by frequently buying new ones. But now she understood that Evalyn was outgrowing her shoes, rather than wearing them out.

Panzella patted Evalyn's feet. Evalyn slid them off Panzella's lap, curling her legs under her. Panzella leaned forward.

"Evalyn, dear one," she affirmed, "everything about you is remarkable." She tapped her index finger gently on the end of Evalyn's nose.

"I don't know how you have managed to be so lucky, but promise me this. If you have even the tiniest bruise or soreness, you will wear your shoes, yes?"

Evalyn nodded seriously, and then flashed her brilliant smile. Panzella returned Evalyn's smile with a hug. Although she tried to hide it from others, Evalyn was her favorite student. She gave her a quick wave, before dashing off to join her husband.

Evalyn watched her walk quickly down the stairs. Panzella's affection for her wasn't the only thing she was attempting to hide. While others might be unaware, Evalyn knew Panzella's right hip often caused her pain. Regretfully she knew she couldn't do anything about it.

It was Sunday morning. Evalyn was getting dressed for church. It could have easily been a Saturday or Friday. It could as easily been a church, temple, synagogue, or mosque. Ever since she could remember, Evalyn and her mother had explored one religious center or another. Her mother called them "spiritual adventures." The places they found particularly interesting they would often revisit.

"It doesn't matter what method of transportation we use or what road we take to get there," Maddy had told her, "as long as Spirit is our ultimate destination."

Evalyn knew about her Texas relatives, but didn't remember them. Her mother had taken her for a very brief visit years ago. Her grandparents in particular were inflexible in their views about how folks should worship. Maddy wanted Evalyn to make her own informed decisions regarding how she wished to worship (or not worship) whatever deity she preferred—God, Allah, Buddha or the goddess Isis. And she wanted Evalyn to have all the spiritual information possible at her disposal.

Although this might seem strange to some, Evalyn found this practice enjoyable. It reminded her of eating at a smorgasbord—so much to chose from! By the time she was seven, Evalyn had attended services at numerous Christian churches, Jewish synagogues, and Hindu and Buddhist temples, just to name a few. She sang, chanted, prayed, and danced, participating in the different forms of spiritual celebration.

She liked meeting new people and many of the ideas she'd heard filled her with a sense of wonder. Sometimes she invited Christopher on these "spiritual adventures." But if they involved too much sitting or too much silence, he got antsy.

She opened her closet door and stared into its disorganized depths. She took out a simple green sundress, slipped it over her head and scrutinized her reflection in the mirror. Most of the other girls in her class were already developing breasts. She sighed. Her breasts were such a disappointment to her. She'd had mosquito bites that were bigger.

As Evalyn and her mother put the breakfast dishes in the sink, there was a knock at the door. Maddy was scouring the living room, trying to locate her frequently evasive keys. Evalyn opened the door to find Christopher standing there. "So ... you're on your way to church?" Christopher asked expectantly.

"Yeah, wanna come?" Evalyn invited. She correctly surmised he hoped to join them. He was neatly dressed—neatly for Christopher anyway-and his blond hair was still damp from his shower.

"Sure, why not?" Christopher responded nonchalantly. "Ace is really getting on my nerves this morning anyway."

Evalyn gave him a sympathetic glance. The possibility of having a brother like Ace made her glad she was an only child.

"Call your mom and ask, first," Maddy murmured, lifting up the sofa pillows, continuing the frantic key search.

Christopher lowered his chin, slightly chagrined. "I already told them I'd be spending the morning with Evalyn at Sunday School."

Maddy stopped searching for a moment, to glance up at Christopher with a short laugh. "Not if I don't find my car keys, you won't."

Christopher pointed to the key holder on the wall next to the door. "There they are, Mrs. Williamson."

She snatched the keys off the hook and herded the children into her very old, but very reliable, car.

"So where are we headed this Sunday?" Christopher asked, familiar with their forays.

Evalyn wanted to return to a Sunday School class on the west side of town taught by a young Asian woman, named Miss Chin. The one thing she particularly liked about Miss Chin was the way she answered her overabundance of questions with grace and humor. "Remember the big white church, the one with the tall steeple?" Evalyn asked. Christopher nodded. "We're going there. I have more questions for the teacher."

Maddy turned on the radio as she drove. She preferred the "oldies" station and sang with gusto, even though she was off key. Twenty minutes later, she pulled up in front of the church to drop off the children, and then drove around to the back of the church to park.

Maddy went to join an adult discussion while Evalyn and Christopher entered the room filled with children in the ten-to twelve-year-old age group and took their seats. Evalyn glanced around for Ms. Chin, but didn't see her.

To Evalyn's disappointment, a bony man with red, thinning hair, sporting a sparse goatee, walked to the front of the room. In a stern, loud voice, he introduced himself as the assistant minister, Pastor Murphy. With a dour expression, he informed the children that Miss Chin could not be there today so he would conduct the class for her. Christopher lifted a shoulder and sent the dejected Evalyn a sympathetic glance.

Pastor Murphy clasped his hands in front of him and smiled at the children, thin lips spreading over yellowed teeth. Evalyn sensed he really wasn't happy to be teaching this class. In fact, by the way he glared at them; Evalyn felt he didn't like children much at all.

She couldn't figure out why he bothered teaching them if he didn't like them. And besides, he talked much too loud. She squinted, studying him. She was sure she had never seen him before, but there was something familiar about him, especially the close- set eyes.

"Christopher," she asked, "Doesn't he look like somebody we know?

"Yeah," Christopher retorted. "A red ferret. Or maybe a red devil."

Evalyn covered her mouth with her hands to stifle the laugh that was dangerously close to escaping.

"Today's Sunday School lesson is on the story of Jacob," Pastor Murphy boomed. "He was sold into slavery." He droned on and on.

"Now there's a thought," Christopher whispered loudly to Evalyn. "White slaves, yeah, I've heard of them. I can get rid of Ace *and* make money at the same time.

Evalyn snorted. "Who'd *want* him?"

Christopher responded in a loud whisper, "Wonder how much he'd go for?"

The Pastor scowled in the direction of their loud murmuring. "Did you have something to say to the class?" he asked haughtily. "Questions, perhaps?"

"Ah...er.. .do you think they got a fair price for him?" Christopher stammered, at a loss of what to say.

Pastor Murphy glared at him. "What's that?"

"When they sold their brother..." Christopher muttered, "I just wondered if they got a fair price." One of the boys sitting in the back snickered; Pastor Murphy scowled."You're missing the point of the story," Pastor Murphy snapped, sending a dark look in the direction of he boy.

"Hmmm...I don't think I've seen either of you before," Pastor Murphy said,

looking at Evalyn and Christopher. "What church do you go to?"

"Well, I don't go to one church," Evalyn piped up.

The pastor scowled and blinked several times. "What? You don't go to one church?" His scowl deepened. "What do you mean?"

Christopher volunteered, "She goes to a lot of different places—not just churches—temples, synagogues, mosques..."

The assistant pastor was blinking faster and turning an interesting shade of dark pink. Christopher's eyes widened, fascinated. He wondered if the pastor could blink any faster or turn any redder. He decided to give it a try.

"And one time she went to a pagan dance ceremony celebrating the winter solstice. I went too. It was fun."

Pastor Murphy turned deep red. "P...p...pagan?" He stuttered. Christopher was amused. Evalyn's eyes darted from the pastor's face to Christopher's, confusion marring her pretty features.

The assistant pastor took several deep breaths in an attempt to compose himself before proceeding to another activity. He ordered one of the children to pass out paper, crayons, and a few other art and craft items.

"Let's work on an art project in the time we have left," he voiced loudly. "In keeping with today's lesson, let's draw Jacob and his coat of many colors,"

"Good," muttered Christopher under his breath. "Now maybe he'll stop talking for a moment and give my ears a rest."

Evalyn spread crayons, markers and glitter between them for them to share. "He's got the name wrong anyway—it's Joseph," she said. Chris shrugged. 'Maybe Jacob is his last name." Evalyn looked doubtful.

She loved art and easily ignored Pastor Murphy while her attention focused on the project at hand. She began to draw enthusiastically. She used every color in the box to make a circle full of bright sparks. She sprinkled the colored sparks with gold and silver glitter.

The pastor walked around scrutinizing the children's work. He paused by the table where Christopher and Evalyn were working diligently. He leaned over Evalyn's shoulder, and grimaced.

"What's this?" he barked, pointing. "It doesn't look much like a coat at all."

Evalyn sprinkled a little more glitter on her drawing, biting her bottom lip as she concentrated.

"It's not," Evalyn candidly replied. "When I'm finished with this, I'll draw Joseph Jacob's coat... or whatever his name is." She blew away some of the glitter that hadn't stuck.

Preoccupied with the task at hand, she tried to ignore the pastor as she added the finishing touches to her masterpiece. He stood a little too close, peering over her shoulder.

"It's the Supreme Being," Evalyn offered, since he appeared to be waiting for an explanation.

"Young lady, no one knows what He looks like.'" Pastor Murphy responded smugly, rocking back on his heels.

Sliding her drawing towards the pastor, she exclaimed triumphantly, "Well, they will now!"

Christopher and the other children in the room laughed. Pastor Murphy fumed.

"How dare you make fun of *God!*" he roared. Spit collected in the corners of his mouth.

"I'm not making fun of Him!" She crossed her arms across her flat chest. *Not that He would care,* Evalyn thought. Even if Pastor Murphy didn't have a sense of humor, she was certain It did. After all, It made the platypus, living rocks, and mint that came in chocolate and orange just to keep human beings on their toes.

"And just because you don't know what The Sparkler looks like doesn't mean no one else does!" she added.

The Pastor was shocked. He struggled to find words. His mouth opened and closed, his eyes blinked rapidly. With the bushy eyebrows and goatee, Evalyn thought he really did resemble the devil, all he needed was the red suit and forked tail.

"The Sparkler?" he roared. "You called Him *The Sparkler!* Why that's blasphemy!"

"People call God by many names," she shot back. "And all of the names are beautiful!" She thought of all the places she and her mother had visited. "Jehovah, Yahweh, Allah…" She thought hard, "God or Goddess. Today—I called It the Sparkler, tomorrow I just might decide to call It something else."

Within seconds the pastor's face changed from fuchsia, to crimson to deep maroon—far surpassing its previous shade. Christopher stifled a laugh, pretending to cough as the pastor scowled at him, narrowing his eyes and pressing his thin lips together over his yellowed teeth. The pastor pointed a menacing finger in front of Evalyn's face.

"Do you know what He does to bad little girls?"

She may have been only twelve years old, but she realized a threat when she heard one.

"The Sparkler would *never* hurt me!" she exclaimed vehemently, jumping up out of her seat, pointing her own small finger in front of his face.

"And *nothing* you could ever say will make me afraid of It! Besides, my mother told me He loves me even more than she does, and my mother loves me a *lot!*"

Christopher had never seen Evalyn get so mad. He hadn't known she had it in her.

She wasn't finished. "Even Einstein said the Almighty may be tricky but *never* mean! And Einstein was a heck of a lot smarter than you!" She placed her hands on her hips in a perfect imitation of Maddy.

Abruptly, Pastor Murphy raised his hand as if to strike her. Christopher froze in place, ready to spring to Evalyn's defense. Realizing he had an audience of a dozen children, the Pastor's hand smoothed the sparse hair covering his head and lowered his hand. His expression changed from anger to one of feigned piety.

"Young lady," Pastor Murphy clasped his hands together in front of him, "what you need to do is pray."

Evalyn's breathing had slowed as she calmed down. But her eyes glittered mischievously. "Oh, I will," she offered, cheekily. "I'll pray for *you!*"

She grabbed her drawing and nudged Christopher out the door, ignoring the glowering looks Pastor Murphy aimed in their direction.

"Way cool!" Christopher exclaimed, grinning. He loved nothing more than a good argument. "Evalyn—you rock! This was the most fun I've ever had in Sunday School!"

She rolled her eyes at him "Fun? Ugh!"

Christopher stepped outdoors to wait while Evalyn went through the lobby to use the restroom. When she returned to the lobby, she saw Pastor Murphy speaking with her mother. He was making angry gestures—her mother looked grim. Neither of them seemed happy.

"My daughter has the right to worship in whatever way feels right to her." Madelyn said evenly, her voice soft, yet firm. "Unless things have changed, Americans have the right to religious freedom."

"Nevertheless, my decision still stands."

Having had the last word, he turned on his heels and marched quickly away, averting his eyes as he stormed past Evalyn.

"Well, I bet this is a first!" her mother remarked, shaking her head. "The pastor seems to think you and Christopher are a bad influence on the other children. The two of you have been expelled from Sunday School!"

Chapter 4

*B*enson Cunningworth III hoped to find the public school building open on a Saturday, and luck had been on his side. This Saturday a maintenance crew was replacing light fixtures in the administrative offices and a side door had been propped open. He slipped in unnoticed.

He walked down the long, empty hallway with his schedule of classes in hand, matching the numbers on the doors with the ones on his list. He wanted to make sure he knew where each of his six classrooms was located. Knowing exactly where things were made him feel less anxious.

Benson's previous school had been an elite private boarding academy in the east, the same one attended by untold generations of males in his family. He had been born in a local Omaha hospital, but except for his very early years, which were spent on the grounds of his family's prestigious Dundee estate, he resided at the academy, returning home only on holidays.

During most summers, he traveled through Italy or France with his mother, who he adored. She, on the other hand, treated her son as an afterthought. After a week or two she would deposit him with English relatives.

Although he attended the academy for most of his young life, the academy's board of directors suggested to his parents it would be better if he did not return the following year. Benson was not a poor student, quite the contrary—he was brilliant—he always made straight A's. It was his rather odd behaviors which had grown steadily worse over the years.

Benson wouldn't miss the other students. He never fit in anyway. However, he would miss the familiarity of the routine to which he had grown accustomed. He knew what time the meals were served, which teachers were best avoided, and what day his clean laundry would be delivered to his room.

Finally satisfied he had located all the rooms on his list, including the gym and the cafeteria, Benson returned his class schedules to his monogrammed leather portfolio and left the building.

It was the first day of Junior High for Evalyn and Christopher. They wanted to arrive early, so they had walked to school instead of waiting for the school bus. This would be the first time since they had started school that they would not be together all day. At first, this had bothered them—they were closer than many siblings—but after studying their schedules, they discovered it wouldn't be as bad as they thought. They shared the same homeroom class, where they were headed now, as well as chemistry and Spanish.

"Hey," Evalyn checked Christopher's schedule. "We have the same lunch period too."

"I hope the food is better here than it was at Bethune."

"I wouldn't count on it, but they do have snack machines. I already spotted them outside the double doors."

"Emergency rations" Christopher nodded. "Cool."

They walked into their homeroom. Another student had arrived before them, a tall thin boy wearing glasses. Straight. jet black hair almost reached his shoulders. He was wearing clear plastic gloves and he was wiping off his desk with hospital-strength disposable wipes. Evalyn and Christopher exchanged glances.

They walked over and stood quietly beside the boy, curiously watching as he wiped off the top and sides of the desk. Benson ignored the bystanders. He was used to other children's meanness, expecting the worst as a matter of course.

Evalyn bent down and peered under the desk. Sure enough, some errant student had stuck a piece of chewing gum under the bottom.

"Gum." She pointed to it.

Benson hesitated; the girl was probably teasing him. He was no stranger to ridicule. Cautiously, he reached under the desk with his gloved hand. His fingers touched the offensive piece of last semester's bubble gum. He pried it loose and slowly lifted his eyes.

Instead of being met with the derision he had expected, her smoky green eyes held such deep compassion and understanding it left him momentarily off guard. He glanced quickly at the boy standing next to her. The boys' blue eyes were filled with curiosity, but not contempt.

"Hi," Evalyn gifted him with her bright smile and held out her hand. "I'm Evalyn."

Benson stared at her outstretched hand, and then back to his own gloved one. Uncertain, he swallowed hard. Benson had rarely experienced friendliness —and he was so desperately lonely. Hesitating a moment more, he pulled off both of the plastic gloves and tossed them into the nearest trash basket.

He shook Evalyn's warm hand and introduced himself. "I'm Benson Cunningworth III." He spoke with formal politeness. "Very nice to meet you."

"Call me Chris." Instead of shaking hands, like Evalyn had done, Christopher gave him a knuckle bump. Benson frowned slightly. This was a first. He'd never knocked knuckles with anyone before. Seen it done, yes. Done it? No. Awkwardly, he returned the gesture.

"Benson Cunningworth the *third*... there are two more of you floating around somewhere?" Christopher asked jokingly.

Benson smiled slowly, as though his face wasn't quite used to it.

"There's just one more actually—my father, Benson Cunningworth II."

Christopher nodded in response and wondered how they kept track when all the men in the family had the same name. Maybe they just called one another the First, the Second or the Third. One day he'd ask him about it .

Benson laid his schedule sheet on the desk. Evalyn leaned over, studying it.

"It looks like we've got a few of the same classes," she announced.

They compared their schedules and found they shared homeroom, chemistry and lunch periods.

"Oh, but you're not taking Spanish with us." Evalyn pouted. "It looks like you're taking French instead." She was obviously disappointed.

Benson flushed with pleasure. This was another first. No one had ever cared whether or not he shared a class with them, or been disappointed if he didn't.

"I... I could switch and try to see if I can get in Spanish." He stammered, hesitantly.

Evalyn's dark eyes held a glimmer of hope.

"It's intermediate Spanish." Christopher mulled it over, shaking his head. "You'd have to have taken Spanish already to be able to get it."

"Not a problem," Benson replied eagerly.

"But you're taking advanced French." Most thirteen-year-olds were usually in beginning or intermediate language courses. Very few were in advanced language courses.

"And you're in an advanced class, no less." Christopher added, peering over Evalyn's shoulder at Benson's schedule.

"I can speak Spanish, too. So…maybe, if there's room, I can try to add it."

Evalyn studied him, shaking her head slowly. "Why do I think there's something you're not telling us?" she suggested with a slight smile.

Benson flushed, embarrassed. "I … um… speak fluent French, Italian, Japanese … and Spanish," he murmured. His shoulders slumped. He so liked these two, he didn't want them to think he was bragging.

Christopher chortled and slapped Benson lightly on the back. "Please! See if you can get into Spanish—we need all the help we can get!"

Benson grinned. He agreed to try to add the class before the school day ended. Christopher, Benson and Evalyn agreed to meet later during lunch.

Before long other students entered the room, slamming books on desks, yelling greetings across to friends they hadn't seen all summer. Soon the teacher appeared, and the class quieted down. Junior High had officially begun.

Although coming from different directions, Christopher and Benson arrived at the cafeteria at the same time. They spread their things on an empty table and sat down to hold their places while Evalyn headed for the hamburger line.

Evalyn returned with her lunch tray and began methodically opening the mound of ketchup packets she'd placed on the table. One by one, she emptied the contents on a plate next to her fries. As Benson watched her, he meticulously wiped his fingers on a disposable germ-killing cloth. He laughed, amused more by Evalyn's intense concentration than by anything else. Her pretty face puckered, and she was biting her bottom lip between her teeth. His cook would have a stroke if ordinary ketchup were put anywhere near the *haute cuisine* which regularly graced their dining table.

"Get used to it, Benson." Christopher snorted. Evalyn ignored them and kept squeezing and emptying her stack.

"You'll never get them all opened before lunch is over," Benson admonished. "And even if you do, your hamburger will be cold—if it's not already."

"Hmmm," Evalyn began sardonically, "a hot hamburger without ketchup versus a cold one with ketchup. Wow. *Really* tough decision." Evalyn rolled her eyes at Benson, without pausing from her squeezing and emptying routine.

Benson thought to himself that Evalyn would probably be thrilled if she tasted French gourmet catsup containing Bordeaux, roasted garlic and fresh thyme. He'd have to remember to bring her a bottle.

Looking around for the vending machines, Benson spotted them near the cafeteria doors. "Would anyone like a Coke?" he asked politely, rising from his seat. They declined, shaking their heads.

Benson carefully counted out the exact change and put the coins into the machine. He watched as the soda bottle made the journey downward before falling into the well at the bottom. He reached down to retrieve it. Quickly, a hand shot out and snatched the bottle from the slot. Benson looked into the face of a sneering, redheaded youth.

So now it starts, sighed Benson, wearily.

Wondering what was taking Benson so long, Christopher looked over his shoulder. At that moment he saw Randy, the redheaded bully, approaching the vending machines. Other than growing larger, it didn't seem he had changed much since the fourth grade. Christopher's eyes narrowed as he saw Randy grab the Coke. "Be right back," he murmured, easing from his seat. He went over to Benson.

"Give him back his Coke, Randy," Christopher ordered roughly. "Now! Unless you want me to *break* your nose this time." Randy paled, the freckles standing out in sharp contrast to his white face. Holding one hand protectively over his nose, with the other hand he shoved the soda at Benson. Snarling, he stomped away.

Benson wiped the top of the bottle, took a swig of Coke. He watched as Randy made a hasty retreat. Christopher and Benson grabbed burgers and fries from the food line and joined Evalyn.

A few others had come to sit at their table. Some of them were kids they had known from elementary school, others were students they met during their morning classes such as the tall, raven-haired girl who introduced herself as "Yolanda Esperanza Zimarripa," rolling her r's.

"What a beautiful name," Evalyn complimented. "It sounds like music."

The girl laughed. "Thanks, but call me Yoli, everyone does."

"Your name is almost as long as his," Christopher mumbled, his mouth stuffed. He gave a jerk of his head in Benson's direction.

"Don't talk with your mouth full," Evalyn chided.

"As I was *saying*," Christopher continued, ignoring her, "Benson Cunningworth the Third *is* a mouthful." He looked at Benson thoughtfully. "We're calling you Ben—just Ben."

Pleased, Benson grinned. He'd never had a nickname before—at least not one which hadn't been an insult. *Ben.* He liked it. Surrounded by noisy, bantering new friends, he found he had an appetite. Suddenly he was *starving*. He bit down into the burger. Cafeteria fare had never tasted so good.

Evalyn stifled a yawn. After several weeks of school, it seemed the only lesson she was learning was that procrastination never paid. Staying up late the night before trying to finish a Spanish assignment meant she hadn't received the tem or more hours sleep she always needed in order to function well. Maybe she'd

69

splash cold water on her face on the way to class—it might help wake her up.

She slid into her seat in the rear of the classroom only seconds before the bell rang. Christopher sat to her right and Benson in front of her, having managed to add the class the day after school started.

Exhausted and struggling to stay awake, Evalyn kept nodding off. She took deep breaths and lightly slapped her cheeks. Finally, unable to keep her eyes open, she lay her head on her crossed arms and promptly fell asleep.

Christopher gently poked her when Mrs. Reyes' back was to the students. Evalyn scowled in her sleep, but didn't awaken. Benson, trying to hide her from the teacher's view, placed his elbow on the desk, put his chin in his hand and leaned to one side. He knew Mrs. Reyes habitually walked from one side of the room to the other, so he shifted in his chair, tilting first one direction and then the opposite.

It proved impossible to hide the sleeping girl. Mrs. Reyes spotted her and walked briskly down the aisle. Tapping the desk, she quipped, "*Siestas* are not allowed in class. Pay attention, Evalyn."

Sleepily, Evalyn sat up and rubbed her eyes. She pouted, irritated at being disturbed but slightly embarrassed to be caught dozing. She had been having such good dreams. Mrs. Reyes walked to the front of the classroom and continued writing at the blackboard.

Evalyn tried not to fall asleep again, but lost the battle. Her head nodded on her chest. Christopher shot Evalyn a sympathetic glance. He knew she needed more sleep than most kids her age. He also suspected the reason.

Benson left his seat and walked to the front of the room. He inclined his head toward the teacher and whispered something in her ear.

Mrs. Reyes gawked at him, and then her eyes turned to Evalyn. Hastily she scribbled a pass and had Benson deliver it to Evalyn.

As Benson slid back into his seat, Evalyn opened her drowsy eyes. "I told her you may have stomach poisoning from the cafeteria food at lunch." He whispered conspiratorially. "And I added you might throw up all over the place at any minute." He grinned, handing her the pass. "Take this to the nurse's office. They have beds in there and they'll let you lie down and sleep."

Evalyn collected her things and staggered from the classroom.

The school nurse was preoccupied with another student, a rather green looking boy with a thermometer in his mouth. Shoved near his feet was a plastic-lined wastebasket. Perhaps Benson's food poisoning story was true after all. The nurse waved Evalyn over to an empty cot in a brightly lit corner of the infirmary, and returned to care for the boy.

Evalyn pulled the curtain around the cot for privacy. She fell asleep as soon as her head touched the pillow. The ringing of the last bell of the day awakened her about an hour later. She peered through a slit in the curtain. The nurse was nowhere in sight, evidently having forgotten about her. Evalyn grabbed her things and slipped out. She would remember to thank Ben for this. She owed him one. Christopher was dropping by later, and she'd invite Ben to come too.

Maddy was in the kitchen singing along to her favorite oldies on the kitchen radio. She was enjoying every minute of her day off.

Evalyn called after school to say her new friend, Ben, as well as Christopher, would be coming home with her. Earlier Evalyn told Maddy a bit about Ben, saying his parents traveled a lot and he, too, was an only child.

Maddy figured if Ben was like the average adolescent male, the depths of his stomach most likely resembled the elevator shaft of the Empire State Building. Luckily, a large Crock-Pot on the counter held thick Texas chili that had been simmering all day, perfect food for cool autumn weather. Honey cornbread and a batch of cookies were baking in the oven. She would invite Evalyn's new friend to dinner. Christopher usually invited himself.

Hands on her hips, she examined the kitchen table, covered by a red and white checkered tablecloth. White napkins lay folded, ready for use. *Chili and white napkins … a recipe for disaster*, Maddy thought. She opened a nearby cabinet, took out dark red napkins and quickly replaced the white ones.

She heard the front door open to the happy noise of laughter and bantering, which often accompanied her daughter and her friends.

"Hi, Mama," Evalyn hugged her mother warmly. Maddy kissed her daughter's cheek.

"Sure smells good in here, Mrs. Williamson," Christopher commented, slipping out of his jacket and tossing it over the back of the sofa. He bent to give her a perfunctory hug before heading for the sink to wash his hands.

"Will you be staying for dinner, Christopher?" Maddy asked, to the sound of running water.

Grinning, Christopher dried his hands on the towel hanging below the sink.

"Why thank you, ma'am." He drawled, "It's mighty nice of you to invite me."

Maddy shook her head, chuckling. Then her attention settled on the gangly teenager standing quietly next to Evalyn. He was a couple of inches taller than Christopher. Next to him, Evalyn looked like a doll. He wore a bomber jacket, like most of the boys, but his jacket was made of buttery soft leather and his jeans artfully faded. She mused that the cost of his wristwatch probably equaled her annual salary.

Behind the eyeglasses, however, the expression in his dark gray eyes made Maddy's heart ache. He looked weary, as though he wasn't quite sure if he was welcome here or anywhere, for that matter. Something about his demeanor reminded Maddy of a stray dog—one that had been kicked far too many times.

"Mama, this is Ben," Evalyn introduced, pulling him toward her mother as she tossed his jacket unceremoniously on top of Christopher's.

"You know, I told you about him."

Benson put out his hand formally, "Pleased to meet you, Mrs. Williamson."

Ignoring his outstretched hand, impulsively Maddy hugged him tightly. *My, he's so thin!* She looked up at him and smiled warmly. Benson grinned shyly and returned her hug awkwardly, as if he wasn't quite sure how to go about it. The desperation in his eyes faded ever so slightly as Maddy's motherly ways poured a bit of love into his empty heart.

"Welcome to our home, Ben. Are you hungry?" She asked, gesturing toward a chair.

Benson sidled toward the sink, pointing. "May I use your sink? I need to wash my hands."

Maddy watched as he ran the water, and beamed when he used the nailbrush and germ killing hand soap. Twice.

She dished up large bowls of chili for each of them, and placed warm squares of cornbread in the center of the table. Within moments, the sounds of eating, random teenage conversation and laughter filled the cozy kitchen.

On this Friday after school, Ben, Christopher and Evalyn decided to walk instead of catching the bus. The weekend forecast promised blue skies. Their walk home wasn't long, not more than a few miles and they planned to stop by the mall on their way.

The three friends entered the mall and headed for the pizza place near the indoor climbing wall. Lately, Christopher was getting into rock climbing. He enjoyed it more than playing the speed racing game at the arcade—which he enjoyed *a lot*. Even though a safety harness was secured to a guy on the ground controlling the tension whenever he climbed, Christopher felt euphoric. Occasionally he managed to convince Ben to join him. Evalyn preferred to watch from a safe perch on the ground.

"I'm hungry," Christopher announced.

"Like that's news," Evalyn retorted. "Since when are you *not* hungry?"

"Yeah, I could eat now too." Ben agreed. His stomach rumbled in sympathy. "The food in the cafeteria today was worse than usual. What was it anyway?" He had given up trying to guess what was in the casserole and had only eaten a bag of potato chips.

"The menu listed it as the "Friday Surprise." Evalyn interjected.

"Some surprise" Christopher retorted. "I've thrown up stuff that looked better."

"Yuck, Christopher!" Evalyn exclaimed, stopping to slap him sharply on the arm. "I didn't need a visual!"

Ben laughed at the expression on Evalyn's face. She truly looked disgusted and horrified.

"Let's order the pizza first," Evalyn remarked, resuming her pace. "Cause once Christopher starts playing *High Speed Racers*, or *Mario Brothers*; he won't stop until he's stuffed every dollar he has into the machine."

Christopher snorted. "Whatever you say, Ms. Pac-man."

"It's a lot better than the ones you play like *Racing Nowhere Fast* or *Bullets for Bambi*." She crossed her arms over her chest, raising one eyebrow. "Besides, what's wrong with Ms. Pac-man?" She demanded.

"Nothing. Except you've been playing it for ages, yet never manage to win."

Evalyn groaned, her arms falling at her sides. "Yeah, I know. I think I'm addicted to it. My mom told me she played it when she was pregnant with me. She and my dad would play it on the base." The boys knew Evalyn's father had been in the Air Force at the time.

They went to the window and ordered a ham and pineapple pizza. Evalyn pulled the crumpled coupon from her jeans pocket and handed it to the teenager working the counter. Ben pulled out his credit card.

It wasn't that Christopher or Evalyn ever asked him to pay for anything—Ben was practical as well as generous. Every month his mother deposited hundreds of dollars into his personal expense account. His allowance went a lot further than theirs did. Besides, what he received from his friends was worth far more than anything money could buy.

Ben handed the cashier his card. The cashier shook his head. "Sorry. Cash only."

"Everybody takes credit cards!" Ben exclaimed, exasperated.

The cashier crossed his arms and cocked his head to one side. "We're not everybody."

Realizing the cashier meant business, they dug in pockets and backpacks, came up with $22.37 between them. They placed the money on the counter—a collection of crumpled bills and sticky coins. "That'll be $11.25, with your dollar-off coupon."

"Cool." Christopher added, "Now we can pay for the pizza and hang out at the arcade for a while afterward."

Taking the money and the coupon, the teen rang up their order, yelling to someone over his shoulder, "Hey, Eddy, one Hawaiian!" He turned back to them, "It'll be ready in twenty minutes."

They headed for the arcade section of the pizza place. Christopher dramatically flexed his fingers. "I think I'll start with street basketball and end with …"

"Oh, let me guess," Evalyn surmised, rolling her eyes as he walked away. "*Need for Speed?*"

Ben played at the machine next to Christopher's. Until he met them, he had never gone to a video arcade, preferring to play alone at home. He had seen them of course, during the rare occasions when he ventured out, but the noise and the crowds had been too much for him.

Twenty minutes later, Christopher wandered over to Evalyn. Her game was just finishing.

He peered over her shoulder at the score. "See, you lost another one," he remarked. "At least you're consistent."

She glared at him, stalking to an empty wooden table and muttering something unintelligible under her breath. Ben went to the counter for their pizza. Christopher carried Evalyn and Ben's sodas and a bottle of water for himself. Evalyn handed out paper plates and napkins.

Steam rose from the piping hot pizza. Christopher folded a large piece in half and bit into it. Evalyn cut hers with a knife and fork. Using the fork, she placed a piece in her mouth.

"I mean really, Evalyn." Christopher contended. "Not even Ben eats pizza with a fork." Ben had folded his piece neatly and somehow managed to avoid getting sauce on his fingers.

"Like you should talk," Evalyn retorted, "with sauce dripping down your chin! Maybe you should take a page from my book."

Christopher grabbed a napkin and wiped at his chin. The napkin came up clean.

Scowling, he glared at Evalyn. Her forest green eyes danced mischievously.

"Gotcha!" she burst out laughing.

They finished the pizza. Christopher and Ben gobbled down twice as much as Evalyn. Ben leaned back against the seat, contentedly sipping his soda until the straw hitting the empty bottom made a slurping sound. He went to the soda machine returning with refills for himself and Evalyn. Questioningly he looked over at Christopher.

Christopher shook his head, holding up his half-filled water bottle. "I'm good. Thanks."

Evalyn turned to Ben, her green eyes bright. "Did you know that today's my birthday? I'm fourteen."

Of course he knew. Unknown to Evalyn, he and Christopher dropped gifts off at her house the previous day and Maddy hid them.

"Do you want to come over and hang out with us?" She asked. She didn't bother to ask Christopher, taking for granted he'd be there. They had spent birthdays together since they'd met.

Ben grinned. Maddy's baking expertise was well known. Birthday cake. His mouth watered just thinking about it. "Wouldn't miss it."

The three of them entered Evalyn's house accompanied by the unusually high decibel levels generated by young people. The house was decorated with balloons and streamers, something Maddy always did for Evalyn's birthday, even when it was only the two of them celebrating. Of course, she had baked Evalyn's favorite cake, red velvet with thick cream cheese frosting.

Looking up from the book she had been reading, she greeted them and led them into the kitchen. She liked these boys. They were good kids.

On the kitchen table, next to the cake, were three gifts—a carelessly wrapped small package held together with mounds of tape and crookedly tied ribbons, and another box professionally wrapped with brightly colored foil and a huge, ornate bow. A certificate edged in gold was propped next to the boxes. Evalyn snatched it up quickly and read:

One free day to do whatever, wherever! All expenses paid! Love, Mom.

Evalyn grabbed her mother, gave her a tight squeeze and kissed her cheek.

"I'm saving this for one of those horribly boring days when I'm broke," Evalyn announced, laying it carefully aside.

Enthusiastically, she opened the smaller package. It was obviously from Christopher—she'd recognized his signature wrapping—lots of paper and half a roll of scotch tape. It was a mint green T-shirt with a caricature of a long-lashed duck wearing lipstick, a pink tutu, and ballet shoes. The caption under the cartoon read, "Quackstep."

Holding up the shirt, she asked, "Is this what you'd call a *fashion statement?*"

"Don't you like it?" he asked, hurt.

She grinned widely. "Of course. I love it! It's my favorite shade of green."

She slipped in on over her head. Even with the shirt she'd been wearing underneath, it was extra roomy and soft, just the way she liked her shirts.

Christopher frowned. "I think it's a little big." He brightened. "Maybe you can use it for pajamas until you grow into it. It's what we do at my house."

She pulled the other box closer. It was quite heavy. Ben's eyes were on her face, watching closely. He'd never given a friend a gift before. Enthusiastically, Evalyn tore off the wrapping. The box held a wooden crate that contained a dozen bottles of French gourmet catsup made with Bordeaux, roasted garlic and fresh thyme.

Christopher groaned, holding his head in his hands. "Ben, you do know—Evalyn has a ketchup addiction. Now she's going to end up in rehab for sure."

Ignoring Christopher, Evalyn giggled with delight. "Oh, Ben!" she gushed, giving him a tight hug. "It's exactly what I wanted! How'd you know?"

Ben flushed, pleased by her hug and embarrassed by her praise.

The boys had second helpings of cake before Ben stood, getting ready to leave. Rather than stay over with his friends this evening, as he often did, he had called for his driver to pick him up early. His father was arriving later, having recently completed a business venture in Argentina, and Ben was looking forward to seeing him.

Maddy carefully wrapped a large piece of cake and placed it in a plastic container for him. Ben cradled the container carefully in his large hands. He'd have to remember to get Maddy's recipe and have his cook make it. On second thought— perhaps not. He would much rather eat the cake at Maddy's table with his friends.

Evalyn and Christopher walked Ben to the door. Leaning companionably against one another, they stood on the front steps, waving to Benson as the driver maneuvered out of the short driveway.

Evalyn looked toward the west. Dusky shades of purples and orange started to fill the horizon. She ducked into the kitchen.

"Mom, Ok if I go to the park with Christopher for a while?" Maddy nodded, unconcerned with the darkening sky. Evalyn could see as clearly at midnight as she could at high noon. A slight chill was in the air. "Take your sweater, honey," Maddy admonished.

Oak Park was one of Evalyn's favorite places. She never tired of the impressive Bur oaks, which were now beginning to sprout new leaves. Although spring was still officially a couple weeks away, today had been unusually warm for early March. It had been weeks since the last snowfall and the scent of crocuses and daffodils blended with that of new grass. The two friends strolled together in companionable silence, the rhythm of their strides falling into place, synchronized from years of being together.

Evalyn looked up at Christopher. He seemed lost in thought, as though he were pondering some weighty subject. He motioned to a nearby bench and sat, pulling her down next to him.

"How do you do it, Evalyn?" His clear blue eyes probed hers intensely.

"Do what?" She asked innocently.

He gave her an exasperated look. "You know."

"Oh *that.* Healing."

Christopher nodded. She paused, thoughtfully considering her answer. "I've done it for as long as I can remember. I healed my mother when I was just a little kid."

Christopher looked startled. He hadn't known ... she'd never mentioned it before.

"Animals too, when I can."

Dogs' tails wagged and cats purred whenever she was nearby. Many of them animals she had most likely healed. *So that explains it,* he thought.

Evalyn continued, pensively. "I know it has something to do with the flow—the energy.

Christopher looked puzzled. "Energy?"

"It's all around us—this energy. I'm sure it's even *in* us."

"But we can't see it?" Christopher asked. "So where exactly *is* it?"

Evalyn laughed. "Well, it's like the funny story about the two fish swimming in the ocean. One fish asks the other fish, "Do you know where the water is?"

Christopher chuckled. "I guess I'm like the fish who asks dumb questions." Evalyn gave him a look and rolled her eyes.

"But *you* can see it?" He pressed.

"Yes, when I focus. But when I need to use it, I don't think about it. I just use it."

Christopher was silent a moment. "What do you think this power is, Evalyn?"

"Hmm... don't know exactly...the Jedi called it 'The Force.'" Her deep green eyes gazed at him solemnly. "My mother calls it God."

"Do you think I can learn to see it?" Christopher asked, his blue eyes earnest.

80

Evalyn nodded. "Yeah, I don't see why you couldn't see it. Maybe even learn to *use* it."

"So you'll teach me?"

"If you're sure it's what you want." Christopher gave a quick nod. "Yeah, it's what I want."

"Ok, one of these days...when we have a lot of time and when no one's around." She shook her head slowly. "I hope you don't regret asking for this."

Chapter 5

The languid Missouri River flowed three miles east of Oak Park. The locals fished off the riverbank almost year round, except during the bitterest cold winter days. The early June temperature was perfect—warm but not scorching and the humidity was bearable. It was the perfect weather for boating or swimming. An unwritten arrangement deemed the boaters kept to the center of the river, the swimmers and fishers stayed fairly close to the shore, away from the currents.

Christopher and Evalyn told Ben about a special shady spot where a few trees had grown close to the edge of the river. Because of the way the trees blocked the view from the road, few others knew about it. Chances were good they'd have it to themselves. They agreed to meet at Evalyn's house on Saturday and bike down to the river.

Benson thought this sounded like great fun. Earlier that morning he asked his cook to pack a picnic lunch for three (complete with lint-free towels and hand sanitizer). It was waiting for him by the front door in a large basket.

Unfortunately, his customized bicycle—a Lapierre—was still with relatives in England. He hadn't gotten around to having it shipped home. He needed a replacement bike. Fast.

An hour before he was to meet Christopher and Evalyn, Ben grabbed one of his father's silver credit cards, along with the fully stocked picnic basket. He summoned one of the gardeners to pick him up in the front of the house in one of his father's vans. Benson Cunningworth II owned several different types of vehicles, although most of them were rarely used, since he was often out of town.

At Benson's request, the gardener drove him to a bicycle shop near downtown Omaha. The owner took one greedy look at Ben, the servant standing respectfully by the door, and figured that someone—the youth's father most likely—had very deep pockets. Immediately he took Ben over to the bikes in the upper price ranges. While these bicycles cost only a fraction of the Lapierre, compared to his friends' bikes, Ben felt they might appear ostentatious.

So, we're playing soak the rich kid, Ben thought. He knew this game and he wasn't playing.

"I need something under a thousand," Ben insisted, looking the owner in the eye. The man looked away, avoiding his gaze.

"Sure thing," he responded quickly, leading Ben to the less expensive models. A shiny black and silver Trek caught Ben's eye. It came with a water bottle and holder. Ben glanced at his watch. He was to be at Evalyn's in twenty minutes.

"I want this one, but I need the seat adjusted and I'd like a rack over the back tire."

"I can have it done in five minutes flat," the owner offered. He wanted this sale and his young customer seemed to be in a hurry.

Ben grabbed a matching bike helmet, handed the man the credit card, and four and a half minutes later, the gardener wheeled the bicycle out of the shop and placed it in the rear of the van. Ten minutes later, Benson's driver dropped him off several blocks away from Oak Park and drove off.

Excited, Ben attached the basket to the rack. He drove through the park to Evalyn's house, where they agreed to meet up. For most people, riding a bike with friends was not a big deal. For Ben however, it *was* a big deal.

Since he'd met Christopher and Evalyn, his life had certainly improved. For the first time ever, he had friends, *real* friends. They accepted him, quirks and all, and since Christopher and Evalyn included him easily, so did most of the other kids at school.

Outside of her house, Evalyn was securing a bundle to a basket on her handlebars. She smiled and waved as Ben rode up. Christopher arrived a few moments later. Together, they rode off toward the river and then headed a few miles south. Fifteen minutes later, they arrived--hot, sweaty and laughing. A dip in the cool water was just what they needed.

Thick grass led down to small rocks at the water's edge. Several large trees provided shade. Ben had the only kickstand that worked. Christopher and Evalyn propped their bikes against one of the smaller trees.

Several speedboats roared down the center of the river. "Looks like fun." Christopher commented, pausing to watch them. Ben looked at the boats, then back to Christopher, thinking much but saying little, as was his way.

His thoughts were interrupted as Christopher asked for help with a strong rope he had brought, the one he used when rock climbing. He threw an end over to Ben and quickly made a tight knot, tying it to one of the largest overhead branches. He grabbed onto the end, swung out over the deeper water and let go, making a splash. Ben swung out next, spraying water on Evalyn as he landed in the river. It looked like fun, but since Evalyn couldn't swim; she kept cool wading in the shallow water.

"We could teach you how to swim, Evalyn." Ben assured her. "It's really not hard, once you get the hang of it."

"Yeah, it's like riding a bike," Christopher smirked, wiggling his eyebrows. "Stick with us kid," he mimicked, "We'll take you places... show you things."

Evalyn groaned aloud at Christopher's lousy Groucho Marks imitation. She really did think it was time she learned how to swim. "Ok, after lunch then."

"Don't worry Evalyn," Ben promised, awkwardly patting her arm. "We'll take it slowly."

They sat on a patch of thick grass by the riverbank and spread out their lunches. Benson's cook had packed several sandwiches made with thin slices of pink ham, in addition to turkey and roast beef. He brought enough to feed an army. It was just as well, since lately both Ben and Christopher were inhaling food.

There were icy soft drinks in an insulated container, and the small linen towels and hand sanitizer as Ben had requested. Evalyn brought enough chocolate cupcakes to share. Also, much to Ben's amusement, she brought along one of the bottles of gourmet ketchup.

"I'm waiting to discover something that she *doesn't* put ketchup on." Ben mused, shaking his head.

Christopher nodded, chuckling. He snatched the bottle and held it out of her reach.

Evalyn grabbed the confiscated bottle and spread ketchup liberally on one of the ham sandwiches.

"Would you like to go out on my boat with me sometime?" Ben asked offhandedly.

Christopher and Evalyn exchanged incredulous glances. "You've got a boat?"

Ben gave a slight lift of his shoulder, not wanting to make a big deal out of it. "Yeah. I'll take you out on it if you like." Evalyn stared at him, amazed.

"Do you think your dad would be able to find time to take us out?" Christopher looked hopeful. "He's usually pretty busy."

"Ah...er... it's my boat, not my dad's."

From the time he was six, Ben sailed with his father whenever he had time away from work—one of the few things they enjoyed together. By the time Ben was twelve, he was adept. He'd received the twenty-eight foot Bowrider as a gift from his father for his fourteenth birthday.

"You've got your own boat? Cool!" Christopher exclaimed.

Evalyn looked chagrined. Ben must have thought riding bikes down to picnic at the river was a silly, childish thing to do. Ben glanced her way, intuitively sensing what was on her mind.

"You probably find this boring," she murmured, gesturing with a quick wave of her hand. "Not at all. This is special to me, Evalyn," he said sincerely. "I've *never* ridden a bike with friends, or eaten sandwiches on a riverbank."

She was surprised at this bit of information, although too polite to show it. Boat or no boat, there were times she felt sorry for Ben. This was one of those times.

When they had eaten their fill, they stretched out on the grass, enjoying each other's company and the warmth of the afternoon.

Suddenly Evalyn sat up. "Listen!" she said sharply.

"I don't hear anything." Christopher looked bewildered.

"My point exactly. Where are all the boats that were here earlier?"

Ben looked at the river through narrowed eyes. True, there wasn't a boat in sight. Even the birds had disappeared. Dark, charcoal colored clouds were quickly blowing in from the north and within minutes, a strong wind whipped up. They could hear thunder and see lightning strikes several miles away. In a matter of moments, the dark sky ripped opened and rain poured down.

In the Midwest, this type of sudden weather change signaled danger. They realized they were too far from town to have heard the tornado warning sirens. The boaters would have heard the report on their radios.

Christopher and Ben jumped to their feet as a large tree next to them began to sway dangerously.

"Look!" Evalyn shouted. The wind was getting stronger, "Over there!" she pointed to the darkened northern sky.

A huge funnel was hurtling toward them. It seemed to be less than a mile away and moving fast. Within minutes, the force of the wind was so fierce they could hardly keep upright. Dirt and brush flew through the air.

They heard an earsplitting crack as a tree nearest them split in two, falling directly toward Evalyn. Christopher and Ben ran to her. Ben got to her first, throwing his body over hers seconds before the tree crashed down on them.

"Evalyn! Ben!" Christopher shouted, his words thrown away by the harsh gales. Frantically, he started tugging at the broken branches, the wind and rain whipping his face. While fighting to keep his footing, he pulled the tree limbs off his friends. Christopher could see blood flowing from the side of Ben's head, trickling down the back of his neck.

As quickly as the winds had started, they abated, leaving an eerie silence. The tornado turned eastward, across the river toward the Iowa side, leaving a dark, heavy cloud cover.

Evalyn struggled to get out from under Ben's weight.

"Evalyn!" Christopher shouted in relief when he saw her looking up at him from the ground.

"I'm all right, Christopher." Evalyn gasped. "It's Ben! He's not moving!"

Christopher pulled Ben off Evalyn and gently laid him on his back. He was still breathing, but had been knocked out cold.

Quickly Evalyn knelt beside him, glancing about to make certain they were not being watched. She closed her eyes, concentrating, allowing the energy to flow through her. She placed a hand gently on Ben's head; her fingers lightly brushed his eyes. Her other hand she lay lovingly over Benson's heart. Instinctively she sensed he also needed healing there.

Gently a shimmering radiance surrounded her. She breathed slowly and deeply. With each breath, the light increased. Amazed, Christopher watched as she leaned over Benson, awestruck by the beauty of Evalyn aglow. She seemed illuminated from inside.

Christopher could feel the peace, love and compassion flowing from her into Ben. She exhaled deeply, once again and slowly removed her hands. The glow subsided.

Benson stirred, moaned softly. "He should be fine now," Evalyn whispered.

"What happened?" Ben asked, dazed, sitting up, leaning on one elbow. "And what are you two whispering about?"

He felt inexplicably wonderful—better than he could ever remember feeling in his life. He felt calm, comforted. Somehow, he knew *everything* was going to be all right. Instantly and easily, he released the notion of his world falling apart. He no longer felt as if he had to control everything. The compelling, exhausting impulses, which had always been with him, were *gone*. The way he felt them float away reminded him of a bundle of balloons released into the clear summer sky. He felt incredibly light, free. He felt wanted. He felt... *loved*.

"You saved me, Ben," Evalyn marveled. "You threw yourself over me and saved my life."

Looking about, his head cleared. He saw the fallen tree and remembered covering Evalyn with his body. He also remembered feeling an intense pain—then total nothingness. He touched his head where he'd felt the pain. There was no pain now, not even a cut. Through his thick hair, his hand touched a sticky wetness. Puzzled, he held his hand in front of him, staring at the blood. He turned his head and saw blood trailing down onto his bare shoulder.

'What the ...?" Ben stared at the blood. It couldn't possibly be his—he felt no pain.

"Evie! Where are you hurt? The blood …?" Ben looked perplexed. Evalyn had no blood on her, only he did. But he wasn't hurt. Christopher appeared to be unhurt, as well.

So whose blood was it?

There was an uncomfortable silence. Evalyn's eyes were on the ground. Christopher was staring up at nothing. They were keeping something from him. He realized beyond a shadow of a doubt that the blood was his.

Sighing deeply, Evalyn sat on the damp ground and placed her face in her hands.

Ben didn't know what had happened, but he knew Evalyn had something to do with it.

She didn't say anything, but her forest green eyes gazed up at him, filled with compassion and caring, as always.

She glanced at Christopher. He looked away clearly leaving the decision to her.

"Okay, guys." Ben admitted grudgingly. "I know there's something going on here, and I know that both of you know what it is. I figured out it involves Evalyn because there's blood on the tips of her fingers. She had to have touched me because she's not hurt."

Hastily, Evalyn tried to hide her hand behind her, but was too late. He'd already seen it.

Getting to her feet, she walked over to Ben and hugged him tightly. She was relieved he was well— that she had been able to help him. So far, she healed when she needed to, but she feared a day would come when her ability might not work. Only time would tell if she had managed to heal his other problem. She reached for a crumpled towel lying on the ground and gently wiped the blood off him. She walked to the river's edge and dunked the cloth, rinsing out the towel.

"Trust us, Ben." Christopher eyed his friend intently. "You're better off knowing as little as possible.

Although Ben didn't know what was going on, he did know these were his friends—his first friends ever. He trusted them.

"Ok, it's alright. So… you're an alien or something. Don't worry, your secret's safe with me." He grinned at Evalyn and winked. "Hey, what planet are you from?"

Evalyn slapped him playfully. "I'm not an alien."

"It doesn't matter to me if you are, but *if* you are, when the mother ship comes for you, count me in!"

They all laughed then, mostly because they were young, and safe, and glad they had escaped the worst of the storm.

"Our families will be worried," Evalyn speculated, her eyes bright with concern. She started salvaging stuff that hadn't blown away into her basket. Christopher and Ben were looking around and packing what they could. It wasn't until Benson spotted his broken glasses on the ground, that he realized he didn't need them. For the first time in his life, he could see perfectly.

Their bicycles had been blown several yards away, had a few dings and scratches where they had been knocked around a bit, but were otherwise intact. They rounded up what they could salvage of their belongings and quickly headed home. They entered Oak Park from the south. They could see Becca frantically looking around. Broken tree limbs and other debris were scattered about on the ground.

"There you are!" she exclaimed, with obvious relief. "We've been searching everywhere! Evalyn, your mother's at our house worried sick!"

Ben seriously doubted anyone from his house was concerned about him. His parents were abroad as usual, his father on business, his mother jet setting or trying to outsmart the paparazzi. But this unpleasant part of his reality no longer bothered him. He felt a part of the Boldsen clan and also connected to Evalyn and her mother in a way in which he never had been with his own family. He cared for these people as much—if not more than those to whom he was connected by blood. He realized there were bonds as strong or stronger as those of family —the bonds of true friendship.

Becca looked them over, her gaze resting on Ben, her brother's friend. He returned her scrutiny, his gray eyes placid despite the destruction surrounding them. Something about him seemed different. Becca brushed the thought aside. It was probably just her imagination.

The remainder of the summer was uneventful, August was hot and unbearably humid. The mosquitoes were out in droves. Christopher and Ben spent a lot a time swimming in Ben's pool or on the river diving off the side of Ben's sport boat. They enjoyed the long, languid days on the river, with Ben at the helm. His boat had spacious seating in the open bow and a platform at the stern. Sometimes Becca would join them, which Ben enjoyed tremendously. He found her a total contrast to Evalyn.

Whereas Evalyn was petite and dark, Becca was almost as tall as her brothers, fair and freckled. Evalyn was gentle and quiet, Becca was boisterous—and despite her mother's best efforts—her speech was occasionally peppered with profanity. Her dives off the side of the boat were almost as good as Christopher's. She was four years older than they were and Ben and Evalyn both admired her. Christopher however, wasn't impressed.

Evalyn still hadn't gotten around to finding the time—or the courage—to learn how to swim. She knew her fear of swimming was irrational—she loved being near the water, enjoyed going out on the boat. Each time Ben would offer lessons, Evalyn would make excuses.

"I know how busy you are." Ben would say good-naturedly, laughing away her embarrassment. "Don't tell me—you've got to rearrange your sock drawer again."

With four children, the Boldsen's were used to a noisy household, and none of them minded having Ben around except

Christopher's brother Ace, of course. Except for a couple of weeks in July when Ben had flown to Italy for a holiday with his mother, Ben spent more time at the homes of his friends, than he did at his own.

On one particularly hot day, Ben was hanging out at the Boldsen's when Christopher overheard Ace make a snide remark about Ben under his breath. Pretending he didn't hear his brother's rudeness, Christopher 'accidently' spilled a glass of water in his brother's lap 'to cool him off'.

"Why don't you watch what you're doing, you clumsy..." When Ace abruptly left the room to change into dry pants, Christopher followed him.

"If you ever say or do anything to hurt Ben's feelings, I'm going to hurt *you*." Christopher was almost as big as Ace now and refused to accept his brother's bullish behavior, particularly when it was directed towards his friends.

Christopher and Darnell, a classmate who happened to live a few blocks away, were shooting hoops at Oak Park. Last year their school's basketball team had won the regional championship and since school was starting in a few weeks, they were practicing to make sure they'd be good enough to make the team. As they were finishing up, Ben sat on one of the benches, watching. He had stopped by the Boldsen's looking for Christopher and his mother had told him where he could find him. She asked Ben to tell him to come home for dinner and invited Ben to join them.

"Hey Ben. You gonna try out for the team?" Darnell asked, studying his tall friend's long arms enviously. "Tryouts are in six weeks."

Benson mulled it over a moment, "Sure," He shrugged. "Why not?"

Christopher looked at him in surprise. Other than a ballpoint pen, he had never seen Benson hold a ball of any kind. He seriously doubted if he had ever watched an NBA game—would bet his life that he'd never *played* basketball.

"Gotta go," Darnell announced, giving high fives before taking off. Christopher and Benson cut across the park.

"Basketball tryouts, Ben?" Christopher raised one eyebrow. "Really."

"There's a first time for everything," Benson chuckled. "Hey I got a lot to do—thank your mom for me, and tell her I'll take a rain check," he added. He was much too polite to say that eating at the Boldsens' was often a test of endurance.

When Christopher arrived home, Becca was setting the table and the rest of the family gathered round.

"I'm starving," Bob exclaimed. "What's for dinner? Whatever it is it smells great!"

Emily smiled. "I tried a new recipe—Brazilian bean stew. I know you'll love it." Her children exchanged wary glances.

She scooped the stew out of a large pot and passed steaming bowls around the table.

Bob took a large spoonful. Everyone at the table heard a loud cracking sound as he bit into something hard.

"I hope it wasn't my tooth." He made a wry face and looked at his wife.

"What's wrong?" she asked.

"Ah….Honey… the beans. They're almost as hard as stones."

Christopher peered suspiciously into his bowl. His spoon hit something hard. Maybe it *was* stones. With his mother's cooking, one never knew what to expect.

"But this time I followed the recipe exactly." Emily wailed. "I cooked the beans for thirty minutes."

Becca ran to the kitchen. The cookbook lay on the counter. Cookbook or not, Becca thought her mother was the worst cook on the planet.

"Hey mom," Becca yelled into the dining room, "the recipe says 'simmer the beans for two hours and thirty minutes'—not thirty minutes."

Emily looked chagrined.

Bob stood up. "Kids, go finish your homework," he directed. Accompanied by the sounds of scraping chairs and the clattering of silverware on dishes, the children exited from the dining room, glad to make their escape. Christopher paused a moment, to pat his mother on the hand.

"It's Ok, Mom," he said, comfortingly. "It may not be as good as Mrs. Williamson's chili, but I know you did your best."

Bob started to chuckle. Emily shot a fiery glare in his direction. In an attempt to stifle his laughter, he only managed to laugh harder.

"I'm glad that you find me so amusing," his wife replied dryly.

"I didn't marry you for your cooking." He winked, and leaned over to kiss her on the lips.

"Good thing or you'd be disappointed most days." Resignedly she reached for the telephone. "Guess I'd better call for Chinese take-out. Again."

As soon as Benson got home, he went find the manager of the Cunningworth's household.

"Max, please order an NBA regulation basketball hoop."

"Basketball hoop?" The house manager blinked in surprise. Other than the piano or video games, he had never seen the boy do anything athletic, although the mansion boasted a full gym, complete with machines as well as free weights.

"Ah...where would you like it to be installed?"

Benson paused a moment to ponder this. "On second thought, order two of them. Place one at each end of the tennis courts. No one uses the tennis courts anymore."

"When do you want this done?"

He grinned. "This week. And extend the tennis courts about twenty feet."

Max looked at Benson in exasperation. "That would be almost impossible. I'd have to arrange for contractors…" Max stopped short at Benson's determined look, and sighed. "I'll see what I can do."

Next, Ben went to his computer and researched the top NBA players of all time and ordered video tapes. He also ordered several books geared towards developing basketball techniques. In one of the books, he read how Michael Jordon, one of the greatest players of all time, would visualize making the basket with each shot before he went to sleep each night. Ben pondered this awhile. If visualization worked for Jordan…

By the end of the week, the equipment had been installed and the books and videos had arrived. After school and on weekends, Ben spent four to six hours every day practicing or studying ways to improve his game. He sweated like a horse and ate like one. At night he fell into bed exhausted and slept hard. For the first time in his life, his grades dropped. But he made the team.

With determined steps, Christopher took a shortcut through the park, on his way to Evalyn's house. She had promised to help him discover if he had the ability to feel the energy or tap into the source, as she called it and he was eager to discover if he had any such talent. But summer had come and gone and the only thing that Christopher had felt was annoyance. Evalyn had been unusually busy with ballet practice and trying to keep up with her homework. School had only been in session a few weeks and she had already fallen behind. Evalyn procrastinated almost as much as he did about assignments, usually putting them off until the last moment.

There was another thing he also found irritating. She was spending a lot of time with Yoli, one of their classmates, who joined them at lunchtime now and then. There wasn't anything wrong with Yoli—she was pretty and smart and funny, too. It was that he wasn't ready to have *anyone* move in and try to usurp his 'best friend' status, even if they were in high school. It was a rank he'd held since first grade. He shared Evalyn with Ben, perhaps begrudgingly at first, but this was where he drew the line.

By the time he arrived at Evalyn's front door, he had worked himself up into quite a state. Noticing Maddy's car was not in the driveway; he gave way to his aggravation and rapped loudly on the door. Without waiting for an invitation, he opened it and stomped in, scowling.

"What's with you?" Evalyn demanded. She was comfortably curled up on the living room sofa, watching television. Muting the sound, she gazed up. And up. Christopher had gotten taller. He was almost as tall as his older brothers. When had that happened?

"Evie, it's been months since you promised to help me," he ranted, glaring at her. "I've been trying on my own, but I can't seem to figure it out."

"Figure what out?" She asked, gazing at him with wide eyed innocence.

Christopher glared at her. Evalyn lowered her dusky, green eyes.

"You can't pull that innocent look on me, Evalyn Williamson. You know exactly what I'm talking about." Christopher used her given name, which meant he was in one of his rare moods.

Evalyn huffed, and turned off the television. She headed for the kitchen to check on a baking casserole. "So you really *are* serious."

She had hoped Christopher had changed his mind, or forgotten about it. Having this gift had only served to limit her choices, not expand them. She didn't know what could happen to Christopher if he achieved even a smidgen of success. There was no way of knowing in which direction the energy might lead him. The only thing she knew for certain was that the direction was chosen for the person and not the other way around. She also suspected the possibilities of using the energy were endless.

"So are you going to teach me or not?" His scowl deepened. He followed her back to the living room, flopping down next to her on the sofa.

"Christopher," Evalyn murmured resignedly, "I don't think this is something you have to learn, I think it's a part of us really."

"Huh?"

"I think we all have it, we just need to reconnect with it."

"It? What do you mean *It*?" Christopher gestured impatiently with his hands.

"I don't know exactly... but I have figured out a couple of things." She stared at the rug on the floor, as though the answers lay hidden in the intricate design.

"Ok! What things?" Christopher asked impatiently.

"Well, I do know it starts with the energy field...the power we all have all the time.

"Energy field?" His eyebrows furrowed. "What energy field?"

"Well you know, kind of like when you get an unexpected electric shock when walking across a carpet or touching a door handle... it's a part of it—a really small, but very important part.

She spoke slowly, trying to put her thoughts into words. "There are basically three steps involved. The first step is getting in touch with the energy, feeling it... to know it's there and search for it. The second step is harder."

Christopher listened intently to Evalyn's words, trying to grasp the meaning behind them. "Ok... so the first thing I have to do is to look for the energy...?"

"No, you're not listening to me. This is not a scavenger hunt—you don't have to look for it anymore than you need to search for the air your breathing right now. *Know* it's there, even though like air, you can't see it."

"So… just know it's there," he said impatiently. "Ok. It's there. *Now* what?"

"Get still enough to feel it flowing around and through you."

Christopher sat quietly, looking straight ahead, trying to focus on feeling the energy Evalyn tapped into so easily. After ten minutes he began to fidget.

"I don't feel anything, Evalyn."

Now it was Evalyn's turn to sigh. "Christopher, what you're trying to touch in a few short minutes, mystics have spent lifetimes searching for." She gave him an exasperated look. "I know you're a quick study but you'll need to give this some time."

"How much time?" he badgered. "How long will it take?"

She gave a slight lift of her shoulder. "It takes as long as it takes."

"I'm going to work on this, but …." He hesitated, not wanting to seem impetuous. "But what if you're busy—like you've been lately and we don't get a chance to talk about this for a while. What is step two?"

Evalyn smiled. "Step two is where the hard part starts. Once you connect with the energy, you have to become aware of your own thoughts."

"Thoughts?" Christopher was genuinely puzzled. "What thoughts? You mean the junk rattling around in my head?" Geez, he'd hate for anyone to see inside his mind… it would probably look like someone's great-aunt's attic, dusty and full of clutter.

"More specifically, it's about being aware of *what* you're thinking at the moment you're tapping into the energy." Evalyn spoke slowly, as though clarifying for herself. "I've noticed if my thoughts are not quite right, if my thoughts are selfish, doubting, or negative somehow, then I feel bad, and it just won't work."

"Bad? Describe bad."

She paused momentarily, trying to find the right words.

"Well, for me…kind of sick… nauseous. Like I need to make a mad dash for the nearest wastebasket. The more negative my thoughts are the worse, I feel." She made a face. "But in your case, the bad feeling might take a different form. You might feel dizzy or achy or something else. But whatever you feel, you'll know it if you're off center."

Christopher mulled this over. It was hard to imagine Evalyn thinking mean thoughts about anybody. She was undoubtedly the gentlest person he knew. It was one of the reasons he felt so protective of her, he didn't think she would recognize danger if she tripped over it. But then again, she didn't have Ace for a brother. Growing up with Ace had taught him to always keep looking over his shoulder. Imagining Evalyn being nasty towards anyone was almost as difficult as imaging Evalyn heaving. He'd never seen her sick, not even a sniffle. He also strongly suspected she could see better in the dark than others could. He'd been meaning to ask her about it. But it would have to wait until later; right now he had enough to wonder about.

"So any negative thought entering your mind, makes you feel bad?"

She laughed. "Thank goodness no! Not every thought—only those capturing my attention. So I've learned to let the negative thoughts just float on by, like the bubbles we used to blow when we were little kids. Remember?"

He nodded.

"But if I dwell on it, it becomes stronger. More *real* so to speak."

"Real, like how?" Christopher shifted in his seat.

"Close your eyes," she ordered.

"Now?"

"Yeah, right now."

Christopher closed his eyes.

"Tell me what you see."

"Well, it's dark…"

"See anything else?" she prompted. "Look closer."

Christopher was quiet as he scanned the blackness behind his closed eyelids.

"Yes!" he exclaimed. "It's like hundreds of tiny fireworks…"

"That's it! Now… watch closely. What are they doing?"

"They're vibrating! Christopher exclaimed, excited. "Like the silvery white and gold stick sparklers we hold on the fourth of July!" Christopher's eyes popped open.

Evalyn smiled, triumphantly. It's what I see and use when I heal. *Everyone* has this energy *all* the time. The more you use it the stronger it grows."

Christopher mulled this over, thinking about what he had just experienced when he had focused.

After a moment, he raised his head, his brows knitted together. "Ok, you said there were more parts to this. Give it up, Evalyn. What's after part two?" he demanded.

"First things, first," Evalyn replied adamantly. "Learn how to tap the energy at will, become aware of your thoughts, and then later you can learn how to focus it where you need it."

Christopher didn't know for sure, but somehow Evalyn's spiritual adventures—as she referred to their fieldtrips to various places of worship—contributed to her adeptness at using the energy. Since it had been a while since he'd gone with her and her mother, it might be beneficial if he invited himself along more often. Using the help of Spirit when tapping into the energy made sense. After all, as Maddy had once told him, "The worst thing that could happen from frequent prayer, was that one might possibly develop callused knees."

Ben was aware of Christopher's newfound fervor, although he wasn't aware of what was behind it. And like a good Jewish Catholic, as he referred to his faith when asked, he was open to new ideas and asked to join Maddy and Evalyn when he'd learned they were visiting the Transcending Yoga temple the following weekend.

The spacious whitewashed building was designed with wide archways. The windows were high in the walls, allowing light, but blocking distractions from outside. Maddy, Evalyn, Ben and Christopher removed their shoes, as they observed others doing, before entering the main room.

The floors of the sanctuary were littered with large, soft, satin cushions in a rainbow of colors. At the front of the temple was a simple alter decorated with fresh flowers. Sitting cross-legged on a large blue pillow below the alter, was a small man wearing a white linen robe. His eyes were closed and he chanted words in a language unfamiliar to Christopher.

"I think it's a Hindu dialect," Ben whispered.

Evalyn picked up a card placed on the pillow where she sat. Written on it was the English translation of the words, as well as how to pronounce them in the dialect. Maddy and Evalyn closed their eyes and murmured the simple chant which they had quickly memorized. Ben and Christopher followed suit.

Ben had never meditated before and he found the practice extremely soothing. Time passed quickly, and soon the simple service had ended.

"Ben, would you shake Christopher, please." In the quiet room, Christopher had fallen asleep.

"Hate to ruin a good nap, Christopher, but it's time to go," Ben chuckled. Christopher rubbed his eyes and yawned.

Evalyn pursed her lips. "Thank goodness he didn't snore this time." She and her mother exchanged knowing glances.

On the way out, Ben grabbed a brochure with schedules for meditations and services. He might look into this—maybe it might be something he could use.

He studied it in the car on the ride home, Christopher looking over his shoulder.

"What about levitating?" Christopher asked, pointing to a box on the flyer. "As in the-defy-gravity kind of levitating?"

Christopher was astonished. "Can people really do that sort of thing?"

Unconcerned, Maddy shrugged, "Well obviously someone can. How else could they teach it?"

After their first visit to the Transcending Yoga temple, Ben occasionally returned alone. Doing so seemed to strengthen the composure he had acquired since the tornado. Ultimately, it made him feel serene, peaceful.

Chapter 6

It was Saturday morning and when Christopher called Evalyn, he was happy to discover she didn't have dance practice today—she had the morning free. It had been weeks since Christopher had had his first lesson and was eager to meet with her. Although they saw one another often, usually they were surrounded by other people. They rarely got the opportunity to be alone. He had a full house today—all the Boldsens were in residence, even Matt who was home from college. Maddy was home working on a sewing project so Evalyn agreed to meet him at the park. Christopher was relieved. He wanted to talk to her again without being interrupted or overheard.

It was a perfect autumn day, the oak leaves were turning into molten gold, and the few maples interspersed throughout the park, were aflame with fiery red leaves. The air was fresh and crisp and smelled of fall. They both wore lightweight jackets and jeans. Evalyn had a bright green scarf wound around her neck. The leaves crunched underfoot as they walked across the wide expanse of lawn towards an empty bench.

Evalyn turned to face him, gazing intently into his eyes, She'd never realized it before, but his eyes were a mysterious shade of blue—a deep indigo flecked with sparks of silver.

So beautiful—like sunlight shimmering on deep lake water. She wondered why she had never noticed this before. But it was more than just his eyes, it was Christopher himself. There seemed to be something unusual about him— a sense of something moving, something almost fluid. Evalyn couldn't quite figure out what it was.

Christopher waved his hand in front of her face. "Earth to Evalyn. Come in, Evalyn." He demanded jokingly.

She smiled, forcing her eyes in another direction, stalling, trying to recall what they had been talking about before she lost herself completely in the depths of Christopher.

What had they been talking about? Yes, tapping into something...

Christopher continued, "It's like you're making some sort of connection. You light up like you were plugged into a socket."

Evalyn laughed. "You make it sound like I'm a lamp."

"Well, you do glow."

"I do?" Evalyn was surprised. She hadn't realized this.

"You mean you didn't know?" Christopher asked.

Evalyn shot him a direct look. "What? Do you think I do this while staring into a mirror?"

"A soft light flows around you that gets brighter the longer you stay connected ... or whatever it is you're doing," Christopher explained. "I notice it's easier to see in dim light. More noticeable."

"Oh." Evalyn was stunned. No wonder Maddy had worked so hard to protect her when she was younger, keeping her close during the daytime, never letting her spend the night out. A glowing child would be difficult to explain.

Oh, great. Other people talk in their sleep, I glow!

"I've fasted, prayed, meditated, and twisted myself into yoga postures that practically put me in traction." His brows knit together in a deep scowl. "And I'm still not getting it."

"I think you're making it harder than it is.

"But you can do this!" Christopher exclaimed in exasperation. "Why can't I?"

"You're not listening—you're trying too hard. You're trying to force yourself to go in my direction when you need to find a direction of your own."

"But maybe it's just you," Christopher argued. "You're special." He studied her, thinking. "Maybe there was a star shining in the east when you were born, or something."

Shocked, Evalyn stared at Christopher. Then abruptly she broke into uncontrollable peals of laughter. She laughed until tears came into her eyes, her shoulders shaking with convulsions.

Wiping the tears away, she gasped, "Christopher, three wise women didn't visit our house bearing gifts." She added, "And although frankincense and myrrh may have their place, there were times when gold sure could have come in handy."

The junior year had started. With each passing season, Evalyn grew lovelier and more graceful. Christopher and Ben grew taller—Christopher's arms were hard and muscled from swimming; and due to regular basketball practice, as Benson grew taller than Chris, he had become quick and wiry. The attractive trio would have been surprised if they had known they were often the envy of others.

Invariably, when girls found out Christopher and Ben were 'just friends' of Evalyn's a few of them would try to get close to her as a way to get closer to the boys. Occasionally one of the girls would catch Christopher's eye, others he would laugh off; but the attention from girls made Ben feel unsettled and shy. The only girls that Ben felt comfortable being around were Evalyn and Becca. Lately, Megan, a curvy redhead, was quite persistent and she had her eye on Christopher.

"She's known as 'Ms. Red-headed and ready," Yoli informed Evalyn in the girls' PE locker room. According to Yoli, who knew enough gossip floating around the school to start her own tabloid, Megan had dated most of the guys at school.

"Ready for what?" Evie asked, innocently.

Yoli rolled her eyes. "Chica, tu sabes nada!" she muttered in Spanish. "You probably don't know how babies are made!"

Evie placed her hands on her slim hips. "I do know! I paid very close attention in health class!"

Yoli chortled. "Health class is sex 101. Megan's operating at the college level." Yoli jerked her head to the left, spotting the red-head walking quickly in their direction. "Speaking of Megan, here she comes now."

Yoli slammed the locker shut and darted off to class leaving Evalyn with her.

"So…you and Christopher are best buds…?" Megan asked, watching as Evalyn shoved her gym clothes into the bottom of her back pack and placed the books on top where she could reach them easily.

"Oh yeah, I've known him since first grade."

"He's not your boyfriend—you guys aren't going together or anything?" Not that Megan cared—she had broken up many a happy couple—prided herself on it in fact. After getting the guy, she'd drop him faster than a worm ridden apple before going on to the next unfortunate.

"Uh…no. We're just friends. Best friends." This was getting tiring. Lately too many girls had been asking her the same question.

"Well…gotta go." Evalyn gave Megan a short wave and disappeared from the locker room.

Megan leaned against the lockers. This was going to be easy, she thought smugly. To her, boys were like an ice cream parlor and Christopher was the newest flavor of the month.

For a day or two, Megan followed Christopher to see where his classes were, and to find out with whom he spent his time. Usually he was with either Ben or Evalyn. The only girl she saw him with regularly was Evalyn, or Evalyn's friend Yoli, who joined them at lunch with several other friends. Megan managed to show up wherever Christopher was and if anyone else was in earshot, she had a clever way of making it sound like he was interested in her. She fell into step with him on the way to class, and leaned in close, slowly sliding her hand down his arm.

"Nice biceps!" she purred, tossing her thick red mane. "Bet you're a good ...hugger," she added in a husky whisper. Christopher grinned, and stepped around her to go to class.

Megan's eyes narrowed. She wasn't used to being overlooked and it didn't sit well with her. She'd have to try a little harder— make it impossible for him to ignore her.

The next day, Christopher was at his locker which was located on the top floor, near the corner. Several students were milling around, others were heading into classrooms. As he played with the combination, he heard the staccato sound of high heels on the tile floor. He glanced up to see Megan carrying a large stack of books. She met his eyes, feigning surprise as the stack of books crashed to the floor. Christopher, as well as a few others nearby bent to help her retrieve them.

"Oh, don't bother," she chimed to the others, "Christopher is helping me."

She bent over him while he knelt on one knee gathering her books. She wore a tightly fitted black sweater which showed lots of cleavage. A short skirt set off her long legs which ended in four inch heels. The hallway had cleared, leaving the two of them alone. Megan knew an opportunity when she saw one. As they stood, she leaned closer. Christopher caught the scent of her perfume. It was strong, bold.

She pressed closer to him. "I need to thank you properly," she purred softly.

Christopher turned his face towards her. "That's not..." he was about to say 'necessary', when Megan pressed her lipsticked mouth firmly against his. His body responded immediately but despite the flash of heat surging through his groin, he turned his face away angrily.

Megan was stunned. Never had she been rebuffed by any male over the age of five.

"Oh, I understand." She retorted, tossing her head. "You like those dark, exotic types."

It took Christopher a second to figure out to what she was alluding. He flushed, grasping her hidden meaning. Then his eyes glinted like blue steel.

"Incorrect assumption," he responded through gritted teeth. "I'm not into *types*. My best friend happens to be a girl, who *happens* to be Black. I'd feel the same way about her if she were green."

Displeased and disgusted, he stepped around Megan. *Oh, I'll make you pay for ignoring me, Christopher,* she vowed silently. Christopher took the steps to the floor below two at a time while her eyes shot daggers into his retreating back.

The smell of Megan's heavy perfume clung to him. Unconsciously he thought of Evalyn, comparing the red-head's garish perfume to Evalyn's soft, warm scent. Evalyn would never wear anything like that, he thought. She always smelled delicious—like spring flowers after the rain.

Christopher slid into the empty seat between Ben and Evalyn. Evalyn studied him momentarily, and then glanced away quickly, baffled, by the tears that flooded her eyes.

What's wrong with me? Why should I care? She began scribbling notes furiously, in an effort to ignore him.

Ben tapped Christopher lightly on the shoulder. "That lipsticks' not your color," he said humorously, handing him one of his fine monogrammed handkerchiefs. Christopher wiped his mouth. He looked at the flame colored smear on the white linen and swore softly. Evalyn turned her head, inconspicuously wiping away an errant tear, a gesture that didn't go unnoticed by Ben.

Evalyn trudged down the block to her house. It had been a miserable day. This morning, she'd packed a lunch which she'd forgotten to bring and the food in the cafeteria had been worse than usual. She'd flunked the Spanish quiz, and then—when she thought her day couldn't have gotten any worse—she watched Christopher wipe Megan's lipstick off his mouth. Even without the lipstick, it would have been clear to anyone with a nose that he'd been with Megan—he reeked of her signature fragrance. Evalyn wondered if he really liked Megan or if he was just another one of Megan's many flings. But now she just wanted to get home, get something to eat, take a long soak in a hot bubble bath, and forget this day ever happened.

She opened the white picket gate into her yard. Loretta Alexander, a neighbor from across the street, called out and beckoned to her. The young woman looked frantic. Evalyn dropped her backpack on the lawn and crossed the street to see what was going on.

"Hi Loretta, what's up?"

"Could you please look after Brandon while I run to the pharmacy to pick up a prescription for him?"

The young, single mother had dark circles under her eyes, and looked like she hadn't had a good night's sleep in several days.

"His asthma's been so bad lately and on top of it, he's caught a cold and is running a fever."

"Sure, I'd be happy to help out." Evalyn followed her through their sparsely furnished home, into her son's room. The toddler was asleep in his bed, his cheeks brightly flushed.

"I'll sit here and keep an eye on him for you, don't worry."

Loretta threw a grateful glance in Evalyn's direction, slung her purse over her shoulder and hurried out. Evalyn heard the car pull away from the house. The vaporizer in the room was turned off. She checked it—the medication chamber was empty. It must be one of the things Loretta was picking up at the drug store. Several inhalers were strewn across the top of the dresser.

Evalyn smiled at the sleeping boy. He looked like such an angel—although she knew he could be a little imp on occasion.

He was flushed and his breathing seemed slightly ragged. She felt sympathy for him and his mother. According to neighborhood rumors, her husband had abandoned them both. Most of her meager salary was spent on medicines and doctors, but in spite of dire financial struggles, she was a good mother.

Evalyn sat on the bed next to Brandon and placed her cool hand over his forehead. He seemed to be running a slight fever. She sat quietly and bowed her head as a soft shimmer surrounded her. Ever so gently, she allowed the energy to flow from her into Brandon. Within minutes she felt his temperature drop and watched his coloring return to normal. Evalyn placed her hand over his small chest. She could feel the congestion in his lungs, as he struggled to breathe. Again she allowed the power to flow into the child. Within moments his lungs were cleared. She removed her hands and the radiating glow diminished.

Taking a deep breath, Brandon open his eyes, stared at her a second before recognizing her and rewarding her with a bright, dimpled smile. She opened her arms and he scampered into them.

"Your mommy will be right back," Evalyn offered. She noticed a battery operated 'Sing Along' on the top of his toy box and went to retrieve it.

"Why don't we sing until she gets here?"

Together they sang, Old McDonald and were into 'Twinkle Little Star," when Loretta returned. She entered her son's room in time to hear the last chorus of "Twinkle."

"Mommy!" Brandon scampered off the bed and ran to her. Stunned, Loretta scooped up her son in one arm and sat him on her hip. Amazed, she looked at Evalyn.

"His fever has broken! He hasn't been able to breathe this clearly for days! He's been to the emergency room twice this month because of the asthma."

Evalyn shrugged nonchalantly. "Seems like he's taken a turn for the better."

Brandon took several deep, clear breaths and smiled. His mother placed the bag on the dresser and kissed her son on the cheek.

"Sorry, Evalyn, rather than trouble you, I guess I should have been patient and waited for this thing to turn. But with kids, you never know."

"Oh, it's no trouble, we had fun, too."

Brandon tugged his mother's sweater. "Mommy, I'm hungry."

Loretta laughed. "Good! I'll fix you something yummy."

They walked Evalyn to the front door and Loretta thanked her. Evalyn hugged her before darting across the street. She picked up her backpack where she had dropped it in the yard. Her mood had lifted and she entered the house singing. Brandon would never have an asthma attack again.

Chapter 7

*A*s the school year progressed the group at their table grew larger. Like most teens, lunch was their favorite period. Some of them were kids they knew from elementary school, like Darnell Thomas and Andrew McCauley, others were boys Christopher had met on the basketball or swim teams. Occasionally, a group of them would hang out after school at the mall or at Oak Park.

Evalyn thought it was a good thing Yoli sat with them now and then. She enjoyed the guys company, but sometimes there was just too much testosterone buzzing around the table. A few of the guys had PE right before lunch and there were days when their table smelled like a locker room.

"*Please* shower before sitting here," Yoli ordered, digging through her backpack. "I've got spray deodorant and I'm not afraid to use it!" she threatened, pointing the metal cylinder at the closest offender.

The boy leaned away from her, laughing. When the bell rang, the group scrambled for books and backpacks, rushing out of the cafeteria.

Walking several paces behind the girls were Christopher, Ben, and Darnell. Darnell let out a soft whistle. "Keats was right!"

Ben agreed, "A thing of beauty *is* a joy forever."

Christopher smirked. "Yeah, Yoli sizzles."

"Yoli? She's not bad—but Evalyn's the sexiest girl in school." Christopher felt a hot flush of anger, which surprised him. Like most things, this didn't go unnoticed by Ben. Quickly Christopher cooled down.

"She is?" he asked, astounded.

Darnell shook his head, laughing. "I know you two have been friends forever, but my man—are you *blind?*"

Christopher watched, scowling. Evalyn turned the corner, her hips swinging gracefully in a short denim skirt. *His Evalyn, sexy? No way!*

"I was a real happy guy when I found out she wasn't your girlfriend. Nice to know she's up for grabs." Darnell grinned widely and winked. "I get first dibs." Christopher's scowl deepened.

He doesn't know he loves her! Ben was astonished, watching as anger and jealously simultaneously flitted across Christopher's face.

'C'mon,' Christopher admonished gruffly, changing the subject, "or we'll be late."

The days were getting warmer and the daffodils she had planted with her mother last fall were blooming by the front steps. Through the kitchen window, she could see pale green leaves starting to sprout on the trees. She loved spring mornings like this, particularly after having such a harsh winter.

Christopher knocked on the front door and opened it, calling out as he entered.

"In here, Chris," Evalyn shouted from the kitchen. She arranged the Easter eggs she had just colored, prettily in a bowl, adding silk flowers. Christopher turned the chair around backwards and sat on it, resting his arms on the top of the chair back, watching her. He thought she could make anything took artistic, even eggs in a bowl. After adding a few finishing touches, she stood back admiring her handiwork before peeling the shells from a couple of them and placing them onto a plate. She reached for the ubiquitous ketchup bottle.

"Want one?" She asked, offering him a multicolored egg from the bowl.

"No, I'll pass." He watched as she dumped a blob of ketchup onto her plate.

"What are you doing, creating a new Easter tradition? It looks like some type of bloody sacrifice."

Evalyn daintily dipped a boiled egg into the ketchup. "Yum!" she smacked dramatically as she bit into it.

Christopher stuck his index finger down his throat, pretending to gag. Evalyn snickered, before taking another bite.

Rising from his chair, he opened a cabinet and took out a bowl. He found a box of cereal in another cabinet. Juggling them both in one hand, he opened the refrigerator and took a carton of milk and grabbed a clean spoon out of the dishwasher.

"Make yourself at home, why don't you?" Evalyn mumbled sarcastically.

Christopher grinned. "Don't mind if I do." He poured the cereal into his bowl and piled on the sugar.

"Do you really think so much sugar is good for you?"

"Probably not, but it sure tastes better than eggs and ketchup." Evalyn looked at him doubtfully.

They ate in companionable silence for a while, each deep in their own thoughts.

"I'm not sure what's real anymore," Christopher mused. "What I once thought was real seems dreamlike and the things we talked about before seem more like reality."

Evalyn had paused, listening.

"I feel like my body is just the container for what's real. Just something to keep the energy contained in one place." He reached for more cereal and poured it into his bowl. "It's like the frosted flakes are the real me and the box is just my body."

She nodded. "Yeah, like packaging." She understood him perfectly. She'd felt this way her entire life.

"At first I thought it was something I needed to do, but that's not it," turning his head slightly to look at her. "I really don't need to do anything, do I?"

Evalyn agreed. "It's more like... being receptive, open. The only thing we *really* need to do is to get out of the way and let it flow. Just be."

Christopher was pensive.

"Just sleep on it," Evalyn advised. "It'll come to you."

After a while, their conversation drifted to other topics. They discussed teachers, Ben, and others.

Evie hesitated for a moment, before casually saying, "I think Megan is into you." After hearing the rumors, and seeing her lipstick on Christopher, she had to know if the attraction was mutual—although she wasn't quite sure why it mattered to her. But it did.

Christopher flushed, thinking about how the well-endowed dazzler had cornered him by his locker.

"All the guys seem to think she's so hot she sizzles." Evalyn said, pushing for Christopher's response.

Not this guy, Christopher thought, scowling. Besides, he had regularly caught guys staring at Evalyn, watching her as she moved gracefully through the halls. This bothered him more than he liked to admit. He wished they'd focus their eyes on someone else, but her dark, delicate beauty was hard to ignore.

Evalyn pushed her plate away. Christopher had finished eating too, and stood up to take his dish to the sink. Opening the dishwasher and noticing it was full of clean dishes, he began to unload them and put them away. Evalyn came up behind him and slipped her arms around his waist.

"Thanks for helping me. And besides, a guy working in the kitchen is a wonderful sight", she teased, squeezing him tightly.

His reaction took him by surprise. Heat surged to the pit of his stomach as he fought an unfamiliar urge to pull her into his arms. *What's this?* He wondered, confused. He let his breath out slowly, his back still to her, struggling to regain his composure. Evalyn had always hugged him—she hugged everybody. But her hugs had never had this effect on him before. Why now?

It had been weeks since Evalyn had seen Megan's lipstick on Christopher, but she continued to wonder if there was anything to the rumors—not that it mattered.

"So what about Megan?" she asked, stepping around him. Evalyn's scent unnerved him. She smelled good—she always did, but today he noticed that she smelled innocent and sweet—like rain-drenched flowers.

"She's telling everyone that you're going to ask her out." Evalyn continued. Her soft body brushed against his chest and arms as she reached up to put the rest of the things away. A second blast of heat surged through him.

"Are you?" she asked, a slight frown marring her pretty face.

"What?" Christopher snapped. "No, I'm not going out with her."

Evalyn felt relieved, although she wasn't sure why. He wiped forehead with his hand. "It's hot in here. Gotta go."

Evalyn shrugged. He did look warm, although the temperature felt fine to her. She finished putting the last of the dishes away. The door banged as he left.

Evalyn was deep in thought, as she and Yoli walked to PE together. Thoughts about Christopher, that is. He was on her mind as usual, but her thoughts about him seemed to flow in a different direction—kind of dreamy and soft. She wondered if he ever thought about her differently, or if he only considered her in the same way as he did Becca, as a sister.

She never had a brother, but lately her thoughts about Christopher were anything but brotherly. She had no experience with romance, no other feelings she could compare it to. Yoli, on the other hand, seemed to excel in the boy department.

"Yoli," Evalyn began hesitantly. "If you wanted a boy to notice you, and he didn't, what would you do?"

Yoli laughed, "That's an easy one, Evalyn. *Not* getting them to notice is a lot harder."

"For you, maybe."

Yoli stopped. "You're not serious."

Evalyn stared at Yoli blankly.

"Boys look at you all the time!" Yoli exclaimed. By the look on Evalyn's face, she realized Evalyn didn't have a clue.

Evalyn gave Yoli an impatient scowl. "So...what do I do to get a boy to notice me?"

Yoli flipped her dark hair over her shoulder. "You flirt with him."

"Flirt? How?"

Exasperated, Yoli shook her head. "*Chica*, I can't believe you're sixteen and don't know how to flirt!" Astonished, Yoli started mumbling to herself in Spanish. Evalyn looked chagrined; she picked up enough of the inflection to know she was being chastised.

"Ok, ok. Do it like this," Yoli ordered. She lowered her chin, glanced out of the corners of her eyes at Evalyn and batted her long, sooty lashes.

"That stuff works on guys?" Evalyn asked, doubtfully. Surely, it couldn't be that simple.

"Every time." Yoli smirked.

Evalyn couldn't wait for school to end so she could get home to practice in the mirror.

Another Friday rolled around. Chemistry was the last class of the day. Christopher, Evalyn, and Benson hustled through the halls toward the classroom. Their homework assignment had been to read the chapter about atomic structure. Unfortunately,

Christopher had forgotten to take his chemistry book home. He'd left it in his locker yesterday, so he wasn't prepared. He just hoped Mr. Kinsley didn't surprise them with a pop quiz. Benson and Evalyn were ready. For once Evalyn hadn't procrastinated.

Unlike Benson, who found chemistry fascinating, the subject bored Christopher to death. Just thinking of the word 'science' gave him the urge to climb into a coffin, close the lid, and beg someone to throw dirt over him.

"I don't know what the problem is," Ben chided. "Science is cool." Christopher totally disagreed. Girls were cool, swimming was cool. He hoped he could make it through class without nodding off—not that Mr. Kinsley would notice.

He and Evalyn had planned to hang out at Benson's after school so he was particularly eager for school to end. Benson's father had given him a new portable gaming system purchased in Japan on a business trip. This one wasn't for sale in the United States yet. Called the Nintendo Rage, it had two screens. Christopher had read about it and couldn't wait to give it a try.

Christopher considered Benson extremely lucky—his parents weren't around often enough to nag him and they were extremely generous with money and gifts. At the Boldsen's there was an entertainment center with an outdated television and stereo. Benson's house had an entire room for entertainment. It held an Xbox, a PlayStation 3, *and* a Wii plus the largest television he had ever seen recessed into one of the media room walls. On one side were desks holding computers with light-speed Internet access. When Christopher first visited this media room, as Benson called it, he didn't want to leave.

The three of them headed for the back of the classroom, rather than in their assigned seats. The absent-minded Mr. Kinsley often forgot to call the roll anyway. The instructor had the stereotypical demeanor of the mad scientist. His hair was wiry and unruly; his plaid bowtie was askew. The suit he wore hadn't been in style in twenty years, but in spite of his idiosyncrasies, the students liked him.

"As most of you learned while in junior high, all elements are made of atoms," Kinsley lectured, his voice raspy. "And although they may have different weights and different organization, their basic structure is the same."

Christopher could see Ben, leaning forward at his desk, engrossed. Evalyn was taking notes. Good, he'd get them from her later and Ben would be able to explain anything he couldn't decipher from her scribble. He leaned back, crossed his arms over his chest, and closed his eyes. He was sorry he didn't have sunglasses with him or he'd have put them on and been able to have an undetected nap.

Kinsley droned on, "Whether we're viewing the smallest particles of matter or huge ecosystems, it's basically the same." He paced back and forth at the front of the room. "Take water, for example. At least seventy percent of the human body is composed of water."

At the mention of water, Christopher opened one eye.

"Water molecules are constantly moving in relation to each other, and the hydrogen bonds are continually breaking and reforming at incredible speeds—one millionth of a nanosecond."

"What would something moving at such speed look like, if you could see it under a microscope?" Benson asked, interested.

Mr. Kinsley paused. "Well for one thing, unless it was a very high-resolution type of microscope, it would appear to be a blur, more like vibration," he answered. "In order to see it fully, we'd need an atomic force microscope. Unfortunately, that's not in the school budget," he chuckled.

Mr. Kinsley resumed his pacing. "This energy creates an incredibly strong bond. In fact, it's this strength that gives water its unique properties."

Properties of water? Christopher opened the other eye and sat up. The chemistry teacher had his undivided attention. Water was his element. He drank quarts of it daily, loved to swim in it, and compared to most of the teens he knew, showered more often. While many others took it for granted, he appreciated it deeply. Although he would never admit it to anyone, he suspected that this high regard was mutual.

Mr. Kinsley spoke as he wrote on the blackboard, "water is quite receptive and it's a known conduit."

A conduit for what? Christopher wondered. What did it channel?

"…additional properties are adhesion and cohesion. And one other important thing to know is that water has a high level of surface tension," the teacher scribbled a few additional points just as the bell rang, signaling the end of the day.

Most of students headed for the door in a mad rush, eager for the weekend. Lost in thought, Christopher sat in his seat, trying to make sense of what he had just heard.

He had always felt water held some mystery—some secret he felt compelled to discover. He would read over the chapter carefully so he could better understand Mr. Kinsley's lecture. Perhaps these properties held the key. He'd ask Benson about them when he had the chance. He tucked his chemistry book in his pack and headed for the door to join his friends.

They piled into Benson's Jeep and headed for the exclusive Dundee estate. This was Evalyn's first visit to Benson's place and she was excited. She'd heard from Christopher how awesome it was—the kind of house she and her mother would drive by and wonder who the occupants were.

Radio blaring, Benson drove onto a sedate, maple-lined street. He pulled up to a tall wrought iron gate, which parted slowly as the Jeep approached. He continued up the long, curved driveway lined with maples, coming to a halt in front of a stately brown and white Tudor, surrounded by an immaculate expanse of lawn with carefully tended gardens.

There was a patio off to one side and balconies protruded from several rooms on the upper floors. On opposite ends of the manor, two large chimneys towered above the roof. Benson parked directly in front and led his friends up the wide stone steps, to elegant double doors beneath a beveled glass transom. A servant opened the doors for them, while another servant discretely drove the car around the drive to the rear of the house to the large garage.

A mahogany grandfather clock chimed softly as they entered. Evie slowly looked around, eyes widening with each step. She looked up. The ceiling was so high that it almost made her dizzy. Christopher laughed aloud at the stunned expression on Evalyn's face. He was sure he wore a similar expression the first time he hung out at Benson's. She looked around in amazement.

The foyer's floor was made of black and white Italian marble. High above their heads, hung a huge gilt and crystal chandelier that sparkled like diamonds. The walls were papered in subtle shades of beige and cream and one wall held an original *trompe l'oeil* painting of a garden within a garden. Several pieces of red upholstered furniture were arranged in front of the huge fireplace. Winding staircases on each end of the foyer led to the upper level. Off the entry was a large, sunny music room. She felt like she had awakened in Disneyland.

"I told you it was awesome." Christopher chided.

"Ben, your home is beautiful!" Evalyn exclaimed, turning to him. Benson blushed graciously. She pointed to a grand piano visible through an archway. Benson's blush deepened. Of course he played—with such long elegant fingers, it would be a shame for him not to.

"Would you like to see the music room?" he offered, leading the way.

The music room was light and sunny with large windows facing west. The muted colors of the walls and furniture matched those of the entry. The focal point of the room was an ebony grand piano, polished to perfection. On a far wall was a large portrait of a couple dressed in stylish clothing from a century ago. The man was fair with dark brown hair, grey eyes and a mustache. Evalyn moved closer to stand directly underneath the portrait. The woman had raven hair, ebony eyes and olive skin. Evalyn turned to Benson questioningly.

"My great-grand parents," he responded to her unspoken question. He laughed and added, "Family history has it that my great-grandmother was a gypsy and it was through her suggestions my great-grandfather made his fortune."

"Ben!" Evalyn teased, "You've got gypsy blood!"

Benson laughed, "If the story is true, then perhaps I do."

Evalyn turned away from the portrait and ran her hand over the smooth, cool surface of the piano. "You'll play for me?" Evalyn asked. She loved music. Benson nodded.

"Yeah, yeah," Christopher interrupted, "but not now."

"I'll play for you the next time you visit. I promise." He led the way through the house to the media room. The media room had polished wood floors, covered by a thick oriental carpet, and comfortable suede and leather chairs.

Christopher rubbed his hands together as he entered, "Now let the games begin!" he announced dramatically, flexing his fingers.

The sounds of laughter coming from the room caused the household staff to pause and smile. Laughter was the one thing the mansion lacked.

The family cook had outdone himself. The small kitchen alcove in the media room held three kinds of pizza, and a special bacon burger with cheddar cheese on freshly baked buns. There were crispy onion rings, fries, and a wide-mouthed cruet filled with gourmet catsup, which Evalyn found delightfully delicious.

The cook could always be certain when Benson would be out for the evening as Benson considerately called him whenever he knew he wouldn't be home for dinner. He often enjoyed the rowdy fun at Christopher's house as well as the warm comfort he found at the Williamson's.

Many mornings when the Cunningworth's housekeeper tidied Benson's room, she noticed his bed had not been slept in. She wondered where a sixteen-year-old could possibly be spending so many of his nights. These friends of Benson's solved the mystery. The boy always looked so lonely—she was glad he had friends now.

Later, after playing several hours of games and eating, it was time to leave. Evalyn was reluctant to go but she promised her mother she'd be home by midnight. Benson and Christopher had to be up early the next day; they were going rock climbing on Saturday and Benson was staying over at Christopher's house tonight.

As Evalyn walked through the elegantly furnished rooms, she understood why Benson spent so much time at their homes. As beautiful as the mansion was, it felt empty, cold. She didn't mind visiting, but it wasn't the type of place where she would want to live.

She also sensed the real reason Benson's parents lavished him with so many things—they thought it would be an effective substitute for what he really needed and for what they failed to give him—their love and affection.

All of a sudden, Evalyn was in a hurry to get home. She could hardly wait to give her mother a big, tight hug.

Christopher and Benson went out to the Bluffs. While the Bluffs didn't offer the best climbing, they were the tallest hills in the vicinity and would have to do. They drove across the river into Iowa, past cornfields, through Crescent—a town of about three hundred people. Benson drove, glancing around dubiously. Not a mountain in sight, just a few very low hills.

"They aren't very big," Christopher acknowledged, "although people do ski there in the winter, when there's a good snowfall."

"Skiing. Here. Please tell me you're joking." Benson pleaded, parking near one on the larger of the small grassy mounds.

"No, I'm not kidding." Christopher laughed and climbed out of the jeep. "At least it's a change from the rock climbing wall. Let's check it out."

They sported climbing boots, and brought ropes, chalk and a crash pad with them. After an hour or so, they were sweaty and tired, but unfortunately, they didn't find the challenge they had expected. Rather than the rock and stone, the Bluffs were mostly dirt clods and clumps of grass.

They settled themselves at the bottom and pulled out the sandwiches they'd fixed at Christopher's house earlier. Christopher sat cross-legged while Benson stretched out his long, lanky frame, enjoying the warmth of the sun.

"Fontainebleau would be great this time of year," Benson muttered thoughtfully, his mouth full.

"Where?" Christopher queried, and then took a guess, knowing there probably wasn't a continent to which Benson hadn't traveled. "In the Swiss Alps, maybe?"

"Close," Benson smiled. "Fontainebleau, France, actually. Great climbing. Not too dangerous."

"Where's the fun in that?" Christopher retorted, grinning. His expression grew more serious as he began to think about the lecture the chemistry teacher had given on the properties of water.

"Hey Ben, did you get what Kinsley was talking about?" Christopher asked nonchalantly, pretending to pick grass off his shirt.

"About atoms, about water quality or whatever?" Benson was brilliant, of course he understood, Christopher was banking on it—Ben always got A's in chemistry.

Benson nodded. "Yeah... properties of water. Pretty interesting stuff when you think about it."

Christopher decided to give it up—so what if he looked stupid—Benson was his friend and accepted him warts and all.

"So what was Kinsley ranting on about this cohesion, adhesion stuff. Sounds sticky—like gum or something."

Benson laughed, "You're close. Cohesion refers to how water sticks to itself easily, beads up."

"Like it does on a waxed car?" Christopher asked.

"Exactly. Adhesion simply means that when water comes into contact with certain things, the adhesive forces are stronger. Instead of sticking together in a ball, it spreads out."

Christopher mulled this over for a moment.

"So what did he mean exactly, about surface tension?"

"Just that the molecules on the surface of the atoms are different than the molecules on the sides," Benson explained patiently.

Christopher nodded, "I think I'm getting this. It's why cohesion is possible." He finished his sandwich and reached for a bottle of water. He held it high, noticing how the sunlight danced when he shifted the bottle in his hands.

Everything in existence had certain common components. In reality, there were only slight differences between him and water—differences that came down to arrangements of atoms. He wondered if it would be possible for him to connect and strengthen the bond. He knew, without a doubt, it was what Evalyn did effortlessly.

"Ok, one more question." Christopher held up an index finger. "Why is water blue?"

Benson laughed, "That's an easy one. Because water molecules scatter blue wavelengths, absorbing them and then rapidly flinging them off in different directions. It's why mostly blue wavelengths are reflected back to our eyes."

He turned to Christopher grinning triumphantly, "Told you science was cool."

Chapter 8

M addy and Emily were walking together in the park, as they did on rare occasions when the weather was reasonable and their households didn't demand their attention. This was about as likely as finding a four-leaf clover in the Sahara.

Today they had the unexpected opportunity to enjoy one another's company, so they talked about their jobs, and about local politics, until the conversation drifted to their children.

"Matt seems to like college, he's doing well," Emily reported proudly. "I wish he'd influence his brothers. Ace mentioned joining the military, instead of going to college. Christopher will be a senior in the fall. He's been offered two swimming and diving scholarships but can't seem to make up his mind about what he wants to do. Bob and I encourage the kids to make their own decisions, but…"

"Panzella thinks Evalyn's good enough to be accepted into Julliard, but she'll need to get a scholarship, keep her grades up. The tuition there is light-years away from my budget." Maddy sighed and shook her head. "I've talked to her about several other choices, but like Christopher, she can't seem to come up with plan 'B.' It's not like her to be this indecisive."

Both women paused and stared at one another.

"They don't want to make any plans until they know what the other one is doing." Emily offered slowly.

Maddy nodded slowly in agreement. For the past year or so, she had begun to notice subtle changes in the relationship between Christopher and her daughter.

"Do you think they …?" Emily let the unspoken question hang in the air.

"Maybe." Maddy surmised.

Emily smiled, and they resumed walking. "The best romances usually begin with friendship."

The women knew their children loved one another. Over the years, they had watched their love shift, change and grow. They also felt Christopher and Evalyn were, as yet, unaware of these changes.

"You know we already think of Evalyn as part of the family." Emily said, touching Maddy's arm.

"Let's see where it goes. They're still so very young."

"Do you remember being that age? What it was like?" Emily smiled with chagrin.

Maddy laughed, and then shuddered. "Oh yeah. Only too well."

"Whatever happens, let's hope they always remain friends."

Evalyn had been practicing her flirting for a couple of weeks. At first, she practiced in her bedroom mirror and then later tested her newly acquired skill on a boy at school.

Her random target was walking in the hallway when she smiled coyly in his direction and batted her lashes. He tripped over his own feet, bumped into the wall and dropped his books. Evalyn smiled, pleased with her success.

Next, she was ready to try it on Christopher. He was coming over after school. They were due to take the college entrance exams soon so they had planned to study together for an hour or

127

so. Later, she was going to the studio and warm up for her private lesson with Panzella.

Surrounded by snacks and drinks, they made themselves comfortable and got to work. After they had studied the material for about an hour, Evalyn leaned in close to him. She tucked her chin, gave him a sidelong glance and batted her eyelashes provocatively. Ignoring her efforts, Christopher continued talking. She repeated her routine again, this time sidling closer and batting her eyelashes madly.

He stopped in midsentence. "What's the matter?" He peered into her face, concerned. "Got something in your eye?" He reached across the table and handed her a box of tissue.

Frustrated, Evalyn snatched the box from his hand and threw it at him.

"Christopher Boldsen, you're such an idiot!"

"Hey! What's wrong?" Chris cried out. "What did I do?"

Evalyn grabbed her sweatshirt and ran. She was late for ballet anyway.

Panzella choreographed all of the dance recitals for her students. However, when practicing in the studio, the instructor often noticed how Evalyn created moves and steps of her own. The amazing thing was that her improvisations worked. Beautifully.

"I'd like to do something creative at our next recital." Evalyn suggested. Panzella studied her prize pupil thoughtfully. "What did you have in mind?" she asked.

"Something different...unusual." Evalyn's face lit with enthusiasm. "I want it to have elements of classical ballet, but with modern dance interpretations."

"Have you thought of the music?"

"Violins, brass—classical but with a modern twist." Evalyn's brows puckered wistfully. "Is that asking too much?"

Pondering, the dance instructor's eyes shifted toward the ceiling. "Let me think about it during class and I'll get back with you."

After class, Evalyn was wiping the sweat off her face with a towel when Panzella rapidly marched toward her, her face lit with enthusiasm.

"I've got an idea about your music for the recital. Come with me," Panzella commanded, leading the way up the stars to her office. She opened the lower drawer of her file cabinet and shuffled rapidly through disks.

"Something by John Barry, I think."

"Don't think I've heard of him."

Exhaling dramatically, Panzella slammed the drawer shut, coming up empty-handed.

"He writes for cinema, mostly. Great stuff. Innovative. Combines a classical feel with a twist. First of his type to use synthesizers."

"Cool."

She opened another file cabinet drawer and pulled out sheet music. "Ah, yes! This piece is for piano. Do you know anyone who plays?"

Evalyn started to shake her head when she remembered seeing the piano at Benson's. She remembered he did say he'd play for her.

"Yes, I have a friend who plays."

Panzella handed her the sheets. "Have your friend play it and tell me what you think."

As soon as Evalyn saw Ben at school the next day, she approached him about the music.

"Hey, Ben. Can you play this for me?" she handed him the sheets of music. "I'm thinking about using it at my recital this winter."

Benson took the sheets from her outstretched hand and looked at the cover page. He quickly flipped through the sheets, nodding; humming a bit to himself.

"Barry... he's written some really good stuff for cinema." Interested, he looked over at her. "Sure, I can play this. Give me a day or two to mess around with it. Maybe we can get together after school on Friday?"

Evalyn beamed up at him. "Friday's good." "Hey, thanks," she added over her shoulder, before running gracefully down the hall to class. Ever watchful, Benson's eyes followed her.

Late Friday afternoon, Benson and Evalyn were in the Cunningworth's spacious music room. Benson turned on recessed ceiling lights, which emphasized the polished ebony surface of the piano.

The tall, arched windows faced west and mirrored the vibrant indigo and blazing orange hues of the setting sun.

While she leaned against the piano, Ben slid onto the bench and began playing the piece Evalyn gave him a few days ago. He was good. Very good. His long, pale fingers moved effortlessly over the keys; his attention focused. The pages rustled softly, as he turned them. The piece began simply and became more complex as the music flowed. He hadn't played as much as he used to and found that he had missed it.

"It's so beautiful, Ben," Evalyn breathed. He smiled in answer, his pewter gray eyes shining. It felt good having her here, playing for her.

Evalyn slid off the bench, stepping out of her shoes. Gracefully, she pirouetted away from the piano toward the window, floating to the music. Even in faded jeans and a simple cropped T-shirt, she was the epitome of grace.

As Benson looked up from the piano to watch her, he mulled a twist on one of his favorite poems by Byron. *She dances in beauty, like the night ... she's all that's best of dark and bright.*

His hands continued to move quickly over the keys. He had never seen her dance before. She was good. *Very good.* She would dance a while, and every now and then, she would ask him to repeat the last few measures. After he did so, she would modify the moves according to her whim, trying different steps. He had always thought Evalyn was attractive, but as she danced, she became beauty in motion. He realized she was probably one of the best dancers he had ever seen.

Christopher once mentioned he'd attended one of Evalyn's recitals when she was in elementary school. He told Benson he'd been bored to death. As Benson watched her float across the floor in her bare feet, her arms raised in a wide arch, he seriously doubted Christopher would be bored if he could see her now.

Benson felt happy and proud that she was his friend. She was compassionate, she was lovely, and today he discovered she was talented as well. He would have been thrilled to have a girlfriend like her, but he had a hunch about something that neither Evalyn nor Christopher realized—that it was quite possible that they were in love with one another.

Smiling as he caressed the keys, Benson wondered how long it would take them to figure it out. They were his best friends and he didn't begrudge them their happiness, but a part of him envied them.

He looked over at the gilt-framed portrait of his great-great grandparents. Their obvious love for each other shone down from the wall. His heart ached to have someone care for him as deeply. His eyes returned to the keys.

What if he was wrong about Christopher and Evalyn, he wondered; or what if their love wasn't mutual? Could Evalyn make room in her heart for him? Hastily he shoved these precarious speculations to the deep recesses of his mind and returned his thoughts to the sound filling the room.

Seated at his desk on the second floor, Benson's father heard the music and walked out of the office. He knew his son to be an excellent pianist, although he hadn't heard him play much lately. The piece his son now played captivated him. While he didn't feel musically inclined, he appreciated good music, counting it among the finer things in life. He paused at the door to the room and noted that Benson wasn't alone.

Impressed, he leaned against the doorway. *Both of them have such talent,* he thought, as he listened to his son and watched Evalyn move gracefully across the floor. With each passing year, he became more impressed with his son.

He wondered if Benson and the girl were romantically involved—he hadn't gotten that impression when he'd met her before, but then again, he would probably be the last one to know such things.

It didn't matter to him that Evalyn was black. She could be purple for all he cared. Unlike his wife, Mariam's family, he would never stand in his son's way, no matter whenever and with whomever he found his life's love.

He never knew what angered Miriam's family more—that he wasn't Jewish, or that he had gypsy blood. A year after they married, Benson was born. It was then that he realized his wife married him out of rebellion. He'd like to flatter himself by believing that she remained married to him out of love, but he was a practical man. And apparently she was a very practical woman. She stayed with him because his family had more money than hers did.

Evalyn stopped abruptly, "Oh!" her hand flew to her mouth. Benson's father stood in the doorway.

"Father!' Benson stood, surprised. "I didn't know you were home. I hope we didn't disturb you."

"No, you didn't disturb me at all. I was enjoying the performance actually."

Evalyn walked gracefully toward Benson's father. "Hello, Mr. Cunningworth," she murmured softly, her small hand outstretched.

"We've met briefly before ... Miss Williamson, right?"

She smiled prettily. "Evalyn's better."

"Evalyn it is then." He waved his hand toward his son, "don't let me interrupt you." He looked down at Evalyn. "Will you join us for dinner?"

"That's kind of you sir," Evalyn politely responded, "but it's getting late and I really should be going."

"Perhaps some other time, then," Ben's father replied graciously, before walking back to his office.

Evalyn slipped on her shoes and Ben helped her with her jacket, before putting on his own coat. "Ben, can you record this for me?" She figured he could, since she had seen lots of technical equipment in the media room on previous visits.

"Sure, be happy to. When do you need it?"

"By next week, if you can find the time."

He drove her home and, gentlemanly as always, he walked her to the front door. Evalyn thanked him and hugged him tightly then went inside to join her mother.

Christopher, Ben, and a couple of friends from Christopher's swim team—Darnell and Andrew—decided to meet at the mall and give the rock climbing wall a try. Since their attempt at climbing in the Bluffs had proved to be disappointing, this was better than not climbing at all. Besides, today they had finished their senior midterms and needed a well deserved break as well as an opportunity to release pent up energy.

Evalyn and Yoli were going to do some shopping and the entire group planned to meet for pizza afterwards.

After the customary kidding around, the guys got serious and gave themselves to the sport. Christopher was the best, always managing to find footing where none seem to exist for the others.

After practicing for almost an hour, they decided to start at the bottom and race for the top. Triumphantly, Christopher was the first one to make it to the pinnacle.

Unexpectedly one of Christopher's safety lines split. Instantly, his expression changed from exultation to alarm. He heard the line snap, scrambled to grab hold of the wall. The stone scraped against his hands. Darnell swung to Christopher's side of the wall straining to reach him, but was unable to catch him in time.

As if in slow motion, he felt himself fall, aware of the loss of tension in the line, of colors blending in a blur, of the roughness grazing his palms.

Evalyn and Yoli finished shopping and were several yards from their friends when they heard a loud gasp from the crowd of watchers behind the fenced off area in front of the climbing wall.

Evalyn pushed her way through the crowd. She emerged in time to see Christopher plummet to the bottom, one leg pinned under him. Evalyn, as well as the other bystanders, heard the sharp snap of bone. Christopher's eyes rolled back in his head as he passed out.

Immediately the attendant began to shout into a phone, demanding emergency medical help while simultaneously insisting that the onlookers back away. Within minutes, the paramedics arrived. Christopher came to, moaning in pain. His leg, bent at an odd angle, was swelling rapidly. Efficiently the paramedics loaded him on to a stretcher.

"Evie!" Christopher called out, reaching for her.

"I'm here, Christopher." Her face contorted, she squeezed his hand, watching helplessly. Christopher refused to release her hand.

One of the paramedics moved towards her, "Sorry, Miss. Only immediate family allowed in with the patient."

"She's my—my sister," Christopher's voice was hoarse with pain. "She comes with me or I'm not going anywhere," he added, with characteristic stubbornness.

The paramedic looked back and forth between them for a second, as his mind struggled to grasp this. Families were adopting children from difference races these days.

He nodded, "Ok, get in."

Evalyn jumped in, sitting close to Christopher in the tight space. She placed his hand in hers and the vehicle sped off, sirens screaming.

Christopher began to feel a tingling, the pain ebbing slightly. The ambulance passed through a street shaded by a canopy of leaves. Almost imperceptibly, Evalyn began to glow. The medic paused as he was preparing a syringe. He glanced toward them and frowned. "Stop it!" Christopher whispered hoarsely.

Focused only on Christopher and his pain, she hadn't considered that she might be observed. When the paramedic regarded her suspiciously, Evalyn dropped Christopher's hand. As the resurgence of pain seared through his leg and sweat poured off of him, Christopher shut his eyes tightly, his lips pressed together.

The ambulance swung into the emergency drive entrance. The staff scurried around. One of them wheeled Christopher into the Emergency Room as the receptionist inquired about his parents' names and telephone number. Before getting an answer, a doctor barked orders for x-rays and a nurse pushed Christopher's gurney into the hallway near radiology, awaiting a turn.

Looking carefully up and down the empty, brightly lit hallway, Evalyn firmly grasped Christopher's hand. Anyone in pain evoked her sympathy but knowing Christopher was suffering was unbearable. Her entire body trembled in empathetic misery. She would stop this—now.

Focusing on the source, she summoned all of her strength. Christopher's clear, blue eyes flew open, staring into her warm, green ones. A jolt of energy surged into his body. As power flowed to his leg, the pain gradually diminished to a soothing flow. He relaxed, sighed and slowly closed his eyes. In a few moments, Christopher breathed a deep sigh of relief and opened his eyes, letting them linger on Evalyn. He stared, awestruck by the almost imperceptible glow that transformed her lovely features into something surreal and angelic. Then he smiled, thinking, *Whatever this power is that she uses, she is still, and always will be, my Evie.*

Watching him watch her, a responding smile played around the corners of her mouth. Within minutes, the swelling in his leg disappeared, as did the pain and the bruising. The bone knit instantaneously.

Earlier, in order to examine his leg, the paramedics had cut a long slit in the fabric of Christopher' jeans. Now, he swung his legs over the side of the gurney, pushing the torn denim aside to remove the temporary splint.

"I really liked these jeans," he muttered regretfully, shaking his head.

"What'll we tell our friends?" Evalyn asked, eyes widening in alarm. "They were there; they knew something happened to your leg and now it's perfectly fine."

Christopher thought about it for a moment then grabbed a large piece of the bandage used to hold the splint in place. "I'll wear this for a couple of days—maybe even limp a little—until they forget about it," he responded wryly. "C'mon, let's get out of here before they come back."

He spotted his chart on the door and stuffed it into his jacket. Looking in both directions to make certain no one was nearby; they hurried down the hallway, leaving the emergency room through a side exit.

The nurse received a call from radiology. They were ready to do Christopher's x-rays. The receptionist never received a telephone number for his parents but the physician on duty claimed emergency priority and ordered the images taken without further delay.

The nurse stepped into the hallway, glanced around and noticed the empty cot. Mystified, she picked up the splint carelessly tossed against the wall and returned to the nurses' station. "Anybody know ... where's the kid with the broken tibia and his sister?"

The nurses shook their heads. Some of the nurses checked the hallway, one called the radiology department to see if a technician had taken the patient. Nobody had seen either the boy or the girl.

"Who were they?" the receptionist asked. "Are they from around here?"

"Can't tell you," snapped the nurse, "And I can't find the chart. I could have sworn I left it on the door by the gurney."

The paramedic who had been in the back of the ambulance was leaning over the countertop flirting with a student nurse. He deliberated a moment or two, trying to fit all the pieces of the puzzle together, but wasn't quite getting it.

"Are you talking about that blonde kid?" he asked.

"Yes, he was with a black girl—his sister, I think."

"Well he couldn't have walked out of here, that's for sure," the nurse quipped. "That was one of the worse fractures I've seen in a while—broken in at least two places."

They called in security to conduct a thorough search. A patient's disappearance was not totally unusual—it occasionally happened in hospitals. However, a patient who is unable to walk—that would be quite a disappearing act, one of unparalleled prestidigitation.

A security guard ran up to the nurses' station, looking around for the paramedic. Spotting him, he rushed up, waving a video tape.

"You thought that there was something up with those two," he said excitedly. "And you were right!"

The paramedic snapped his fingers. "I knew it! There *was* something fishy going on."

137

The security officer stepped into a nearby lounge, beckoning the paramedic to follow. Hearing the commotion, the nursing supervisor joined them.

"Get a load of this." He pushed the tape into the slot in the bottom of the television.

The tape showed Christopher lying on the gurney, Evalyn standing next to him, holding his hand. They could see the swollen leg, but Evalyn's back was toward the surveillance camera, blocking the view. In the well-lit hallway, it appeared as though there was a slight shimmering around Evalyn, reminding them of heat waves coming off an asphalt road on a hot day.

"What's that? Is something wrong with the lighting in that hallway?" The paramedic asked.

"Nothing is wrong with the lights. Keep watching."

Within a span of a few moments, they could see the swelling disappear. Dumbfounded, they watched Christopher sit up, shake his head try to pull his torn pant leg together. They watched as he swung both legs over the gurney, take the chart, and walk out under his own power.

"Hand me that tape," snapped the nursing supervisor. Snatching it from the officer's hand, she marched past the nurses' station, and headed for the administrator's office.

The nursing supervisor rapped once sharply on the door before opening it. Seated at his desk, the administrator looked up in surprise. The expression on the supervisor's face brought him up short.

"What is it? Did someone call a code? I didn't hear a code."

'No one's coded."

She walked past him to a television set in the corner above a wet bar.

"What's going on here, Doris?" he demanded.

"A picture's worth a thousand words." She slipped in the tape and stepped back.

They watched the tape in silence, the administrator's mouth agape.

"Is this some sort of trick?" he asked angrily. "I'm too busy...."

Placing both hands on his desk, she leaned over, her face even with his. "It's no trick."

"Then what the...."

The nursing supervisor shook her head. "I have no idea what happened. All I know is that kid came in here with one badly broken leg and walked out of here on two good ones!"

With a deep sigh, the administrator placed his head in his hands. In his entire career in hospital administration, he had never come across a situation like this one. He leafed through the disaster preparedness manual; there was no precedent to follow.

He didn't know whether to call the Center for Disease Control or the Bureau of Stateside Security. Deciding to err on the side of caution, he called them both.

Chapter 9

here is a nap mat when you need one? Evalyn wondered. Healing Christopher had exhausted her. Coming home the night he fell, she slept for sixteen hours straight. Several days later, she continued to sleep more than usual.

Eight hours of sleep was below her necessary quota—she usually needed at least ten or twelve hours to feel rested. If she couldn't manage to get enough sleep at night, she'd catch a nap as soon as she could.

She wished North High School had a nap room where she could take power naps, like the Japanese. Who knows, maybe it would help improve her grades, which had dropped lately.

She was amazed when she heard her classmates grumble about staying up all night studying for exams. If that's what it would take to get high marks, her academic future looked grim. Since she required so much sleep, she didn't care to spend all of her waking hours studying. She preferred to use her free time to hang out with friends or practice at the studio.

Tired as she was, Evalyn still agreed to meet up with Christopher right after school. He had a stop to make, and then he was dropping by. That meant they would have about an hour before Maddy arrived home from work.

Evalyn had no idea how far they'd get today, but maybe she could share with Christopher what little she understood and try to answer his questions. She curled up on the couch and Christopher sat in an easy chair across from her.

She didn't know if her mother would approve of the coaching she'd been providing for Christopher, so she hadn't mentioned it. If by chance, Maddy found out and did not approve, Evalyn decided she'd beg for forgiveness. That would be considerably easier than asking her mother for permission.

Other than talking with Christopher, she never discussed her gifts—not even with Maddy. When she was younger, she noticed that whenever she mentioned it, a pained look crossed her mother's face. She would do nothing intentionally to cause her mother misery. Writing about it in her diary helped her feel less alone and isolated.

She tried to explain how she used her mind, to focus her thoughts. Christopher's brow furrowed. "I'm trying to get this... it's not so easy to understand."

"Actually, it's quite easy," she retorted. "You do it all the time. Everyone does, only most people don't realize it. It's automatic."

"So you're saying that our thoughts go floating by like bubbles, and when we pull them in and think really hard on them, they become real?" Christopher's eyes brightened. "So if I were to focus on mountain climbing and use the energy, then say...I could climb to the top of a mountain, a *real* mountain?"

Evalyn laughed. "You know, just the thought of heights makes me dizzy, but yes... the basic principle of combining the energy with focus is what works best."

She hesitated, realizing she might be sounding a bit too clinical. She tried to think of the best way to explain it so that he'd easily understand, but she didn't want to talk down to him.

"Or you could think of thoughts like light switches. In the "off" position they're neutral, although you know that the power is there, waiting to be used."

"So the power is there, at our service, so to speak." Christopher pondered this.

Evalyn nodded. "And each switch is a separate possibility, based on your natural desires and inclinations. Focusing is like clicking the switch *on*."

"Sounds easy enough."

She laughed. "Easy in theory, hard to do in practice."

"Ok, what's the hard part? You do it with healing."

"It's not as easy as it seems. For one thing, you have to monitor your thoughts carefully, particularly discarding any doubting thoughts..."

"Doubting thoughts?"

"For an example, let's use your dream about climbing a real mountain. Doubting thoughts would be something like, "I'll *never* have the money to travel to Mt. Everest. That sort of thing.""

"So doubting squashes it?"

"Yeah, for sure. Remember the light switches are neutral, but each switch holds a different possibility. One switch says, *Yes, I'm going to climb a real mountain*, the other switch says, *I can't afford to travel to the mountain*.

"And I get to choose which switch I turn on? You mean the choice is mine?"

"Yeah, big time. You've got to believe in what's possible, even when you can't see it."

"This sounds too good to be true," he protested.

"Nothing is too good to be true!" Evalyn responded emphatically.

"So what about things like grades? Will focusing on energy help that?

Evalyn snickered. "Oh, yeah. But it has to be something that *you* care about, something that's really important to *you*—not important to your parents or your teachers."

She became serious. "When I heal, I touch the energy. Then I think about the person being well, I don't dwell on the sickness for an instant."

"Kind of hard to do when the person's face is crumpled in pain or blood is running from a cut. How do you do it?"

"I concentrate, and ignore what may seem like sickness. I know that sickness isn't the strongest—wellness is stronger. Just like I know that love is stronger than hate."

"But what about dwelling on negative thoughts?" he asked. "You mentioned that when you think negatively for too long, you feel sick."

"I do, yes—but not everybody does."

"So what about someone who thinks negatively a *lot*?" Christopher asked. "Won't that make negative things happen for them?"

"Yes, of course. You see it happening to people all the time. But they prefer to think that it's 'fate' or that 'life sucks.' They don't know that the majority of it is coming from them—that they're the source of their own misery by *choosing* to flip the misery switch."

"So you're saying that everyone is choosing something all the time, even if they don't know they're doing it?"

"Exactly. It's about knowing you have choice, or free will to make a choice." She tilted her head slightly, "Now you just have to learn to focus and to do it deliberately."

He leaned forward in his chair.

"And how would you recommend that I do that?"

"Just like I do with healing," she admonished. "Practice."

She took a deep breath and sat very still. She closed her eyes and breathed deeply. In a moment. Christopher began to see a

softly diffused light surrounding her. It vibrated subtly, like the
sparks he saw when he closed his eyes.

She opened her eyes and saw him staring at her.

Closing her eyes once again, she commanded softly,
"Practice!"

Evalyn got off the school bus, tied her sweatshirt around her
waist and rapidly walked the block to her house. Her mind was
on ballet practice—she was having trouble with double pirouettes
and fouettés, especially in pointe.

Maddy's battered old car was parked in the driveway. Evalyn
opened the front door and saw her mother, wearing an apron
over her work dress, standing in the kitchen doorway. A stern
expression clouded her face. Evalyn rarely received *the look* from
Maddy, but when she did, she knew she was in trouble.

Uh-oh. The report cards went out this week. That must be it, Evalyn
thought guiltily, her stomach sinking. Her mother didn't insist
that her grades be all A's, but she refused to accept less than a C.

Evalyn knew that lately schoolwork had been her last priority.
Now, seeing the disappointment on her mother's face, she
regretted that decision.

"Hi, Mom," Evalyn smiled weakly.

Maddy pointed to a kitchen chair. "Sit." She ordered.

Evalyn laid her backpack on the floor and sat down. Her
mother sat across from her.

"One D and an F, Evalyn! What's that about?" She asked
angrily.

"I'm sorry, Mama," Evalyn murmured, her eyes downcast.
She knew she had let her mother down.

"Evalyn, you know I have never insisted that you make the
Honor Roll, but this!" Madelyn was furious. "This is inexcuseable!
Until now, your grades were good enough to get into college. If
you don't pull these grades up now, you'll have to repeat those

classes. You may not be able to graduate in June with the rest of your friends."

Two classes. It was worse than Evalyn thought. She knew she'd been struggling but she couldn't believe she had managed to flunk a class. She had never done that before.

"You are grounded from any activity other than school."

"But what about dancing? What about—"

Maddy interrupted her, putting up her hand. "If your grades are up on the next report card, you'll get your privileges back." Maddy spoke firmly. "And not until then."

The telephone rang loudly on the wall. Maddy stood up to answer it.

"Yes, I've just told her." she said to the caller. "Ballet is definitely out until her grades improve."

She handed the phone to Evalyn. "It's Panzella. I spoke with her earlier and told her your lessons are cancelled until further notice."

Evalyn was devastated. Dancing was one of the best things in life. It *was* her life. Numb, she walked to take the phone from her mother's outstretched hand.

"Hello," Evalyn whispered hoarsely.

"A dumb ballerina is worse than a dumb jock." Panzella snapped, without preamble. "At least people *expect* jocks to be dumb." When Panzella was irritated, her accent became more pronounced, and she was very irritated now.

Evalyn understood the message clearly. There had been occasions when Panzella had spoken sharply to her students, but never with Evalyn—until now.

"A commitment, Evalyn. It's what you promised me. Get those grades up and get back in this studio!" The line went dead.

Evalyn hung the phone up, picked her backpack off the floor, and went upstairs to cry. "Dear Diary, I really blew it..."

She felt her life couldn't get much worse. How mistaken she was!

Christopher headed for the public library; he needed to finish the research for a Political Science paper that was due in two days. Evalyn's grounding was enough to make him knock the dust off his books.

He assumed he'd find everything he needed on the Internet, but the paper still fell short of being acceptable. Well, it was acceptable to him but his teacher was an uncompromising tyrant and he needed to make an A on this one.

The history section was on the top floor. He laid his pack on a fairly secluded table near the stacks of books about American Political History. He hunted through the shelved books, searching for information on the cessation of states in the Pacific Northwest.

He jotted down notes and photocopied a few pages from several different books. Most of it bored him, except for Alaska. It was one place he'd always dreamed of visiting.

He turned the pages of the book and studied the photos of white-capped mountain peaks outlined against vivid cobalt blue skies. He stared at a photo taken at night during winter in Barrow, the northernmost American city. He'd be sure to check this book out so he could read more about it later. He wondered what it would be like to gaze upward and see brilliant swirls of drifting green, white, and deep pink floating against the blackness.

Evalyn mentioned that energy was the primary cause of everything but thought most people didn't recognize it as such. For instance, she said if someone takes aspirin for a headache and the headache subsides, the person might think it was aspirin that healed them. But really, the energy force is the healing agent.

For some, taking the aspirin is the only means they have of triggering the energy force. Evalyn had found an adept way to eliminate the "middle man," the aspirin, and trigger the energy source directly.

Christopher's cell phone vibrated. He picked it up, glanced at it to see who was calling. "Yeah Becca, What's up?"

"Mom asked me to call to let you know Matt's home for the weekend and dinner's on the table in fifteen minutes. If you're late you know Ace will eat everything in sight."

He could hear the smirk in her voice. She was right—Matt would be fair. Ace would be a hog. It would be at least a half hour before he could make it home.

"What're we having?

"The *one* thing Mom makes really well—Lasagna." Becca hung up.

As Christopher put the phone in his shirt pocket, he froze. He pulled the phone out slowly, feeling its weight in his hand. He stared at it.

That's it! The cell phone was an intermediary device. Becca wanted to get a message to him and this was the means she used.

He thought about all the ways people have always used to get messages to others. Smoke signals, drums, carrier pigeons. There were telegraphs and telephone landlines. And now, the cell phone.

A slow smile spread across his face. *We're getting better at communicating with one another as time goes on*, he mused.

If he was right and the cell phone was the go-between, then people should be able to communicate with one another by going directly to the energy.

Water appeared to be his natural element, perhaps he could use it—even in the most minute amounts—to act as a conduit to direct the energy. Since he was already going to be late for dinner, he figured he might as well put his theory to the test.

The library had gotten quieter and he was in a secluded corner. He sat very still, closed his eyes and focused on touching the energy. After a few moments, he could feel the surge of power building deep within him, flowing from the top of his head, into his chest—filling him.

All of his senses became sharper, heightened. This had never happened before and he found himself reveling in the sensation. He focused, visualizing the thought flowing from his mind to the water in the cells of his body, traveling to the most minute particles of water in the atmosphere.

Like an arrow passing through air directly to its target, he shot Ace a crystal-clear message.

Christopher walked in the door, greeted by the delicious aroma of tomatoes and spices. He headed for the kitchen, and laid the library book on the countertop before washing his hands at the sink.

He felt a bit drained, which was uncharacteristic—usually he had energy to spare. He attributed his tiredness to a missed lunch. He was hungry, starving actually, and was sure he'd feel much better after he'd eaten. That is, if there was anything left.

His parents, brothers, and sister were sitting at the table, finishing their meal. Ace gave Christopher an uneasy glance.

"Sorry I'm late," Christopher murmured apologetically to his parents. "Took a while to find the books I needed." He eyed the baking dish set in the middle. A hearty portion had been left for him.

It worked! He thought exultantly. He helped himself and smiled, turning to Ace.

"Nice of you to leave me some, Bro," Christopher murmured in a tone meant for Ace's ears only. "Guess you'll sleep well tonight after all," he added cryptically.

All the color drained from his brothers' face.

Christopher put a forkful of lasagna into his mouth.

Emily leaned across the table, examining Ace closely, concerned. "You're not feeling well son?" she asked. "Suddenly you've gotten so pale."

Ace regarded Christopher nervously. He hastily pushed away from the table. His chair scraped across the floor.

"No," he stammered. "I'm fine. Just need some air." He quickly exited the kitchen before they had time to respond.

Puzzled, Bob and Emily exchanged glances. Matt and Becca seemed as perplexed as their parents. Christopher, fully aware of what was going on around him, kept his eyes on his plate, seemingly preoccupied with his meal.

"What's up with him?" Becca asked, staring at the closing kitchen door.

"Maybe there's a fire somewhere he forgot to put out." Matt chuckled.

Christopher struggled to hide a grin. The message he had sent his errant brother was: *If there's no dinner left when I get home tonight, you'd better sleep with one eye open.*

In a high-rise conference room overlooking the city, several doctors and scientists at the Center for Disease Control in Atlanta were viewing a copy of the video tape forwarded by the hospital in Omaha a week ago.

Leaning back in a leather and chrome swivel chair, Dr. Robert Jamison, the center's director, rubbed his chin, perplexed. In his entire career, he had never seen anything like it. The others in the room appeared to be confused as well.

"It's hard to believe the hospital doesn't know who she is and that that chart was the only record. I don't know what's going on, but we need to find out who she is and get that girl in here pronto," Jamison ordered.

"Under what prerogative?" asked Andrew Clarke, a young African-American doctor, sitting at the director's right.

"We don't need one. We've passed the flashing yellow and got the green light on this one," Jamison responded brusquely, swinging his chair upright. "We're acting under the auspices of Stateside Security—and that's a bureau that can do what they damn well please."

"Within reason," Clarke murmured.

Jamison registered Clarkes' comment, nonchalantly flipping papers in front of him. He pushed the papers aside and looked around the room at the staff he had assembled. He knew every detail about each of them. Knowing about their personal lives made them vulnerable and gave him the advantage.

He made it his business to know that Jody Smith, the geneticist, was gay. He had absolutely no interest in him, although he could feign interest if it served his purpose.

He knew the reason Mickey Rodriquez had dark rings under his eyes was due to exhaustion; he had recently become the proud father of triplets.

Jamison recently learned from HR that Clarke had married an Asian woman he'd met on an assignment a few years ago.

The details of his staff's life were important to him. Not because he was a caring man—actually he couldn't care less—it was because he never knew what other leverage he might need when bribes would no longer work.

"I'm meeting with the Stateside Security tomorrow to discuss this further and to put together an investigative team." He turned to Clarke.

"You're heading this investigation, Andrew. Too much time has already passed. Pick whoever you'll need to assist you."

In addition to his medical degree, Dr. Andrew Clarke had an extensive background in law enforcement, making him the best man for the job.

"We'll conduct experiments then?" the geneticist asked hopefully.

The director grimaced. "Not experiments...ah... research. Yes, we need her for research purposes."

Jamison didn't want to waste time on semantics. Research, or experimentation—it mattered little. He was expecting a dossier delivered from the hospital in Omaha. It contained additional information that might prove useful. He knew they were on to something; he could hardly wait to begin research, particularly DNA testing. The possibilities were endless.

The next afternoon, Dr. Jamison and Dr. Clarke met with Jim Richards, a top administrator with the Atlanta division of Stateside Security. Global espionage and media investigations were a few of his areas of expertise. Richards had already viewed the video tape several times and verified it as authentic. Richards also had a reputation for using strong-arm tactics when an opportunity presented itself.

Jamison introduced the two men. Clarke and Richards shook hands (sizing up one another as alpha males are prone to do) as they took their seats.

Tall and handsome, Andrew Clarke had recently turned thirty. He looked more like a model than a medical investigator.

Jim Richards, on the other hand was short and stocky, his face deeply etched with lines from decades spent in the field. His eyes reflected the jaded expression of someone who has seen the worst and expected nothing better.

"Dr. Clarke here," Jamison explained, "is going to be in charge of the CDC angle of the investigation. He has experience which I think will be helpful."

Richards tossed a sharp glance in Clarke's direction. Clarke returned his look with a level one of his own.

"I think it will take both of our departments to get to the core of the problem," Richards affirmed in his low gravelly voice, rough from years of smoking a pack a day.

"We have to work together in order to find this girl...fast. We can't risk having another country find out about her ability. Think how this could affect military operations," Jamison snapped. He was irritated. He still hadn't received the dossier containing eyewitness reports from the hospital—he expected it yesterday.

"According to what I saw on the tapes, she could heal a fracture. What else might she be capable of?"

"We'll need to get to her before anyone else does." Richards reiterated. "Of course, it's for her own safety." He coughed in his hand.

"Yes, of course," Jamison responded quickly, his mind on the myriad of ways she could prove useful. "How soon can you fly out to the Midwest?" he asked Clarke.

Clarke tilted his head to the side, noticing how Jamison phrased it as a question rather than an order, which was his customary style with subordinates.

"I can be in Omaha by tomorrow morning," he replied. He always kept a suitcase packed since he often had to travel at a moment's notice. Winter was cooler in the Midwest than it was in Atlanta; he'd bring warmer clothing. "The rest of my team will be there by nightfall."

"Good. I'll expect a report by the end of the month."

Clarke shook hands with Richards once again before leaving the room, his eyes steely with determination. He would make certain he found the girl first.

It was after hours and Jamison was still in his office. This wasn't unusual since he usually worked twelve to fourteen hour days. The intercom on his desk buzzed. It was Hendricks, his office manager, asking to speak with him. Jamison looked at his watch; he could spare a moment or two.

The manager, a young ambitious intern entered, carrying a slim, padded envelope. "The dossier from the hospital arrived an hour ago, Sir. I went to Dr. Clarke's hoping to catch him, but his wife said he had already caught a flight out of town."

"Well then, overnight it to his hotel in Omaha." Jamison turned back to the work on his desk. The manager coughed slightly. Jamison looked up. "Is there something else?"

Hendricks knew Jamison appreciated any information he could provide, particularly when it concerned other employees. The office manager was privy to the files Jamison kept on his staff—in fact, he was often one of the primary sources of information. Jamison paid well to keep the information coming.

"When the doctor's wife came to the door...ah... she didn't seem quite herself."

Did the new Mrs. Clarke have a drinking problem? Or drugs, perhaps? Jamison listened, waiting. He had met her at the center's annual holiday gala.

He remembered she was tall with almond-shaped eyes and waist-length raven hair. She had twirled the crystal flute in her slender fingers, barely sipping the expensive champagne.

No, she didn't seem like the type to imbibe indiscriminately. In fact, she appeared to be the perfect mate for Clarke, elegant and sophisticated.

"Spit it out, Hendricks." Jamison was getting impatient.

"After I rang the bell, I waited a while. I was about to leave—I thought no one was at home, when the door opened slowly. Mrs. Clark apologized for the delay. She said she'd given the housekeeper the day off. She looked very tired—exhausted—and pale. And I noticed she leaned against the door for support, as though she barely had the strength to stand."

Jamison stroked his chin, mulling this over. Maybe she was expecting—some women have a difficult time with pregnancy. He would check with his source in the Human Resources department. Offering seasoned tickets to a sporting event would get him all the information he needed.

"Thank you," Jamison said brusquely signaling the intern's dismissal. He returned his attention to the stacks of papers on his desk.

Hendricks was smug knowing he could expect the usual bonus in his next paycheck.

Chapter 10

Christopher walked down to the river and settled himself comfortably on one of the larger stones. The river was a symphony of sound and color, a moving kaleidoscope of purple and orange, reflecting the brilliance of the setting sun.

He zipped his jacket and pulled his hood over his head; there was a cold wind blowing off the river. He studied the surface a few feet from where he sat, listening to the sound of the water. He looked around at the nearby trees, stripped of their leaves, striking in their starkness. Intuitively he sensed that this separateness—between himself, and trees, rock, and water was an illusion—that everything was connected.

Under Evalyn's tutelage, he had begun to practice—with limited success. At first, he could only feel a slight tingling, but as he practiced, it grew stronger. Still, he hadn't managed to diffuse light the way Evalyn could. He chewed his lower lip, mulling it over. He didn't know what *it* was, but he did suspect this energy could do many other things. Evalyn thought the manner in which energy was directed, depended upon an individual's inclinations or talents.

He thought of things he had never considered before. Rumor had it that a man once walked on water. Fragments of the conversation he'd had with Ben—about the surface tension and cohesion of water—floated through his mind.

The bright colors of the sunset faded to deep indigo as dusk fell. He could hear an owl hooting nearby. Christopher sat motionless, deep in thought, watching the rising moon as its beam streamed across the river.

Then in one fluid movement, he jumped off the rock to the water's edge and stood. He'd made his decision, he had to try. Reaching down, he slipped off his shoes and tossed them on the dried grass behind him. He felt the icy water shyly, invitingly, flow over his bare feet.

Evalyn was curled up on the living room sofa catching up on her reading assignment for Lit class. Her mother had gone to bed an hour ago but she wanted to finish the chapter before she turned in for the night. She heard a soft rap at the front door. The door opened and Christopher walked in and stood in the entryway. He was dripping wet—jacket, jeans, everything except his shoes.

"Christopher," she murmured, barely glancing up from her book. "Most people take *off* their clothes when they go swimming."

He glared at her, daring her to ask questions. Of course he knew she wouldn't—it was the reason he'd come here instead of going home where any member of the Boldsen household would have drilled him mercilessly. Had she been up, Maddy might have raised an eyebrow but he knew she always went to bed at ten. You could set a clock by her.

With a deep sigh, Evalyn laid the book aside. "Stay there and take off those wet things. I don't want you dripping everywhere."

She went into the laundry room, pulled a large blanket from the linen closet and returned to the living room where Christopher had stripped down to his boxers. Christopher in boxers, she had seen before. However, even wet and scowling, this new and improved six-pack version made her heart do a triple pirouette. She couldn't help but stare.

"I'm freezing here, Evalyn!" he snapped, shivering.

Making a face, she wadded the blanket and threw it at him. Catching it, he wrapped it around himself. He gathered up his wet clothes, headed to the laundry room, and tossed them in the dryer.

He spent almost as much time at Evalyn's house as he did in his own. He knew where things were kept, and how to operate everything. He started the dryer without a second thought and leaned against it.

He had spent more time at the river than he'd planned and now he was too tired to study. He'd have to pick Ben's brain again tomorrow after school; otherwise he would fail the test.

Benson had given Christopher a ride home from the library where they had been studying for Fridays' test.

"You're invited to stay for dinner, Ben," Christopher offered generously. "But you accept at your own risk."

With good humor, he said, "I'll take my chances." Like everyone else, Benson was familiar with Emily's lack of culinary expertise.

They dumped their things on the floor by the backdoor and walked into the kitchen, their noses assailed by an assortment of interesting smells.

Becca and his mother were bringing the food in from the kitchen. The rest of his family took their seats at the table. Christopher and Benson went to join them.

Becca stared at a baking sheet on the stove. It was filled with dark, round orbs.

"Mom, what's this supposed to be?"

"Biscuits. You know—the refrigerated kind you peel the label to open." Emily was carrying a large soup tureen to the table. "I may have left them in a little too long."

Becca let out a loud sigh, shaking her head. The biscuits resembled charcoal briquettes. She hoped being a bad cook wasn't genetic.

"Mom, we can't eat these." Becca dumped them in the trash and placed a bag of frozen rolls in the microwave to thaw.

Emily sat the tureen in the middle of the table and began ladling stew into her bowl. Ace grabbed the ladle and took a huge helping. Everyone else at the table scooped a bowlful, too.

Bob filled his mouth with a spoonful. "Eh, what type of stew is this?" He quickly added, "Darling." Emily's quick temper *was* genetic. A few of her children inherited the gene from her. All of them in fact, except Matt, who was even tempered like his father.

"Beef stew." Emily gave her husband a blank look. "What else?"

"It... um has a... um... rather unusual taste."

Becca sniffed the stew. "Mom, it smells like cinnamon."

"Silly girl. Cinnamon is not an ingredient in beef stew—but I did add lots of extra pepper for kick."

Becca got up from the table to get the rolls out of the microwave. She glanced at the small spice bottle next to the stove and muttered under her breath. Sure enough, it was cinnamon. Her mother had inadvertently grabbed the wrong container. Although, in all fairness to Emily, except for the words "cinnamon" and "pepper" on the labels, the bottles looked identical.

The Boldsen's knew the rule regarding their mother's cooking. Eat it anyway.

Benson took the ladle and began to serve himself, when he noticed Becca give an imperceptible shake of her head. Noticing the small amount she had placed in her bowl, he took the smallest serving possible. He tasted it. The potatoes in it were still hard. Benson caught Christopher's eye. Christopher gave him the *I told you so* look.

Emily's beef stew definitely made it to the top of the children's secret list: "Mom's Worst Ever."

Bob cleared his throat. "I have some bad news about the cabin." Immediately four pairs of blue eyes—and one set of gray ones—focused on him.

Even though it was still months away, the Boldsens looked forward to spending a long weekend at a cabin in Long Prairie every October during deer hunting season. Plentiful with deer and elk, hunters often booked this particular area in central Minnesota a year in advance.

While the men were deer hunting, Emily and Becca usually went shopping or simply hung out in the hot tub, just taking it easy.

"The cabin is not available," he morosely informed his family. "Although I've looked, I haven't had any luck finding one large enough to fit all of us."

Hearing the grim news, the family became unusually quiet, a stark contrast to their normal rowdiness. All of them looked disappointed.

Ever since Christopher could remember, his family had gone to Minnesota in the fall or early winter. He knew Matt would be devastated when he heard the news. Even Ace was just picking at his dinner, more surly than usual. Next to beer drinking, hunting was one of Ace's favorite pursuits.

Benson glanced around the table at the dejected faces surrounding him. He cleared his throat. "My family happens to have a cabin near there," he announced quietly.

At this hopeful news, the faces all lit up—all except Christopher's. His eyes narrowed as he looked at his friend suspiciously. He'd known Benson for several years, and never heard him mention a family cabin. Anywhere. Ever. While he'd heard Ben speak of his family having several vacation homes scattered throughout the world, from London to Argentina, cabins weren't the Cunningworth's style.

Five pairs of blue eyes focused expectantly on Benson. "I don't think my father's made any plans, but let me get back to you to make sure he isn't using it during that week in the fall."

At this hopeful news, the family began chatting excitedly. Christopher continued to stare at Benson, who innocently returned his look. Christopher knew it would be a physical impossibility for Benson II to be vacationing in a nonexistent cabin.

Christopher' stomach rumbled. Resigned, he looked down at the half-filled bowl in front of him. He glanced down at his watch. It was six thirty.

"I think I may have left something at the library," Christopher announced, looking up. "Ben, would you mind giving me a ride on your way home?"

"Sure. No problem."

Benson stood to leave. Becca jumped up from her chair. "I think I need a book," she added breathlessly. "Mind if I hitch a ride."

Benson didn't mind at all. He always enjoyed Becca's company. She was warm and funny with a bit of her mother's frankness thrown in for good measure. She was pretty in the way many Midwestern girls often are, with clear skin sprinkled with a dusting of freckles.

They piled into his Jeep and Ben headed straight for the Williamson's. Evalyn heard the Jeep and jumped up to open the door. The three of them walked in laughing, welcomed by aromatic smells coming from the kitchen. Christopher knew Evalyn and her mother habitually ate dinner late. Maddy always cooked enough to feed the entire town.

Maddy looked up, smiling. She saw Becca standing behind the two boys and added three extra plates to the table. Dinner must have been especially awful if Becca joined them.

"We're having pot roast," Evalyn announced. She placed a basket of piping hot made-from-scratch biscuits on the table next to the huge platter filled with roasted beef and vegetables swimming in savory dark brown gravy.

They dug in eagerly. The meat was tender; the golden Yukon potatoes were soft and buttery. Dessert was a Midwestern favorite—caramel apple pie.

After dinner they shooed Maddy out of the kitchen, turned up the radio, and helped Evalyn clean up.

"Please don't tell our mom we ate here." Becca's eyes pleaded as they stood in the doorway getting ready to leave.

Maddy laughed, tossing a conspiratorial glance Christopher's way. "I never do."

Benson drove home, lost in thought. His father had been home for the last month, which was unusual. Ben liked that and wished it would happen more often, although he realized his father's travels, unlike his mother's, were necessary in order to maintain the family estate.

His father was a handsome man with elegant, finely chiseled features, jet eyes and black hair turning gray at the temples. Ben had his mother's fairness, but he had his father's features, height and temperament.

This year his mother had only been home for one or two holiday visits. Even then, she spent most of her time entertaining several Dundee neighbors or lounging in her suite in the east wing.

Benson pulled the car up to the front of the house, leaving the keys in the ignition. One of the servants would drive it around to the garage where they would check fluid levels, tires, clean it, and have it ready for his use tomorrow.

He ran up the stairs and entered the foyer, asking one of the servants if his father was in. A servant informed him his father was in his study. The door was ajar, meaning his father allowed interruptions.

Ben knocked lightly and walked through the open door. He sat down in one of the antique armchairs beside the desk.

"I think I'd like some vacation property in Minnesota," he announced quietly. His father lifted one eyebrow, appraising his son. Benson had grown taller, and had put on a little weight. Although he had never mentioned it, he was proud and happy with the changes he had noticed since his son began attending public school. Evidently, his son had a better sense of what was in his own best interest then did his parents.

"Yes, a resort could be a good investment," he murmured before returning his attention to the accounts on his desk.

"I was thinking of something on a smaller scale," Benson persisted. "Say... a cabin with about a half dozen bedrooms, somewhere near central Minnesota. I'd like to find one by October, if possible."

His father studied him for a moment, wondering what had provoked this—his friends perhaps. Benson II didn't mind. He had met a few of his son's friends and found most of them amiable. He was particularly fond of Christopher and Evalyn.

"Call our real estate attorney and tell him what you'd like. Tell him I've already approved it."

Benson II turned his attention back to the work on his desk, dismissing his son.

A week later, his father flew to Europe on another business trip, leaving a large envelope for Benson containing information regarding a rustic lodge north of Long Prairie, which their attorney had purchased.

The Boldsen's piled in the van and headed for Minnesota. Matt had taken a break from college to join them. When Emily asked about supplies, Benson informed her they wouldn't need much—as his family usually kept the lodge fully stocked with linens and kitchen supplies.

Several weeks ago when Benson informed the Boldsen's the Cunningworth cabin was available, he asked Christopher if he would mind if he joined them. The Boldsen's were grateful for the generosity of Benson's family and Christopher was delighted he wanted to come along.

"Do you even know how to hunt?" Ace asked skeptically.

"No, but Christopher offered to teach me." Benson advised.

Ace snorted. "A lot of good that'll do. Christopher has been hunting all his life, and the woods are full of deer, bobcat— we even spot wolves now and then, but he's has never nailed anything yet!"

Curious, Benson eyed Christopher. "Never?"

Christopher lifted his shoulder, resignedly. "I can never keep up with you, Bro, but this may be my lucky season."

"That's what you said last year," Ace cited, "and the year before that".

Earlier that morning, Becca told them she couldn't go. She worked part time at a grocery store and the cashier who planned to fill in for her had to cancel due to an emergency. Without a replacement, Becca had to cover her regular shift. She was clearly disappointed. But not as disappointed as Benson was when he heard the news. He had been looking forward to spending time in her company.

Bob followed the map with the directions Benson had given him. Benson's lodge was about ten miles north of the cabin they usually rented each season in Long Prairie.

They drove through the wooded countryside filled with bare oaks, interspersed with pines and cedars. They turned northwest for a few miles, Benson watching the road carefully. He had never been here, but had seen the photos and layout sent from the realtor to their business manager.

"There, straight ahead!" Benson pointed several hundred yards in the direction in which they were headed.

Bob pulled up in front of a large, two story lodge that seemed to blend in with the surrounding woods. A tall pine tree grew through the upper floor veranda and huge windows reflected the late afternoon sun.

The Boldsens were impressed to say the least.

"What a place! Matt exclaimed.

"It's five times the size of our usual cabin," Ace blurted out.

Bob punched him lightly on the arm. "Be sure and thank your father for us, Benson."

"I'll be sure to send him a card, as soon as we get back," Emily interjected.

They carried their things up the stairs to the porch, dropping bags inside the doorway. The main room had a huge stone fireplace and comfortable furniture in shades of rust and brown. Above was a loft overlooking half of the bottom level. A master bedroom and bunkroom were also located on the main floor. There were four smaller bedrooms upstairs.

Emily wandered into the kitchen, fully stocked with everything they could possibly need. There was a rotisserie and modern stainless steel appliances. She opened the refrigerator and found it full of dairy products, fresh fruits and vegetables. The freezer had neatly labeled packages of meat and poultry.

In the rear of the kitchen was a pantry containing dry staples and canned goods. A cooled alcove within its recesses contained imported beer and wines. Through the kitchen window, she spotted a large, steaming, hot tub and smiled. She could really get used to this.

The early morning was damp. Benson pulled his jacket tighter around him, glad he had put a wool sweater underneath. He didn't understand why hunters had to get up before dawn. Even deer need sleep.

"So let me see if I get this." Benson spoke slowly, as if Christopher's IQ had taken a sudden drop. "You go hunting... but you don't actually *hunt*."

Christopher grinned. "Yeah. I think you're getting it"

"So why do you go through all the trouble of getting up at the crack of dawn, putting on this camouflage, and hauling all this gear?

"Because the Boldsen men hunt. Period." Christopher answered patiently. "Sometimes I feel like I'm adopted or something. I hate hunting."

"It's obvious you're not adopted—all of you look alike." Benson nodded, thinking of the vast number of traditions in his family he didn't enjoy. "You're a bit like Matt, but you and Ace are as different as brothers can be."

"You've been a better brother in the years I've known you than Ace has been in my entire life," Christopher acknowledged, pensive. Suddenly his mood shifted. "Hey! Let's become blood brothers!"

Benson looked a bit apprehensive. "You mean like with real blood and all?

Christopher nodded, as he dug through the numerous pockets of his hunting jacket and pulled out his non-hunting knife. Using the sharp tip, he made a small cut in the palm of his left hand until blood appeared.

"Come on, Benson," he insisted, beckoning, "give me your hand."

Since he was left-handed, Benson put out his right hand. He winced as Chris made the cut.

"I don't see why you have problems shooting. You obviously don't have problems using knives to draw blood," Benson said wryly.

They shook hands; their blood mingled.

Christopher dug in another pocket and found a couple of crumpled Band-Aids and handed one to Benson. He poured two steaming mugs of coffee from a thermos in his pack and they drank the coffee in silence, letting the hot liquid warm them.

"Since you don't hunt, what do you do with the time?"

"I do some target practice, using either the bow or a knife. 'Gotten pretty good at both'" Christopher added, "But I wait until it's light enough to make sure I don't *accidently* hit a deer."

Benson laughed.

Christopher reached into another pocket and pulled out a deck of cards. "...and I play a lot of solitaire." He shuffled the cards and grinned, holding the deck toward Benson.

"Interested in a game of Poker?"

Becca was bummed. She enjoyed going camping and she couldn't believe her bad luck. Try as she might, she couldn't find anyone who didn't have plans. Her family was going to be gone for days and she dreaded staying in an empty house alone. After she finished her shift, she packed a few things and drove over to the Williamsons.

Maddy and Evalyn welcomed her; delighted she wanted to stay over. Evalyn always liked Becca, who treated her like a kid sister.

The three of them applied blue clay to their faces and gave one another manicures and pedicures. Emily was not into such things, so Becca had not experienced this, but Maddy and Evalyn were *girlie girls* and Becca had a blast, ending up with cobalt-colored fingers and toes.

They munched on Maddy's brownies and homemade pizza. They played oldies music and danced in the kitchen.

No wonder Christopher and Ben stayed over so often— Maddy and Evalyn were great hosts and seemed to enjoy having guests.

When Becca heard Evalyn had never been to a skating rink, she offered to take her and teach her how to rollerblade. She caught on quickly—Becca was amazed at her agility and grace.

"It's like dancing!" Evalyn squealed delightedly. "Only faster!"

It was the last night Becca would be staying with the Williamson's. Her family was returning tomorrow. Maddy and Evalyn had gone to bed. Becca lay ensconced in the comfortable guest room.

Becca awakened during the night to go to the bathroom. On her way back to her room she noticed a light shining under Evalyn's door.

"Evalyn," she whispered. Trying not to disturb Maddy, she opened the door to Evalyn's bedroom.

Puzzled, Becca froze. Encircling Evalyn was a soft light. Becca looked around the room, trying to determine its source. Her eyes widened in surprise as she realized the light was coming *from* Evalyn.

Startled but not frightened, Becca paused in the doorway watching her sleeping friend, watching the light shimmer around her before quietly closing the door and tiptoeing back to the guestroom. She lay awake for a long time trying to make sense of what she'd just witnessed.

Evalyn sat on one of the wood and black wrought iron benches in Oak Park waiting for Christopher. She wore a thick green, hooded sweater and her favorite lived-in jeans. It had been more than a week since she'd last seen him and she was surprised by how much she had missed him.

She had just finished ballet class and was softly humming one of the pieces, the music drifting through her mind like colorful butterflies

Eager to see Christopher, she arrived a little earlier than they planned. She didn't mind waiting—she enjoyed people watching. She observed an elderly couple walking their dogs, two boys chasing a soccer ball, a young mother pushing a stroller. It was one of those rare, periwinkle blue-sky days in early winter. The temperature was higher than average for this time of the year and she was reveling in the sunshine.

In the distance, a broad shouldered young man crossed the park in long strides. He seemed vaguely familiar. He wore khaki pants, a blue jacket. A blue plaid scarf was tossed casually around his neck. Dark blond hair fell across his forehead. Fascinated, Evalyn leaned forward, watching him. He had to be the most beautiful man she had ever laid eyes on.

As he strolled closer, his eyes found hers and he smiled.

Evalyn gasped in disbelief. *It was Christopher.*

He had only been gone for a week. How could she have not noticed how beautiful he was? No wonder the girls at school were always staring at him!

"Hi Evie." He slid close to her on the bench. "Been waiting long?" he asked, his voice low.

Staring at Christopher, it took her a moment to find her voice. "Er... ah.. No. I got here a little early."

He leaned back and put his arm along the back of the bench, stroking her shoulder lightly.

"Nice sweater. That color looks good on you."

She trembled slightly at his touch.

"You can't be cold?" Christopher asked, surprised. He took off his scarf and gently wrapped it around her neck. Moving closer, he pulled her next to him.

Evalyn's heart hammered in her chest. Surely something must be wrong—she could barely breathe. She fought with conflicting desires—the desire to flee and the desire to throw her arms around him and kiss him until they were both breathless.

He was looking at her intently, his lake-blue eyes boring into hers. "I missed you," he murmured, his voice low. He kept his arm around her. Missed was an understatement. He had dreamed of her every night he'd been away.

Evalyn couldn't trust herself to speak, afraid that whatever she might say would come out wrong somehow. Or worse, she couldn't bear to kiss him and see rejection reflected in his eyes. This wasn't a risk she was willing to take.

She couldn't risk anything that might mar the friendship she had with him. It would ruin everything. He cared for her, she was certain. Hadn't they always been best friends? It would have to be enough.

Several weeks had passed and a light dusting of snow covered the ground. Evalyn walked through Oak Park, crunching on iced snow, on her way to Christopher' house. He was expecting her and had left the back kitchen door unlocked.

"Hey, Ace," Evalyn walked into the kitchen to find Ace sitting at the table. Of all the Boldsens Ace was her least favorite. "Where is everybody?"

Slowly, Ace put down the beer he'd been drinking and leaned back in his chair; his eyes traveled over Evalyn, lingering far too long. She shuddered involuntarily, as she hung up her coat, fighting the impulse to put it back on. His look made her feel undressed.

"You're lookin' mighty sweet," he drawled, taking a swig from the bottle in his hand. "...like a tasty piece of chocolate candy."

Annoyed, Evalyn shot him a direct look. Ace undoubtedly thought he had paid her a compliment. She glanced into the trashcan by the door. It was just as she suspected. Evidently, this wasn't his first beer. Several empty beer bottles were on top. From the looks of things, he'd probably been at it a while.

"I'm wondering" he insinuated, "If you taste as sweet as you look." He eased out of his chair.

"Shut up Ace," Evalyn snapped. Enough was enough—she'd had it. "You're drunk!"

Ace smirked, slowly walking toward her, backing her into the wall.

"What's wrong, Evalyn? After all you *are*... hot. Way too hot for Christopher."

He laughed derisively, sliding his hand up her arm, making her skin crawl. Leaning close, he tried to kiss her.

"No!" Evalyn said loudly; she turned her face aside and shoved against him hard, determined to push him away. She didn't want to have to live with the horrible memory that the first time she was ever kissed was by *him*.

As hard as she tried, she couldn't budge him. Amused, he laughed at her helplessness. Fear and revulsion coursed through her.

Then, blessed relief. Over his shoulder, she could see Christopher frozen in the kitchen doorway, damp from the shower, wearing only a pair of jeans. He had thought he heard Ace talking to someone and figured it must be Evalyn since he had been expecting her. He had slipped downstairs to tell her he would be with her shortly.

It took a second before the scene in front of him registered—Evalyn protesting— backed against the wall—his brother looming over her, obviously drunk. He saw Evalyn struggling to break away, gripped by Ace who was attempting to kiss her.

Ice-cold fury ripped through Christopher as rage clouded his vision.

Quietly, Christopher he came up behind Ace. "She said, 'No!'" he shouted as he brought an iron-muscled arm down around his brother's throat, hurling him across the kitchen. Ace crashed into the table, sending a porcelain bowl of fruit and the half-filled beer bottle crashing to the floor.

"What's the big deal, Bro?" sneered Ace. He got to his feet, blood dripping from a cut on his face. "You don't even know what girls are *for*."

Evalyn saw the blood and winced, as her anger struggled with her ever present empathy.

Ace continued, grinning. "I bet you haven't even figured out she's female! Here's a hint Bro—girls are the ones with *breasts*."

He lunged toward him and Christopher sidestepped the move, smashing his fist into his brother's stomach, knocking the wind out of him. Ace fell onto a chair, splintering it.

"Enough!" Bob roared, his voice filling the room. Appalled by his son's behavior, angrily he strode into the kitchen, followed closely by Matt. Emily and Becca stood in the kitchen doorway, their mouths agape, the bags in their arms filled with wrapped packages.

Christopher had drawn his arm back for another punch when Bob grabbed Christopher, intercepting the blow. Matt pinned Ace firmly by the arms, forcing the fighting brothers apart.

Stunned, Emily looked around at the destruction they had done in her kitchen, busted chairs, smashed dishes, and broken beer bottles. The brothers had fought before, as all brothers do, but *never* like this.

"I want to know what happened here," Bob roared, waving his hand in the direction of the damage. Ignoring his father, Christopher turned to Evalyn.

"Are you alright? He didn't hurt you did he?" Christopher asked.

Evalyn trembled visibly, shaken by the thought of what could have happened if Christopher had not arrived when he did. "No," she whispered, rubbing her arm where Ace had grabbed her. "I'm…. alright."

Becca ran to her side.

"Evalyn, what happened?" Becca demanded.

Evalyn was flooded with shame and revulsion. "He… Ace tried to kiss me," she whispered. "Christopher pulled him off me."

Ace shook off Matt and stormed out the door, slamming it behind him. They could hear his car peel away from the curb.

Bob and Emily were at a loss about what to say. "Evalyn… we're so sorry about our son's behavior," Bob avowed apologetically.

"Honey, we'll talk to him about this, I promise," Emily assured her, patting her arm.

Becca eased the stunned Evalyn into a chair, where she sat limply. Becca began to help her parents clean up the mess.

Christopher, looking shaken and appalled, said, "I'll finish getting dressed and take you home."

Christopher walked Evalyn through Oak Park to her house. He frequently glanced down at her, but she walked quietly beside him, her arm tucked through his. When they got to the door, Maddy opened it.

"Emily called. She told me what happened." She eyed Evalyn with concern. "Honey, are you alright?"

Evalyn nodded wearily. "I'm Ok, Mama." She gave Maddy a hug. "I'm just tired. Think I'll go to bed. 'night Christopher." They watched Evalyn as she slowly climbed the stairs to her bedroom.

"Mrs. Williamson, I'm so sorry—"

Maddy cut him off, putting up her hand. "Christopher, you've nothing to be sorry for. I'm just grateful you were there and that Evalyn is safe."

Christopher stood in the doorway, feeling helpless and ashamed of his brother's behavior.

"Go on, home Christopher. I'm sure Evalyn will give you a call tomorrow."

She hugged him before closing the door and going upstairs to see about her daughter.

Later that night as Christopher lay in bed, he thought about the words Ace had used. Word that made him as angry as his attempt to kiss her against her will.

His brother had made it sound like Evalyn was a 'thing' rather than a human being. "You don't know what girls are for," his brother said, as though girls were like Kleenex—something you blow your nose on and then dispose of. Ace was *wrong*. He knew exactly what Evalyn was *for*. She was meant to be loved. It was what he had always done and would continue to do.

He threw off the covers and sat on the edge of his bed, focusing. Eyes closed, he breathed deeply, slowly, and sent a telepathic message to Ace.

If you ever touch Evalyn again, there won't be enough of you left to bury.

Chapter 11

This was Christmas Eve. Benson maneuvered his Jeep through the recently plowed streets toward the Williamson's.

Days before, his parents called—his father from Tokyo, his mother from Nice—to apologize for not being able to spend the holidays with him. He had spent far too many holidays alone and felt grateful that Evalyn and Maddy had invited him to join them. In fact, he had eagerly looked forward to the evening.

In preparation for the holiday celebration, Maddy and Evalyn had been baking all day. When he entered their home, he was greeted with warm hugs, as always, as well as the delicious scent of fresh baked treats. There were pies and cakes, gingerbread cookies, and blue and white iced Hanukah cookies that Evalyn had baked especially for Benson.

Other than attending the Yoga Temple, there had only been four other occasions when Benson had entered a place of worship. Once was when he attended his cousins wedding in London, another had been to attend his grandfather's funeral. The last two auspicious events had been his Bar Mitzvah (where he badly bungled reading the Torah) and his Catholic confirmation (where he spilled the entire cup of wine down his white shirt, getting a few drops on the priest for good measure).

Whereas he'd found the former occasions excruciatingly boring, the latter two occasions had been a source of tremendous anxiety. He performed these duties to please his Jewish mother and his Catholic father. With each parent trying to convert him, this seemed the simplest solution.

While the constant arguments over his conversion ended, he found it amusing that converting to each religion had frustrated both of them equally.

Whenever he joined Evalyn and her mother, his experiences, although sometimes unusual, were always enjoyable.

Tonight they were planning to meet up with the Boldsens at a local cathedral and attend midnight mass—which Evalyn had explained really wasn't held at midnight but at eight o'clock. After the service, everyone planned to return to the Williamson's for dessert.

The Boldsen clan, attired in holiday red and green, arrived earlier and were holding seats for them several rows from the front. Maddy, Evalyn, and Benson genuflected briefly before slipping into the pew to join them.

Something was up, Benson surmised. Everyone, including the Williamsons, was courteous yet cool toward Ace. No one mentioned anything and Benson was too polite to ask.

He noticed that Evalyn sat as far away from Ace as possible and that Christopher sent dark looks his brother's way. Whenever he did so, Ace would blanch, although he was sitting on the far side of the pew

All about them children tittered with energy and excitement. Benson felt a bit excited, too, as he looked around at the huge cathedral decorated with poinsettias and evergreen wreaths. The pungent fragrance of pine boughs mingled with incense.

The front of the dimly lit church was arranged similarly to a stage setting. There was a lean-to with bales of hay, and an empty wooden cradle. A guitar was propped against a crude bench.

Soft voices began to sing carols. Benson turned his head to see where the music was coming from. A choir loft was located in the rear; he hadn't noticed it when he entered. The congregation joined the choir, singing familiar Christmas carols.

Instead of the homily, the priest turned the service over for the special celebration. Parents shushed their children, who settled down as the service started.

Heads turned to watch a teen girl walk sedately down the center aisle, followed by several younger children. They wore simple homespun cotton robes and big smiles. The two older children led sheep with rope halters; the youngest boy followed them, carrying a little lamb in his arms and taking small, careful steps.

The congregation stood as a robed young man led a donkey upon which sat a young woman dressed in a pale blue robe, her dark hair covered with a white silk cloth. In her arms, she carried a sleeping baby. She and the man looked so adoringly at this child; there was no doubt they were the baby's real parents.

The man led them to the front of the church, gently took the child from her arms while she dismounted and settled herself on the bench. He kissed the sleeping baby tenderly, before passing the child to her. He tethered the donkey to the side. The children took their places around the woman.

As the congregation quieted, the oldest girl picked up the guitar and began to sing as she played *Mary Did You Know?*

Benson's breath caught in his throat. Her voice was surprisingly beautiful, a powerfully strong contralto in one so young. He had never heard this song before. Her voice and her words moved him deeply. "When you kiss your little baby..."

As she sang, three regally dressed men walked slowly down the center aisle, each carrying a golden box. They placed their gifts at the feet of the child's mother and moved to stand behind the children.

The girl continued the poignant melody, "You kiss the face of God…"

As she finished her song, a hush fell over the church. Even restless children quieted. For Benson, the rest of the service passed in a blur. He usually found the holiday season filled with tension, pressure, and unmet expectations. Tonight he was filled with such peace—a peace he couldn't quite explain—he just wanted it to last for as long as possible.

Is this what Christmas is supposed to feel like? This quietness, this awe?

Perfunctorily, he responded to the others. He even helped Maddy with her coat, but he wasn't completely himself until he was ushered outside where he was met with a blast of the chill night air which smelled of evergreens and snow.

The Boldsens were oblivious, but Evalyn slipped her arm though Benson's and smiled at him warmly, intuitively sensing his mood. He answered her smile with a tremulous one of his own. She patted his arm comfortingly.

Everyone crowded noisily into Maddy's kitchen, laughing and eating her feather-light cakes and munching on buttery cookies. She had also made a sweet potato pie. Christopher promptly placed the pan in front of his place at the table. Maddy knew it was one of his favorites—next to caramel apple pie, which she had also made.

Evalyn was making a pot of coffee when Maddy noticed Benson's absence. She found him sitting quietly in the living room, near the Christmas tree watching the twinkling lights. Maddy placed her arm around Benson's shoulder, and for a few moments, quietly watched the lights with him.

The pleasant sound of laughter floated in from the kitchen. She always thought Benson was a fine boy—she would have been proud to have a son like him. She wondered how many holidays he had spent alone. Just the thought made her heart ache. No one should be alone on Christmas, or Hanukah, or whatever day one celebrated. This was a time to be with family.

She'd have Evalyn freshen the guest room later. Benson would sleep here tonight. After a moment, she returned to her guests, leaving Benson to his solitude.

Christmas morning dawned bright and clear. Coming down the stairs, Maddy smelled coffee and heard laughter coming from the kitchen. Christopher had come over and the three friends were sitting at the table eating pie for breakfast.

"Merry Christmas!" they chorused.

Clad in pink pajamas and bunny slippers, Evalyn jumped up to hug her mother. Maddy kissed her cheek.

"Did Christopher save me a piece of sweet potato pie?" Maddy asked jokingly, taking a seat and pouring a cup of coffee from the carafe.

Christopher slid the last piece of pie in front of her. "I was sorely tempted...."

"Tempted? Guilty would be more accurate. You ate half the pie last night!" Evalyn quipped.

Maddy glanced over at Benson. His clothing looked vaguely familiar before the realization dawned. He wore a flannel bathrobe. It had belonged to Evalyn's father who had been tall, like Benson. The robe and pajamas beneath it fit him perfectly.

Many years ago, Maddy carefully packed away several pieces of her husband's clothing in a cedar chest in the attic. Every now and then, she'd open the chest and lovingly touch his things, remembering the occasions when he'd worn them. One sweater in particular, still held the faint odor of his warm scent. Periodically she'd replace the scented laundering packets she used to keep the clothing fresh.

"Ben needed something to sleep in last night," Evalyn offered hesitantly, "so I put a few things in the guestroom for him to use."

"It's good you thought of it, Evalyn." Maddy reached across the table, patted her daughter's hand. "I'm glad the clothing has been put to good use."

Until this moment, she had no idea Evalyn had known what was in the chest. Evalyn smiled, relieved. She didn't think her mother would mind—Maddy was more practical than sentimental.

"We wanted to wait for you, so we could open gifts together," Evalyn sang out, leading the way into the living room. Maddy laughed. They were practically grown-ups, but when it came to presents, they acted like giddy kids. Excited, they opened presents—untying ribbons—noisily tearing off wrapping paper. It seemed like a few more gifts had been placed under the tree since last night.

Maddy had knitted sweaters for all of them. Christopher's sweater was a deep blue, chunky cable knit. For Benson, Maddy had used fine gauge dove gray wool, which complemented his eyes perfectly. She'd noticed months ago that he no longer wore eyeglasses and suspected that her daughter might have something to do with it, but didn't dare question Evalyn for fear of the answer. Evalyn's sweater was palest green, knitted in whisper soft baby yarn. She had seen her mother working on Christopher and Benson's sweaters in the evenings, but hers was truly a delightful surprise.

Months before, Christopher had taken a candid photograph of Evalyn and Maddy of which they were unaware. He had had it enlarged and placed it in a gilded frame. They thanked him profusely. Maddy looked around to find a place for it. She put it on the mantle above the fireplace where it fit perfectly.

Benson handed Evalyn and Maddy small wrapped silver and blue packages which held soft leather gloves lined with cashmere. He blushed with pleasure when they both hugged and kissed him at the same time.

Christopher and Benson dove under the tree and surfaced with the gifts they had gotten for each another. Unexpectedly, their presents were identical.

Evalyn giggled, "When you both asked me for ideas, I figured I'd make it a 'no brainer'—gift certificates from Computer Savvy." She gracefully lifted a shoulder. "You both practically live there anyway."

After an hour or so, Christopher and Benson left. They were planning to go skating and later, Benson was having dinner at Christopher's. But he had left his things in the guestroom and Maddy and Evalyn knew he'd return to their house later as he often did whenever the Boldsen's boisterousness became too much for him.

Christopher agreed to accompany Evalyn to the local community theatre tonight. She was going to practice for her upcoming dance recital in early spring. Although it was almost a month from now, she asked him to come along because she wanted his opinion first. It was an interpretive ballet she had choreographed herself and no one else had seen it in its entirety.

It had been more than ten years since he had seen Evalyn dance. That particular occasion had been at her first recital, after she had agreed to go to one of his Little League games. She always had been his biggest fan. Sitting in the midst of his raucous family, she had cheered for him enthusiastically. He thought it would be only fair for him to attend her recital, although he thought the little girls running around in pink tutus looked like silly fluffs of cotton candy.

After the conflict of a few months ago with his brother, he felt that being bored for an hour or so while she practiced, was the least he could do. Since the incident, he had been particularly gentle with her and watched her closely for any signs of irreparable damage. Lucky for Ace, she displayed none.

They walked toward the theatre enjoying the brisk late winter evening. Christopher lifted his head, breathing in the subtle scent in the wind, "It's going to snow later," he said matter-of-factly. Evalyn nodded, she had hoped they had seen the last of winter weather and that spring would arrive early but if Christopher said it was going to snow, then it would snow. He was more accurate than the local weatherman. They walked on in companionable silence, their strides matching.

"So… ah… it's called interpretive dance?" he asked, breaking the silence, hoping she would give him a clue—even a small one—so he'd be able to make an intelligent guess. She didn't take the hint.

"What exactly are you interpreting, Evalyn?" He asked directly, afraid of missing the mark and looking like an uncultured idiot. Even after all these years, he wasn't beyond trying to impress her.

Slyly she glanced at him from the corner of her mischievous green eyes. He was fishing and she knew it.

"Watch first and then you tell me. If you get it right, then I've done it right," she quipped. She laughed as his face fell. She wasn't going to let him off easy.

"The stage manager mentioned no one would be here—I could have it to myself tonight," she informed him. "I hope he remembered the lighting," she muttered to herself.

Evalyn noted the manager had left the back door open, as he'd promised. They entered and walked down the dim hallway through the door nearest to the seats in front of the stage.

As promised, the stage manager had arranged the lighting as Evalyn requested. Soft lights in varying shades of blue encircled the floor of the entire stage. From above, a single blue spotlight slanted at an angle, widening into a blue pool across center stage.

"Sit there," Evalyn ordered, pointing at the middle front seat. "And pay attention." She ran lightly up the stairs and slipped behind the curtain.

Christopher slipped out of his parka and settled into the soft cushioned seat. He glanced around the intimate theatre, pleased. The seating was placed strategically—slightly higher than the stage. After a few minutes, he heard soft music flow from discretely hidden speakers. Oboes, piano, violins—he didn't recognize the piece, but it was pleasant—soft, poignant.

Evalyn stepped so quietly into the blue light that he hadn't noticed her until she arched one arm gracefully above her head, the other to her side, lifted slightly from the shoulder. Her head was bowed.

She wore a simple leotard and a diaphanous white skirt barely covering her hips. Her braids were loose, falling to the middle of her back. Her feet were bare. The sight of Evalyn, standing motionless caused Christopher to catch his breath. *When had she grown so beautiful?*

Christopher was fully aware of his feelings for Evalyn. In fact, he believed it was one of his best kept secrets. He couldn't quite pinpoint the moment when his feelings had shifted from those of friendship to those of love. But he knew without a doubt he loved Evalyn more than anyone.

He would just have to be patient, until she learned how to love him the same way. For now, just being near her and being a part of her life was good enough for him. He settled deeper into his chair to watch her.

Gracefully, Evalyn began to sway to the music, moving slowly onto her toes. She glided effortlessly toward the blue light, twirled, and then glided away from it. The white skirt floated gently around her. She quickened her steps with the music, leaping—gaining momentum with the crescendo. She seemed to flow across the stage. The blue lights reflected the contrast of the white chiffon and her dark skin.

She became oblivious to her surroundings. She only heard the music, felt the floor beneath her bare feet.

She flows, Christopher thought, *like water.*

Fascinated, he leaned forward, his hands on his knees, his lips parted. He watched as Evalyn pirouetted into a serene lake and then became the lake itself. She was a raging river, her hair wild and swirling.

With arms outstretched, she burst upward, into a fountain spray. And then, her quick, delicate steps surged into a rippling brook. An ethereal play of light and shadow, she was so beautiful in motion. Tears filled his eyes.

He knew she was dancing for him, telling him of her love, in a language she knew he would understand.

As Christopher watched, Evalyn began to glow. He sat up in his seat, mesmerized. She was a moving, dancing, light. Awestruck, Christopher came to his feet. His heart beat loudly so loudly, he thought the entire world could hear it.

In the pit of his stomach, an inferno blazed, outmatched only by the flame searing through his heart. He wanted to take her into his arms and hold her forever, to show her their feelings were mutual. He had to get to her—to tell her how he felt about her. With two long jumps, he leaped onto the stage. He took a hesitant step toward her and stopped.

Evalyn, I..." he gestured helplessly, at a loss for words.

The music flowed around them, like water.

She stopped dancing and took a few tentative steps toward him, her eyes widening. She held one hand to her mouth, the other reaching for him, pointing.

"Oh! Christopher!" Evalyn whispered softly, "*Look* at yourself!"

Slowly, he glanced down at his body, raised his arms. There was a subtle shimmer, an almost imperceptible radiance.

He gaped at Evalyn in amazement. This had *never* happened to him before. Evalyn rapidly crossed the floor and leaned against his chest, his arms encircled her tightly. A mist of soft white light swirled around them, as their energies combined.

"Evalyn, I...I love you," Christopher declared shakily.

"Yes... I can definitely see that now," she breathed, a laugh lilting her voice.

She raised herself on her toes and pressed her warm lips to his. A shock surged through them. Quickly, they pulled apart, its force taking them by surprise.

Undaunted, Christopher pulled Evalyn back into his arms, enfolding her. He kissed her again more slowly this time, passionately. It had taken years to come to this—he never wanted to let her go.

He was filled with love...wonder...questions. There was still so much he didn't understand—about himself, about her, about the energy flowing between them.

"This... power," he murmured, brushing his lips against hers. He kissed her again, unable to stop himself. His lips seem to have a will of their own.

"I don't understand what it's all about ..."

She stopped his words with soft kisses of her own on his face, neck, lips.

"It's always been about love, Christopher," Evalyn murmured, her breath mingling with his. She looked into his face, her eyes liquid. "This much power could never come from anything else."

Christopher walked her home. They kissed once again in the doorway, finding it difficult to pull away.

Evalyn closed the front door, leaned against it, feeling lightheaded and giddy. Then she flew up the stairs to say goodnight to her mother before disappearing into the sanctuary of her room.

She didn't bother to turn on the lamp—the streetlight down the block provided all the light she needed. She looked into the mirror and studied her reflection. She looked the same, but different. Gingerly, she touched her lips. They felt more sensitive somehow. *So this is what falling in love feels like.*

She pulled her diary out from under the mattress at the foot of her bed and started writing: *Dear Diary, Tonight I had my first kiss. It was everything I thought it would be and more.*

Sitting on her bed, arms wrapped around her knees, she felt like she was floating on air and never wanted to land.

Evalyn awakened to the enticing smell of fresh coffee and the sound of voices in the kitchen below. The voices belonged to Christopher and her mother. She glanced at the clock on her nightstand.

She knew her mother rose early on Saturdays so she could get her errands done before the stores became too crowded. But not Christopher—it would take a bulldozer to move him out of bed at seven thirty on a Saturday morning.

Hurriedly, she tossed the covers aside. She had to see him—to see if last night was real or just a very pleasant dream. She brushed her teeth, wound her hair in a top knot, and decided against getting dressed. She skipped downstairs in her pajamas. He'd seen her in her pajamas so many times, one more time wouldn't make much difference.

The moment they saw one another their eyes lit up. This exchange wasn't lost on Maddy. Speculatively, she looked from one to the other. This explained why Christopher was at her door shortly after daybreak this morning.

"Morning," they chorused in unison.

Evalyn poured coffee into the mug at her place at the table. She could hardly drink it for grinning, her eyes taking in Christopher over the top of her cup.

"I've already finished breakfast. There's bacon and eggs in the fridge," Maddy offered graciously. She grabbed her purse and the car keys from the hook by the door. "See you kids later."

As soon as Evalyn heard the car leave the driveway, she hopped from her chair and wriggled into Christopher's lap. He kissed her until she was breathless and laughing.

Between kisses, Evalyn murmured, "I'd like to sit here forever, but I have to shower and dress." She may have learned how to kiss only yesterday, but she was a quick learner.

"I came over to ask if you would go out with me tonight," he announced, his voice solemn.

Hanging out together was something they'd done most of their lives. Usually whatever they did was on the spur of the moment. A telephone call a hour beforehand was usually all the notice they gave one another.

"Shall I call Benson and see what he's up to? Maybe he'd like to join us."

Christopher slowly shook his head. "Maybe some other time, but not tonight."

Evalyn wrapped her arms around his neck. "Ok then, but why so serious?"

"Cause this is a *date,* Evalyn. I'm asking you on a date. *Officially"*

Oh. A date. She grinned, delighted. "Oh, yes! I officially accept."

Last night she had her first kiss, tonight was going to be her first date. Her life was taking off in an exhilarating direction and she liked it.

Chapter 12

*D*r. Andrew Clarke had a vested interest in this operation. He wanted to make sure the CDC found the girl, rather than the Bureau of Stateside Security. While he couldn't put his finger on it, there was something about Jim Richards he didn't trust. Due to the inherent physiologic component of the case, the CDC had been placed in charge of the investigation rather than the bureau. He suspected Richards was resentful.

Jamison, his director, hadn't placed Clarke in charge because he liked him, quite the contrary. Jamison sent him because perfectionism was one of the few things Clarke and Jamison had in common. Clarke was as meticulous regarding his investigations as he was about his attire.

It was Clarke's policy to have his assistants unearth the information and then he would do most of the fieldwork himself. He was better than anyone else on the team at dealing with conditions in the real world. In addition to being extremely intelligent, and highly intuitive—he was also charming and charismatic. Sooner or later most people willingly provided him information with little encouragement.

The day after his arrival, Clarke's assistants handed him a slim folder with video, photos and information gleaned from supposedly confidential hospital and ambulance records. They didn't have much to go on, only first names.

According to statements from the ambulance driver, the young man was named Chris, which Clark surmised could be short for Christian or Christopher. Also, according to reports given by the paramedic and hospital staff, the girl in the video, who purported to be his sister, was called Evie, probably another nickname, Clarke concluded.

Based on the dynamic played out between the two, his gut told him they weren't brother and sister. There was something in the tender way she touched him, in the way he looked at her with longing.

With descriptions of both Chris and Evie, Clarke checked around town to see if anyone recognized them. He was given several leads but so far, none of them turned up anything. He had one address left.

He located the address on the map and drove around the area for a while, checking out what appeared to be a normal, middleclass neighborhood. As he approached the home, he saw a handsome middle-aged couple get into a car and drive off. Clarke pulled to the curb two doors down from the house. He walked up to the front door and knocked. A young man in his early twenties answered.

"Are your parent's home?" Clarke asked nonchalantly. Of course he figured they weren't as he assumed the couple he watched drive off before he came to the door were the young man's mother and father. Whereas older adults often play their cards close to their chests, he knew kids will often tell all.

Ace shook his head. "Nah, they just left."

"Where's your sister? Is she in?"

"Becca?" *What would this suit want with her?*

"No, your other sister, Evie."

Ace snorted. "Evie. She's *not* my sister. And her name is Evalyn, not Evie."

The investigator knew the type—they'd tell you anything for a price. This kid was young, it shouldn't take too much. He pulled several crisp twenties from his wallet. In a flash, Ace snatched them from his hand.

"Yeah, I know her." He grinned broadly. "Give me another coupla bills and I'll tell you where you can find her." Clarke handed two more twenties to Ace.

Ace pointed toward an area he called Oak Park, then gave Clarke a description of Evalyn's house.

Clarke hesitated a moment, opened his wallet again and took out a crisp hundred dollar bill. Eyes widening, Ace reached for it. Clarke held fast to the other end.

"Ummm, just one more thing," Clarke intoned, "If anyone comes around asking questions about this 'Evie,' tell them you don't know her. Oh, and by the way," he added, his gaze leveled, "I've never been here."

Nodding, Ace closed the door.

Preoccupied with his newly acquired wealth, Ace almost bumped into his sister coming from the kitchen, carrying a tray. Hastily, he shoved the money into his pocket.

"What are you doing standing there?" he demanded.

"Nothing. I live here," she retorted, sarcastically. "I'm Becca, your sister. Remember me?"

"Always sneaking around!"

"I wasn't sneaking anywhere. I was in the kitchen making a sandwich." She eyed her brother suspiciously. "Who was at the door?"

"No one. Mind your own business, Becca!" He slipped past her and fled up the stairs, two at a time.

Balancing the tray holding her sandwich and a glass of milk, Becca peered through the small window in the front door. She saw a man wearing a dark gray overcoat leaving their yard. He walked to a car parked down the street, climbed into the non-descript gray sedan, and drove off slowly. *Who had her brother been speaking with? What was going on?*

Back in the car, Clarke smiled to himself, giving a sigh of relief, thankful he arrived before the Bureau. Clarke figured he would feed Richards just enough information to keep his investigators from coming here—simply tell them he'd found information that turned out to be a dead end.

Jim Richards was a competitive man by nature. He refused to allow the Bureau of Stateside Security to play second fiddle to the Center for Disease Control. He had been doing investigations when this young upstart was still in diapers. Nevertheless, Dr. Clarke seemed to be a powerhouse and Richards had a hunch it wouldn't take him long to find out the girl's identity.

As soon as Richards returned to his car, he made two telephone calls. One was to the airline to schedule the next flight out. The other was a call to the Bureau in Omaha. Richards ordered an investigator from the Omaha branch of the Bureau to find the location of the mall where the paramedics had picked them up, to find the closest high schools to that location, and to get any scrap of information they could unearth. He would handle this operation his way.

The day after the meeting with the CDC, Richards landed in Omaha. He was given the addresses of two high schools in the vicinity—one on Twentieth Street, the other on Thirty-sixth. He would visit them both.

He found nothing of importance at the school on Twentieth Street so he headed to the second high school located about fifteen minutes northeast. He surmised classes were due to be out in ten minutes, so he should be able to catch the students milling around the campus.

He made it to the school in time to park in front just as the bell was ringing, signaling the end of the day. Out of his car and on the way up the stairs, he stopped a gangly teen.

"Hey, Tommy!" Richards boomed. "It's good to see you again! My, how you've grown!"

The boy scowled disdainfully. "I'm not Tommy, I'm Jonas Vincent," and added under his breath, "and you're an idiot." He stepped around Richards and continued on his way.

Richards walked down the hall, mingling through the crowd. He really didn't expect to find the two kids, just get information about them.

A teacher spotted him looking around and walked up to him, "Are you looking for someone?"

Richards smiled, "Yes, I'm looking for my son, Jonas. Jonas Vincent."

The teacher smiled, "He's probably still up on the third floor."

"Thanks." Richards walked up several flights of stairs, arriving breathless at the top, a legacy from his pack a day cigarette habit. Ahead, he noticed a voluptuous redhead taking a book out of her locker.

He walked up to her, using the only names he had from the dossier. "Hey, I'm looking for Chris and Evie. Have you seen them around?"

Megan slammed her locker shut with a bang. Just hearing their names said in the same breath irritated her. She still hadn't gotten over Christopher's total and complete rejection of her.

"Are you a friend of theirs…family or something?" she asked suspiciously. Not that she cared. For one thing, Megan's brother was on probation and this guy looked more like her brother's probation officer—something about him screamed "government."

Richards followed his instincts, honed from years of experience. "They're not friends--just need to bring them in for questioning."

With any luck, Megan thought hopefully, Christopher was in some sort of trouble. If so, it served him right.

"We're having midterms—everybody's studying." She volunteered, "Check out the library. Not the one at the school—ours sucks—the public library."

Maddy's day had been horrific. It was one of those days when nothing seems to go as planned. Recently she had accepted a teaching assignment in an elementary school across town and on the way to work she'd had a flat tire. This meant another teacher had to substitute for thirty minutes until she arrived. After lunch one of the students vomited up her classroom and the students were sent to the gym until the mess could be cleaned up. After school, but before her day could end, she attended a meeting with an irate parent. It hadn't gone very well.

As soon as she walked into the house, she hung her coat in the hall closet, laid her hat and scarf on the closet shelf, and walked into the kitchen. She put the kettle on to boil water and went into the living room to light the fireplace. The late Spring weather had been unusually cold and damp and she felt chilled to the bone. A crackling fire and hot tea would warm her. Hearing a knock at the door, she hurried to answer it.

The smile froze on Maddy's face. In her doorway stood an official-looking, dark-skinned man wearing a finely tailored overcoat. Everything about him screamed "establishment." She felt the blood drain from her face and felt grateful for her dark skin; he wouldn't be aware of the effect he had on her.

She didn't need an introduction. Ever since her daughter's birth, Maddy had been prepared for the day when someone would show up at their door.

The protective instincts of a mother came to the forefront. Her mind raced. It might take a week or more to put her plan in place: She'd quit her job, close out her bank account and head for some place in Central America where they could blend in easily. Panama perhaps, or Belize. She didn't care what she'd have to say or do. She would protect her daughter as long as there was breath in her body.

"Hello," she greeted the man at the door, her voice courteous, feigning curiosity. "May I help you?"

"Are you Evalyn's mother?" He asked pleasantly.

She nodded slowly. "What is this about?"

"I'd like to talk to you and your daughter."

"She's not here at the moment. Is something wrong?" Maddy queried, knowing this would be unlikely.

"No, Ma'am." He pulled out a badge, handing it to her. "I'm Dr. Andrew Clarke from the Center for Disease Control," he stated. "If you can spare a moment, I'd like to speak with you."

The tea kettle whistled in the kitchen.

"Please come in." She held the door open wide, inviting him in. "Would you like to join me for a cup of tea?" Maddy asked politely.

Evalyn was practicing for an upcoming recital and wouldn't be home for at least another hour or two. It would give Maddy time to investigate this man. She knew instinctively he planned to investigate her. She had to find out how much he knew.

Evalyn tucked her arm through Christopher's as they walked down the library steps. In spite of sneaking in a kiss or two when no one was watching, they still managed to study.

While they had been inside, the sky had darkened considerably. Just as they arrived at the bottom of the stairs, the rain began to fall. They searched the nearly deserted street, expecting to see Benson drive up for them at any moment.

A white van pulled up to the curb. The driver rolled down the window and beckoned to them. He had a map in his hand.

"Hey there. Could you help me find an address?" he asked, smiling broadly.

They took steps toward the driver. Just then, the side doors slid open and two burly men stepped out.

"Get in," one of the men ordered gruffly. "Both of you."

"We're not—" Christopher stopped in midsentence. In the same instant, the other man moved his jacket to the side, displaying a gun tucked into a holster. Evalyn gasped.

"We can do this the hard way or the easy way. It's up to you," the man with the gun insisted. "We really don't want to have to hurt either of you. And we *really* don't want to hurt Becca. So don't force our hand." Christopher paled at the mention of his sister's name.

They knew their names! Who were these men?

"Christopher, they've got Becca!" Evalyn said, alarmed. "We've got to do what they want."

Evalyn climbed into the van, Christopher jumped in behind her. The man with the gun got in with them. The other man sat in front, next to the driver.

A fourth man with a crew cut was seated in the back. Christopher and Evalyn sat across from him. Evalyn pressed against Christopher's side.

"Where's my sister?" Christopher demanded hotly.

The man with the crew cut smiled malevolently. "Home, I would guess. We're really not interested in her." He reached his hand toward Evalyn.

Christopher caught his hand in an iron grip. Involuntarily the man winced. "Don't." Christopher warned through clenched teeth.

Christopher could feel the hard metal of a gun pressing into his ribs. He released the man's hand, and angrily flung it away.

The man with the crew cut flexed his pained fingers. "Lose the gun, Jake. The boyfriend here might cause it to go off accidently. Our orders say to bring 'em in unharmed."

Benson looked up at the clock. He had been playing the piano and completely lost track of time. Christopher and Evalyn were waiting for him in front the library. They had plans to take in a movie.

He smiled, wondering what they would see this evening. Evalyn liked romantic comedies, Christopher enjoyed a good horror flick. The two of them seemed closer than ever lately.

Backing the Jeep out of the garage in one smooth movement, Benson scanned the sky. It was overcast and dreary. The air felt heavy. Thick, ominous, clouds hid the sun completely, making it seem later than it was.

The rain began falling just as he stopped at a traffic light a block away. Benson spotted Christopher and Evalyn standing in front of the building. A white van drove slowly down the nearly empty street, coming to a stop in front of Christopher and Evalyn. Benson noticed Christopher turn toward the van, as though someone had called out to him. Probably asking directions.

Other than Benson, no one else was nearby. Before the light changed, he noticed two large men step out of the van. Within seconds, Christopher and Evalyn were hustled inside and whisked away. The men moved so smoothly, so swiftly, that if Benson hadn't been looking for them he would have missed everything. He didn't know what was happening, but whatever it was, it didn't sure didn't seem to bode well for his friends.

He decided to follow the van, staying far enough behind to be unnoticed, but close enough not to lose them. Benson trailed the van to a street in a business district southeast of downtown. He watched as a large corrugated garage door opened in back of a warehouse and the van drove inside. With a clang, the door slid shut.

Dr. Clarke drove away from the Williamson's. Mrs. Williamson had been courteous, but as most adults during initial contact, offered little. Beneath her calm exterior he detected fear. He wondered about this.

His cell phone rang. "Clarke here," he answered crisply. He listened intently for a moment and then his temper flared.

"On whose instruction?" he demanded, yelling into the phone. "I didn't give an order for an interception!"

He threw the phone down on the seat next to him and peeled onto the freeway, heading for the Omaha branch of Stateside Security.

Ben parked several blocks away from the warehouse but in view of the building. It was raining harder, and the sun had set and the little light it had provided disappeared. The dull yellow of streetlights did little to lessen the gloom.

He got out of his Jeep, pulling up his jacket collar. He walked back toward the building, carefully checking out the street. The area held mostly warehouses and factories. There was a large post office, but it appeared to be already closed. Across the street, he noticed a gray electrical cable box half buried in the ground.

Drenched, he went back to his Jeep and slid into the seat, positioning himself where he could keep the garage door in sight in case they decided to move his friends to another location.

The darkness deepened. The few places that were open when he first arrived finally closed for the night and the workers drove away. Except for his Jeep, the street was deserted.

Ben had a sinking feeling in the pit of his stomach. Realizing there was no one he could turn to, he knew he had to find a solution. Fast. He felt sure Christopher and Evalyn's safety depended upon it.

In the glove compartment he found a pocketknife and several boxes of matches, which he stuffed in his pockets. Pulling his hood down low, he grabbed the tire jack from under the back seat.

Under cover of darkness and in pouring rain, Benson crept back to the warehouse and circled around to the front of the building. He peered into the windows on the side. The lights were off in the room; he couldn't hear any noise.

As quietly as he could, he broke the window, grateful the downpour covered the sound of breaking glass. He found the latch, slid the window open and climbed inside. He could hear the murmur of men's voices coming from the back of the warehouse where he'd seen the van enter. He listened closely at the door, but couldn't make out what they were saying. He couldn't hear Christopher or Evalyn either.

Ben struck a match. The room he was in was an office of some sort, with metal filing cabinets and desks. He looked up. In the ceiling was a sprinkler, the kind linked to an alarm when set off by fire. Ben breathed a sigh of relief—this was exactly what he was hoping to find.

He placed a large trashcan on top of a desk directly under the sprinkler, stuffed it with papers from the cabinets, and tossed in lighted matches. He waited a few minutes to make sure it would stay lit before slipping back out the window and across the street to where he had spotted the electrical cable box. As soon as he heard the fire alarm sound in the warehouse, Ben took the jack to the cable box, breaking it open. With a sharp knife he severed all the wires, cutting all the power to the area. The street lights and all the electricity on the street went out, leaving the area in total drenching, darkness.

Quickly, Ben ran back to the building, waiting to see which entrance they would come out of. "Evalyn and Christopher," he whispered softly to himself. "I'm counting on you to take it from here."

Evalyn and Christopher had been pushed into in a small, windowless room. The electric lock clicked shut behind them. The room contained two cots and a table with a lamp.

Through an open door at rear of the room was a stark bathroom containing a sink and toilet. Evalyn looked at Christopher in alarm. *They planned to keep them!* Christopher tried the door. It wouldn't budge. He banged on it until his hand hurt. No one answered.

Time seemed to drag, although it was probably only a couple of hours. Evalyn sat on the bed, knees drawn up to her chin. Christopher paced back and forth.

"Christopher, you're driving me crazy." She patted a spot on the bed next to her. "Come sit by me, please."

Obligingly, he sat close and Evalyn leaned against him comforting them both.

Unexpectedly, a fire alarm sounded and the overhead fire sprinklers went off. Evalyn and Christopher grabbed their jackets and flung them over themselves in an effort to keep dry.

The lamp went out, leaving them in pitch blackness. They heard the click of the electric door lock. Christopher felt his way to the door and turned the handle. It opened.

"Christopher, someone did this—someone's helping us" Evalyn whispered. There was only one person who knew they were not at the library—the person who was supposed to meet them.

"Ben!' Christopher whispered, "He must have noticed the van, seen them snatch us."

In the pitch blackness, Christopher couldn't see a thing, but Evalyn could see perfectly. Taking his hand she pulled him down to the floor.

"Stay with me, and stay down low," she whispered. At the rear of the warehouse, they could hear several men were shouting and crashing about as they stumbled around in the dark. Evalyn and Christopher crawled toward the front of the building.

Ben! Front door!

Ben smiled as he received Christopher's telepathic message. *So that's how he does it,* Ben concluded. He always wondered how

Evalyn seemed to know things when Christopher was nowhere near her, as though she were listening to something.

Obeying the subtle voice in his mind, a voice that unmistakably belonged to Christopher; he started the Jeep. Keeping the headlights off, he drove to the front of the warehouse. Evalyn spotted him first. They tumbled into the Jeep as it slowed. Ben hit the gas hard and headed straight for Dundee.

"Who were those creeps and what did they want—?

"It's me they're after, not Christopher," Evalyn interjected. "But if they found Christopher … Ben, they could just as easily find you. They might connect you to us."

Christopher interjected, "… search your house, or come after you, bring you in for questioning or something."

Benson snorted. "Let them try. Being wealthy has certain advantages. Not only do the wealthy pay fewer taxes than others, in many other ways we're practically untouchable. Few organizations dare to go after anyone who can afford better lawyers than they can. It's an unwritten rule."

In the safety of Ben's family's estate, they were finally able to relax. All of them were soaked through. Ben changed and also found dry clothes for the other two while a servant put the clothes they'd been wearing in the dryer. Evalyn rolled up the sleeves of the robe he gave her, the bottom trailed the floor, but it was warm and soft and smelled like Ben.

They gathered in Ben's bedroom suite. He'd ordered food sent up for them and a mug of hot tea for Evalyn. She curled up on the sofa, while Christopher and Ben sat in easy chairs and put their heads together discussing a plan Christopher had been considering for a while.

Like Maddy, he had expected there might come a time when Evalyn would no longer be able to live a normal life. Still, he never thought anyone would want to kidnap her. Hound her— yes, but abduction never crossed his mind.

In doing some research a few months ago, he and Ben found information about a huge reserve outside of Anchorage, near Mount Saint Elias. The village was accessible only by small plane. If they could manage to escape north, they'd have a chance of surviving the same way many Alaskans had for hundreds of years—by living off the land. Christopher was good with the bow. And they'd be safe.

Later that night, Ben drove Evalyn home in one of his father's cars, circling the block to make certain they weren't being followed. No one had tailed them, so whoever had ordered them kidnapped seemed to have called off the dogs—at least for now.

Christopher followed them in Ben's Jeep. Ben parked his father's car in Evalyn's garage and told her to drive it instead. Her mother's license plate number, as well as the description of her car, was undoubtedly known by whoever kidnapped them.

As Evalyn drove to the ballet studio the next night, she concentrated on ignoring the sadness threatening to overwhelm her. She parked the car and slowly, with heavy steps, walked to the double glass doors. As she pushed them open the receptionist looked up, greeting her cheerfully. Evalyn could only nod numbly in response.

Her eyes stung with tears as she heard the sounds of music from the main practice room and the voice of one of the young instructors. She walked up the stairs, to Panzella's office and knocked on her door.

"Come in," Panzella sang out. She was sitting at her desk shuffling through piles of invoices, glasses pushed down her nose. The comfortable office was dimly lit by a small green Banker's lamp on the desk.

Evalyn pushed open the door. Seeing her dear instructor and knowing she may never see her again was more than she could bear. Tears flooded her eyes and spilled down her cheeks. Panzella quickly ran to Evalyn's side, genuinely alarmed. She had never seen her like this. "Evalyn, *mia cara*, what's wrong? Tell me!" she insisted.

Evalyn wrapped her arms around her instructor, holding her tight. "I can't come here anymore. I have to stop dancing," she sobbed. It wasn't until this moment Evalyn realized dancing was the secondary reason she enjoyed coming to the studio. Panzella was the first. Evalyn loved her dearly.

"If it's about the money…"

"No," Evalyn's shoulders shook with sobs. "I –I have to go away."

"You and your mother are moving?" Panzella struggled to grasp what could possibly have happened to bring her star pupil to tears.

"No, just me." Evalyn clung to Panzella.

Panzella pulled Evalyn over to the small sofa in the corner and sat her down. She sat next to her, placing Evalyn's hand in hers. "Now tell me," she insisted, her accent growing stronger. "What is happening? Why these tears?"

Evalyn was at a loss for words. How could she explain why it was necessary to run for her life? She breathed deeply, her head bowed as she deliberated. She raised her head and looked into Panzella's compassionate, worried eyes, certain the love she felt for her instructor was mutual.

"I know that… your right hip… often causes you pain," Evalyn stammered.

Panzella frowned; puzzled by the direction the conversation seemed to be taking.

"Yes, it's hurting now but …" Panzella replied, haltingly. She always assumed she hid her pain successfully. But not from Evalyn.

"I'll explain it all to you, but first may I show you something?" Evalyn asked cautiously.

"Yes, of course." Panzella responded, thoroughly confused. "Yes, yes. Show me whatever is causing you so much trouble."

Evalyn knelt on the floor at Panzella's feet. Moving slowly, so she wouldn't frighten her, she placed her hand on Panzella's right hip. Panzella gave a sharp gasp, startled by the tingling flowing from Evalyn's fingers. Her mouth flew open in amazement as the tingling accelerated and Evalyn began to glow, her light brightening the room. The tingling coursed throughout Panzella's body, its power intensifying at her hip.

Panzella had never experienced anything like this. It felt like the summer sun in the Italian countryside; she could smell the fragrant scent of the lemon groves she played in as a child. It felt like laughter, and song. It had the power and force of a thousand watts of electricity, yet felt soft, gentle. And the pain in her hip was *gone.*

Panzella's eyes filled with tears. Simultaneously, the tingling in her body and the radiance surrounding Evalyn subsided. *Evalyn was a healer.* For once Panzella was speechless.

Evalyn smiled knowingly, her green eyes fixed on her instructor's startled face.

"*Dio Santo!*" Panzella got to her feet, and rotated her hip—something she hadn't been able to do for years.

"Thank you", she whispered, hugging Evalyn tightly.

"X-rays will show no fracture." Evalyn murmured. "It will be as though it was never broken."

Her dance instructor stared at her in amazement.

"This explains a lot." Panzella affirmed. "Such as why you never get sick, not even during the flu epidemic several years ago, when everyone else at the studio dropped like flies." Smiling, she continued, nodding. "… and why you can dance barefoot."

Evalyn sighed, shaking her head. "Yes, but now others have found out—people in our government, I think—and they are after me."

Panzella regarded Evalyn solemnly. "I don't know the why's or how's of your gift, Evalyn. But I am not afraid of what I don't understand. Most people are. They assume the worst."

Evalyn nodded and stood. "If they find me, I don't know what they'll do—I just know I will most likely be taken somewhere, to some type of place where I'll be detained. Of course they won't call it a 'prison,' but I'm sure once they find me, they'll never let me go. I have to leave tonight."

Panzella walked Evalyn down the stairs and to the front door.

"If you ever need me, *mia cara* ..."

"I know." Evalyn gave Panzella one last hug before getting in the car. As she drove away, in the rearview mirror she could see Panzella in the doorway, waving.

Although it devastated Evalyn to leave Panzella, she felt happy knowing she had been able to give her this one last gift.

Chapter 13

en pulled his Jeep into the Williamson's driveway. Inside Christopher and Evalyn waited impatiently for him to arrive. They were leaving tonight with little more than the clothes on their backs.

Without being obvious, Ben glanced around as he headed for the front door. He didn't see any black sedans or suspicious vehicles on the street, but he couldn't assume they weren't being watched.

Christopher was in the kitchen, speaking with Maddy, trying to comfort her. Ever since Evalyn's birth, Maddy feared this devastating day would come yet accepting the actual leaving seemed unbearable.

When Maddy tried to fill the teapot with water, her hands shook so much the water splashed and spilled onto the floor. Christopher gently led her to a chair and cleaned up the spill, continuing to her in low, soft tones. He put the teapot on to boil, took the cups from the cabinet and set up the tray, as he had often seen her do.

"You know I'll take good care of her, Maddy," Chris assured her.

"You always have, haven't you?" She whispered. Evalyn's secret had been safe with him since he was six and she remembered he'd always protected her from bullies. Yes, she trusted that he would take good care of her daughter. She knew he loved Evalyn, would even die for her. And this frightened her. She loved him as though he was her own son.

Christopher told her he left a note for his parents, saying he would contact them later. He would leave it to Maddy to tell them as much or as little as she would like. Usually Maddy was the strong one, tonight Christopher knew Maddy was doing her best to hold herself together. Evalyn was her life.

While Christopher was talking to Maddy, Ben pulled Evalyn aside and placed two small black velvet pouches in her hand. Baffled, she looked at him.

"A little something for you and your Mom to share," he murmured quietly.

She emptied the contents of the pouches. In her palm were two glistening heart -shaped diamond pendants on platinum chains. Evalyn gasped, shocked.

"Ben!" Quickly Evalyn grabbed him by the arm and stepped out of the view from the kitchen.

"They're beautiful! We could never afford anything like this!" She thrust the pendants toward him, whispering so as not to be overheard.

Her delight touched Ben deeply. He sincerely hoped they would like the gifts. Over the years he had given his mother many pieces of jewelry, as had his father. His mother would brush his cheek with a perfunctory kiss—carefully, so as not to smear her lipstick—and carelessly toss the item in her jewelry cache on top of the mounds of other gems.

"I know Mom would love it. But we can't accept these—it's too much."

"It's a piece of your heart she can keep with her. You'll carry hers as well." Ben looked at her solemnly. Taking her small hand in his, he closed her fist over the jewels. "She's going to miss you Evalyn."

Her green eyes filled with tears. She fought to regain control. She didn't want her mother to see her cry—it would only make things worse.

Evalyn smiled. "She'll never believe it's real—if I give it to her. She'll think they're good fakes."

Ben grinned. "So much the better— as long as she'll accept it. I'll bet that neither of you will take them off anyway—it'll represent the love you share."

Ben planned to keep a close eye on Maddy, to make certain she never lacked for anything. *But who knows,* he thought, *there could come a day when they might want to sell them. The diamonds would fetch a hefty sum.*

Evalyn's thoughts were flowing along the same line as Ben's. The diamonds would provide extra security for her mother. Evalyn didn't know how many years it would be until she saw her mother again. She hugged Ben tightly. "You're like the brother I never had," she whispered. "Thank you."

They returned to the kitchen where Maddy and Christopher were deep in conversation.

"How will you survive?" Maddy asked him. Lines of worry creased her smooth face.

Ben, Christopher, and Evalyn exchanged glances.

"Show her," Evalyn ordered quietly. Christopher opened the large backpack. It contained a few articles of clothing and some food. However, cash filled most of the backpack.

Maddy looked as the neatly stacked bills. Modest as always, Ben's eyes were on the floor. "Thank you, Ben," Maddy murmured squeezing his hand.

"How will I contact you?" she asked Evalyn, fighting to keep her voice steady.

"You won't be able to." Christopher replied. "I'm sure the phone will be tapped, if it's not already. When they realize Evalyn's gone, they'll be watching you closely. But don't worry—we'll get word to you."

Maddy searched his eyes questioningly, "But how…?" None of them answered her.

Christopher focused into the silence enveloping the room. In an instant, a look of astonishment crossed Maddy's face, as Christopher' words rang in her thoughts as clear as a bell.

"You'll be able to hear me inside your mind—like this. And I will let you know how we're doing. I won't tell you exactly where we are but you'll know we're all right."

Maddy's mouth dropped open in surprise

"Of course." Maddy whispered, shaking her head. *So Christopher had unusual talent too. I should have guessed.* His phone calls to Evalyn had lessened over the last year or so. Yet Evalyn seemed to be communicating with him somehow.

Evalyn stepped close to Maddy and fastened the heart-shaped pendant around her mother's neck. Evalyn turned so her mother could fasten her matching one. Maddy fingered the sparkling heart hanging at her neck, her own heart breaking. Tears flowed down her cheeks.

"No matter where I am or what I'm doing, remember I love you Mama." She kissed her mother's wet cheek, her mother's tears mingling with her own.

Ben stepped out the door, glanced quickly up and down the street. The only vehicles in sight were familiar; either parked along the street or in neighbors' driveways. Maddy hugged them tightly before pushing them out the door.

"Go! Be safe and God bless."

The three climbed into Ben's Jeep. Rather than head for Eppley Airfield, Ben drove them across the river into Iowa.

At the moment no one appeared to be following them. Even so, Benson thought it wiser to avoid the major airports. Commercial flights were easy to track. He had arranged for them to board a private plane near the Bluffs that would drop them off at a small airstrip in Wisconsin, near Eagle River.

He didn't know for sure who was after Evalyn, but it had the smell of a government bureau all over it.

During the drive, Ben carefully reviewed the instructions with Christopher. Christopher was tired and had to force himself to listen, but Evalyn was so overwhelmed with grief she heard nothing.

Ben informed Christopher that, in addition to the other items in the backpack, he had managed to get passports as well as drivers' licenses with different names for them. They were identified as Steven Harrington and Alison Baker of Greenwich, Connecticut.

"Greenwich, Ben? Isn't it like... upscale?"

Ben smiled wryly. "Obscenely wealthy, yes. I wanted to make certain that anyone who might check your documents would assume you're just rich kids out on a lark. In the envelope with your passports I included a map of the town, including your Greenwich address. Memorize it."

He took off his watch and handed it to Christopher. "Here, put this on." It was an understated Rose Gold Rolex. Christopher glanced at the huge diamond at Evalyn's throat. Ben wanted to make sure they looked the part. Just rich kids having an adventure.

Christopher fastened the watch around his wrist. His throat tightened.

"It's just a loan, Ben. Ok?" I'll give it back when I see you again."

Ben hugged them both tightly and they boarded the Cessna.

It was nearing sunset when the small plane began to descend near Eagle River. Through the small windows of the plane, Physically and emotionally drained, Christopher and Evalyn barely noticed the flaming red and gold of the magnificent fall landscape. Evalyn's eyes were red, she had cried until she had no tears left to spill.

In the small parking lot, Christopher spotted a yellow taxi toward the side of a bungalow. He shouldered the large pack and headed toward it. Evalyn walked numbly at his side. Christopher tapped on the window to wake the taxi driver. Yawning, he turned on the meter as they climbed into the back seat.

Evalyn huddled in the corner, her blank eyes staring out the window at nothing. Christopher was very worried about her. Other than to blame herself for the danger she felt she had put everyone in, she had barely said more than a sentence or two during the entire trip. There were dark circles under her eyes and she and seemed more fragile and miserable than Christopher had ever known her to be. He was afraid she might break under the strain.

As the taxi pulled away, Christopher noticed a dark gray sedan also left the lot and pulled in behind them. He hadn't notice the car when they left the plane—the dark gray color was a perfect camouflage against the asphalt road.

"Where to, guy?" the cabbie asked.

Christopher didn't answer immediately. Through the rearview mirror, he was watching the gray sedan trailing behind them. Although he couldn't see him clearly, the driver appeared to be the car's sole occupant. *Don't those creeps usually travel in pairs?* Christopher wondered. It could be nothing, but lone driver or not, it seemed odd. They had been the only passengers on the small plane and the airport was practically deserted. The gray car must have been parked behind the building.

Instead of going into Duluth as planned, Christopher decided on the side of caution.

"Does this road have a turnoff into the forest?" He asked the cab driver.

"You must be new around here," the cabbie surmised. "Yeah, the Northwoods has over six hundred thousand acres and thousands of miles of back roads." He noticed the backpack. "You kids going camping?"

"Yeah, camping." Christopher muttered.

"Hope you packed a good tent, or brought a heater 'cause while it's warm enough now, the temperature drops around here at night," he added, looking at Christopher in his rearview mirror.

"Oh, I think we'll be warm enough" Christopher gave him a sly wink. "Ah... hey, could you speed it up a bit? I think the guy following us may have overheard us talking and may be thinking about hanging out with us, but we'd like a little privacy, if you know what I mean."

"Yeah, it looks like we're being followed."

Evalyn sat up and peered out the back window. *They were being followed?*

The cab driver could use a little excitement—business had been slow. He slammed the pedal to the floor; the car raced ahead. The cabbie was familiar with these roads, knew all the curves that lay ahead. Within moments, he lost their tail.

"Pull over," Christopher commanded sharply, when he noticed the other car was no longer in sight. The taxi screeched to a halt. Christopher jumped out, pulling Evalyn after him. He tossed a wad of bills at the driver.

"Thanks. And keep driving, would you? I want to keep him off our trail." The driver returned Christopher's sly wink and took off, wheels screeching.

Quickly, Christopher and Evalyn backed into the trees and crouched down, out of sight. In less than a minute, the sedan whizzed by, chasing the taxi. Checking his compass, Christopher led them westward through the forest, toward Duluth.

If they could just make it there, the car Ben arranged for would be waiting and they would be able to get to the lodge where they'd find details for the rest of the trip. Ben advised Christopher to hide out at the lodge and rest for a few days until they could safely drive across the border into Canada.

Christopher dug in the pack and pulled out a couple of protein bars. He handed one to Evalyn. She shook her head and turned away. Christopher peeled off the wrapper.

"Here, eat it, Evalyn," he commanded gently. She looked at him through tired eyes, but obediently obliged, eating mechanically. He pulled dark hooded parkas out of the pack, and they put them on. The sun was setting and the air was growing colder.

The cold, moonless night was filled with sinuously moving shadows. They didn't talk much, which was unusual. The only sounds were those made by their ragged breaths and their footsteps trampling on the wooded undergrowth of the dense forest.

They had been traveling through the forest for more than six hours and Evalyn was near the limit of her endurance. She summoned all of the strength she had left to keep moving, and concentrated on putting one foot in front of the other, to keep following Christopher who was pushing on up ahead.

Christopher glanced behind. Evalyn stumbled, barely managing to stay on her feet. He knew she wouldn't last much longer. Exhausted, she slowed.

"Please," she gasped, struggling for breath. "Go on without me. I'm only slowing you down."

Ignoring her pleas, he half dragged, half carried her, hoping he had enough strength left for both of them. He couldn't stop now. Not when to do so would mean capture or death. If not physical death, it would mean death of life as they knew it. And they were so very close to freedom.

"Christopher!" she whispered urgently, "Listen!"

They could hear barking hounds in the distance.

"They're tracking us!" Christopher swore.

He dropped the pack he carried, rifled through it for money and passports which he stuffed into his jacket pockets. He reached deep into the bottom of the pack searching for the key, swearing as the cool metal slipped through his fingers into the thick undergrowth. He dropped to his knees, frantically searching. Unhampered by darkness, she spotted it easily, and handed it to him.

The barking of the hounds was much louder now; their trackers were getting closer. Despite the darkness, through the periphery of the trees she can see the lake clearly.

"We're almost there," she murmured.

Nearby they could hear the low, rhythmic sound of lapping water. In the darkness the lake spread across to an unseen shore like an endless expanse of black ink. The barking seemed to fade into the background.

Christopher moved closer to the water's edge. He felt it flow over his feet, beckoning, calming, welcoming. This is the moment he knew would come—the inevitable moment on which everything he had learned, believed, and hoped for was riding.

Evalyn turned toward him, hesitantly, an unspoken question on her lips. And although he couldn't see the expression in her eyes, he knew they were filled with fear. Evalyn couldn't swim.

Christopher lifted her into his arms, felt her relax. He pressed his lips to her forehead. If his life should end with hers, so be it. After all, the best things in his life began with her.

Inhaling deeply, he felt the familiar energy surge through him. Taking a few careful steps forward, he stepped up and onto the surface of the water.

Chapter 14

valyn's eyes fluttered as she awakened, slowly orienting herself to her surroundings. She must have been asleep for hours, although she could tell it was dark outside. The only light in the room was from moonlight filtering through the large windows and from the crackling fire.

She was lying comfortably on the sofa under a warm blanket. Through half-closed lids, she saw the large bearskin rug on the floor and the wood paneled walls. This must be the lodge where Christopher and Benson stayed when they had gone hunting.

She turned her head slightly. Christopher was kneeling in front of the fireplace, placing a log on the fire. He turned when he heard Evalyn stir.

"Hey, sleeping beauty," He tossed a slow smile in her direction. "Did you know you glow in your sleep?"

"So I hear." She yawned widely, stretching. "How long have I been asleep?"

"Almost fourteen hours. It's Saturday."

Still drowsy, her eyes drifted closed again. *How had they gotten here?*

The last thing she remembered was being cradled in Christopher's strong arms, feeling his chest rise and fall with his breaths and his gliding steps as he walked … Evalyn' eyes flew open. *As he walked on water!*

"Christopher... you...you..." Evalyn stammered. Maybe she dreamed it. Or maybe the pressure had gotten to her and she had finally snapped. Yes that was it—she was losing her mind. *No one* had walked on water in two thousand years, if it had ever happened at all. Her eyes filled with tears and her face contorted with sadness. Yes, she was certifiably crazy.

He moved quickly to her side. "Evalyn, my Evalyn." He pulled her down on the rug and held her in his lap while she sobbed. "It's Ok, Evalyn. We're safe now."

She continued to sob uncontrollably. "Oh, Christopher...I've lost my mind...I thought... I thought..."

She looked up into his face. How do you tell someone you're going insane? Especially when they were looking at you with a silly grin on their adorable face?

"Christopher...I thought..." Evalyn's deep green eyes met Christopher's lake blue ones.

He began to nod his head, smiling, "Yes, Evalyn...you thought..."

"Did you walk on water, Christopher," she whispered, "or have I really lost it?"

Her woebegone look was more than he could bear. He broke out into raucous laughter.

"Yes, Evalyn, yes! I did it!" he exclaimed triumphantly. He kissed her firmly on her full, surprised mouth.

Evalyn jumped up and punched him soundly on the arm. "You kept a secret from me!" she exclaimed. "We made a pact in first grade, that we would never, *ever* keep secrets from each other!"

Christopher grinned widely. Evalyn was her old self again. Amid protests, he pulled her back into his lap. He liked having her there; she fit so perfectly. He kissed her again, more tenderly this time.

Evalyn wiped his kiss off. "Don't kiss me. I'm mad at you."
She pouted so prettily, Christopher kissed her anyway.

"Evalyn, I was going to tell you about it. I just wanted to
practice a while first to make sure I could really do it. I didn't
know I'd be put to the test."

"*Humph.*" Evalyn snorted. She turned her nose up and crossed
her arms. "You know everything about me, like where I keep my
diary and ..."

Christopher's face grew serious. "Evalyn—the diaries! If they
find them..."

Evalyn's eyes opened wide in alarm as she grasped the
implication of what he was saying. The diaries held it all—her
thoughts about her ability, her feelings about those she'd helped
over the years, many without the knowledge she was the one
responsible for their miraculous recovery.

By writing about the lessons she'd given Christopher—and
about his success tapping the energy—she'd even put him in
danger. Thank goodness she hadn't known about his newest
"water sport."

"Christopher, send my mom a message. Let her know we're
alright and tell her to destroy the diaries."

Of course Maddy would be worried about them, as would his
parents. He was sure they'd found his note by now. Focusing on
avoiding being captured, they hadn't a spare thought for anything
else.

His arms still wound around Evalyn, Christopher grew
very still. He focused on connecting the water in his body with
condensation in the air, and tapping into the energy flowing
everywhere, always. Using the water as a conduit, he sent Maddy
a message:

*We got away safely. I'll take care... of Evalyn—she sends her love.
Please... tell my folks I'm fine... not to worry. Evalyn's diaries ... bottom
drawer... destroy them.*

Maddy sat at the kitchen table, her hand wrapped around a cup of tea, grown cold hours ago. Her eyes were red and swollen. She hadn't slept or eaten since yesterday morning, not since her daughter left and took away all the joy she had in the world.

She didn't know where they were or even if they were safe, which only made her feel worse. She seriously doubted *they*—whoever *they* were—would not kill Evalyn. She would prove too valuable a commodity for them to destroy needlessly.

It was Christopher's life she feared for the most. She shivered involuntarily when she remembered the look of determination in the eyes of the young black man who had come to her door searching for Evalyn.

She looked at the clock on the wall for the hundredth time this morning. It was almost eleven and still she had not heard from them. They left almost twenty-four hours ago.

The phone rang, startling her. It was Emily. She had been expecting and dreading her call.

She and Bob had read the brief note Christopher left in his room and had called to question Maddy about it, to see if it were true—that their children had run off together.

When Emily heard the dread in Maddy's voice, she and her husband immediately drove over to the Williamson's.

At the door, the two women embraced. Emily and Bob could see Maddy had been crying. Bob ran his fingers though his hair, exasperated. "When I get my hands on Christopher..."

"No, it's not his fault..." Maddy started.

'But why would they run off?" Emily asked. "Evalyn's not pregnant...?"

The question hung in the air. Emily had noticed their children's friendship going to a deeper level. Anything was possible with young romantics.

Bob's voice rose, "If she *is* pregnant, I will wring Christopher's neck." He figured Maddy must doubt their parenting skills—one of their sons tries to kiss her daughter against her will and another runs away with her.

Maddy wished it was as simple as that—that they had run off to elope. She would let the Boldsen's believe whatever they wished. Christopher and Evalyn were eighteen now and could get married without parental consent. She would continue to keep her daughter's secret for as long as she could. Not that it had helped much.

"I'm not sure what's going on," Maddy spoke haltingly, "but I'm sure we'll hear from them shortly."

Emily hugged Maddy again tightly before they left, "I'll call you later, to see how you're doing."

Maddy was taking this very hard. Something felt odd about it, but Emily couldn't figure it out. She'd talk to Becca about it later, maybe she knew something.

As soon as they got home, Emily went to Becca's room to see if her daughter knew what was going on. She sat down on the edge of her bed.

"Do I think Evalyn could be pregnant?" Becca was astounded. "What kind of a question is *that?*" She looked down at her mother as though she had lost her mind.

"Well, they've run off together. Since you're a few years older, I thought maybe she might have confided in you."

Christopher and Evalyn had run off? This *was* news. But Evalyn pregnant. *That* Becca seriously doubted.

"Mom. Wait." Becca put up her hands. "Let me get this straight. Christopher and Evalyn are *gone?*"

She handed Becca the piece of paper. Becca read the words on the brief note.

I'm leaving with Evalyn. I'll call you when I can. Love, Christopher.

Becca looked perplexed. "Mom, let me check around and I'll see what I can find out." A second after Emily left her room, Becca called Benson. He told her he didn't want to talk about it over the phone, but that he'd come over directly. She ran downstairs to wait for him.

When Benson came to the door, Becca took one look at him and realized he knew something. She pulled him inside before her parents knew he was here. They'd drill him, she was certain. She wanted to talk to him first.

"They think Christopher and Evalyn have eloped." She added bluntly, "They believe it's because she's pregnant." At this news Benson make a choking sound.

Becca smiled wryly. "Yes, that's what I thought too. Not likely." Benson said nothing. "But I know it has something to do with Evalyn."

Benson looked at her sharply. "You know about Evalyn?"

"Probably not as much as you do, but yeah…" Becca gave a sardonic grin. "For one thing, she glows in the dark, like she's radioactive or something."

This was news to Benson, but it would explain why she never spent the night away from home. Becca told him about the few days she had stayed over at the Williamson's when the family went camping and what she had seen when she had gone to Evalyn's room, how she glowed softly while she was sleeping.

"Does anyone else know?" he asked.

Becca shook her head. "Probably only Christopher. But it still doesn't explain why they would run away."

"Well… there's more," Benson began hesitantly. "Remember the tornado that blew through here a few years ago?"

"Yes, the three of you had been at the river and we went crazy looking for you."

Benson nodded. "I don't know what happened for sure, but I got hit by a falling tree—I know I passed out. When I came to, there was lots of blood on my shirt, on Evalyn too—her hands were covered with it—as though she had been holding me or touching me. But I couldn't find a wound anywhere. Neither of them will admit to anything but there are a few things I've noticed since that day, for instance, my vision is better than perfect…"

Becca snapped her fingers, "Yes! I remember you used to wear glasses, but..." she continued slowly, "... I noticed other changes... you were different after that. Not so..."

"Weird?" Benson laughed. "I can't explain how, but Evalyn healed me, Becca."

Becca was quiet, mulling this over. She met Benson's calm gray eyes with an even look. "I think we'd better let my parents believe in their 'pregnancy theory'. At least it's something they can understand."

"What I can't figure out is how they knew exactly where to find her." Benson mused. "Maddy mentioned a man came by their house a couple of weeks ago—"

"Wait!" Becca grabbed Benson's arm. "About that same time I saw Ace talking to someone at our front door. A man. When he left, I could have sworn Ace stuffed something into his pocket—it looked like a wad of money."

She turned to yell into the house. "Mom, Dad. I'll be right back." She grabbed her coat from the hall closet. "I'm going out with Benson for while."

Becca took a firm grip on Benson and pushed him out the door.

"Where to?" he asked, backing the Jeep down the driveway.

"To a hole-in-the-wall pool hall where my low life brother hangs out with his low life friends."

They pulled up in front of a dive in a dubious neighborhood. Becca stormed inside, Benson bringing up the rear.

"Hey Blondie," a tattooed man with greasy hair, called out. Becca ignored him. In the smoke filled room, she spotted her brother with a beer in one hand and a pool cue in the other. She marched up to him.

He looked surprised to see her. "Becca—what ...?"

Before he could finished his sentence, his sister balled up her fist and gave him a solid right hook to the jaw. With three brothers to practice on, her punch had power.

"You smarmy bas—"

"Hey! Take your fight outside, Blondie," the bartender yelled, irritated.

Enraged, Ace turned red.

Becca continued, furious, "How could you sell out your own brother, Ace?" She gave him a hard shove. Ace's face paled. She knew she'd hit the mark.

Several friends of Ace's started to laugh. "Ah, man. He's getting his butt kicked by a *girl!*"

Embarrassed, Ace took several steps toward Becca, his fist balled. Benson stepped in between them.

"I wouldn't do that if I were you," Benson said evenly, his gray eyes glinted like frozen steel. Becca tried to push past Benson to get at her brother, but his lean, muscled arms blocked her way. She leaned around Benson and hissed loudly, "If anything happens to Christopher, I will never forgive you! I hope you rot in hell!"

With a warning look at Ace, Benson put his arm around Becca protectively and led her outside.

During the drive on the way to her house, he heard her sniffling and pulled the Jeep over to the side of the road. He reached into his pocket and handed her one of his fine linen monogrammed handkerchiefs, and put an arm around her to comfort her and found that holding her comforted him also.

He was just as worried as she. She leaned against his shoulder, alternately sobbing and swearing. She blew her nose loudly.

"I'll wash it and give it back to you tomorrow."

"Keep it, Becca. I have lots more."

Smiling though her tears, she kissed his cheek. In the darkness his smile matched hers. He kept his arm around her a little longer than necessary before starting the car and driving her home.

Maddy was sitting in the living room. She had been sitting there for a while—so long that the sun had set about an hour ago and the room had grown dark. She hadn't bothered to get up to turn on the light.

They had been gone more than thirty hours now and she'd heard nothing. Christopher told her he would contact her; let her know they were alright. Maybe he was out of telepathic range—she wasn't sure how these things worked. Or... her breath caught. *Maybe they had already killed him and captured Evalyn.* She covered her mouth with her hands and closed her eyes. She prayed, *God, they're Your children, too. Please protect them.*

She stood up to turn on the light, when she felt a thought as soft as butterfly wings drift through her mind, *We got away safely. Tell my folks I'm fine. Evalyn says she loves you.*

Maddy sunk in the nearest chair, weak with relief. They were alright, no one had found them. An additional thought floated to her: *Find the diaries in the bottom drawer... destroy them.*

Maddy put wood in the fireplace and lit the logs. After the fire had caught, she went to collect the diaries.

She smiled as she climbed the stairs, sure that there were at least a half dozen of the small flower-cover books with gold locks. She'd always known where Evalyn hid her diaries; she even knew that the hiding place changed from time to time, but she fiercely believed her daughter was entitled to her privacy and never would have pried. Nor would she do so now.

The stairwell walls were filled with beautifully framed photographs of family and friends. Maddy had begun collecting the photos years ago. She liked them out where she could see them; she wanted them to be enjoyed rather than hidden in a photograph album in a closet.

Her favorite was one of her dearly loved husband—serious, yet handsome in his military uniform. Next to the photo of her husband, and slightly lower on the wall, was their wedding photo. Their love for one another reflected in their eyes. There were photos of Maddy holding Evalyn as a baby. Most of them were of

Evalyn and Christopher together and many taken in the last few years also included Benson.

Before continuing to Evalyn's room, she went to her closet and took out a large, decorated box in which she kept mementos. She found the drawing that Evalyn had given her on her first day of school. On that day she had drawn a picture of herself and Christopher. Maddy turned it over to read what she had written years ago, "Evalyn and Christopher, age 6." At first chance she'd frame it and hang it on the stairwell wall with the others.

Maddy gathered the diaries and returned downstairs. Lovingly, she touched the cover of each one before tossing it into the blazing fire.

Christopher parked the rented car at the rear of the lodge where it couldn't be viewed from the road. As Benson had instructed, he opened the safe hidden in a cupboard. Inside were more bundles of cash and an envelope containing keys and directions to the safe house in Alaska.

For several days the two stayed close to the lodge, recuperating. The lodge was well stocked—Benson had thought of everything.

They ventured out only to gather kindling for the fires they made in the evening. While they felt relatively safe here, they didn't take their current freedom for granted. Despite their precarious situation—or perhaps because of it—they relished every precious moment of this time they had together. They had an unspoken agreement not to talk about recent events, or of how deeply they missed their families. Instead they spoke of the antics of their friends, of the past, and left their concerns about the future. They pushed fear and worry as far from their minds as possible.

Evalyn carried two steaming mugs of hot chocolate into the living room. Christopher reached out for his. They sat close together on the rug nearest to the fire and began chatting about power, energy, and spirit and how it all seemed to connect.

Christopher took a sip, pensive. "How could something so amazing be all around us and we just... ignore it....miss it?"

"I've often wondered..." Evalyn mused. "I also wonder about your bond with water and the way you seem to connect it so easily with the energy."

Christopher tried to explain his connection with water and how he used it for a channel. "I sense it around me... the water... I can even smell it when others can't."

Evalyn knew that this was so. Even as a child, he knew when it was going to rain or snow. He found it hard to describe such an indescribable phenomenon. It felt so natural to him.

"The more receptive I am, the more power flows in." He studied her, and shook his head. "Evalyn, the power flows in easily—all I have to do is get out of its way. I get the impression the more power I can handle, the more flows to me."

Evalyn listened, content to be curled up next to him. She had her own ideas about the source of this power—she wanted to hear Christopher's.

"I don't think the power can run out. Evalyn, I think it's limitless... that it comes from something so immense I can hardly grasp it."

Evelyn knew she sensed an incredibly loving energy whenever she tapped into the inexplicable power. It was greater than love— but love was the only word she knew that could come close to describing it. *Is there a word for something greater than love? Infinite love, perhaps?* She wondered. Evalyn leaned toward him. "But can you can feel the love coming from it?" she pressed.

Christopher nodded, solemnly. "Yes," he whispered. "It's like nothing I've ever felt before." He paused for a moment, shaking his head. "It's unconditionally caring..."

"Sometimes I think it's something we once understood perfectly—in another place or time—but somehow have forgotten."

"Forgotten? How could we possibly forget a love so immense? What do you think happened?" he asked.

"I believe everyone—every human being was able to express this power. Then something must have happened.

"What?"

"I'm not exactly sure," Evalyn murmured. "But understanding human nature as I do, I bet it had something to do with power, or rather about the misuse of power. About the ugly side of humanity, or the need to oppress others, to feel superior. The only way some folks know to make themselves taller is by standing on someone else's head."

Christopher had no response for this, but he sensed her ideas held more than a grain of truth.

Huddled close together, warmed by the fire, they pushed away thoughts of everything, allowing themselves to revel in the sweetness of the moment. Similar thoughts drifted through their minds. *What if we're captured? What if this is the last chance we'll have to be together?*

Gently, Christopher placed a trail of kisses down Evalyn's throat, breathing in her sweet, familiar scent. She trembled slightly. His hand slid around her back, under her sweater. Her skin felt like warm satin.

She turned her mouth to meet his. Partially from passion, partially from their desperate need to find comfort, their kisses deepened. They clung to one another, their legs entwined.

Evalyn was the first to regain control of her senses. She had to believe in the future, to keep hope alive. She placed her small hands on Christopher's bare chest. *When did he remove his shirt?* She gave him a gentle push. "No, Christopher... we can't do this now," she murmured breathlessly.

Reluctantly he took her hand from his chest and kissed her palm, before reaching for his shirt.

"Ok, Evie. You're right." He looked at her through passion filled eyes, watching as she fastened the top of her sweater that had mysteriously become undone, revealing a lacy white bra underneath. He reached out to touch her once again, and then drew his hand back. She had said "No, the timing wasn't right." Unlike his brother, Ace, he realized that "no" meant "no."

"But one day, when all this is behind us we'll finish what we started tonight," he said, his voice husky with unspent passion.

Evalyn's green eyes smoldered, her passion matching his. "Oh, yes. Christopher," she breathed. "I'm counting on it."

Christopher tossed her a lopsided grin and shook his head to clear it. "I think I had better go outside and get some air." She was tempting him more than she realized.

Evalyn watched him leave, fighting the desire to reach for him and pull him back into her empty arms. Instead she held on to the slimmest glimmer of hope that their time would come.

They cooked their meals together and on cooler evenings, they sat on the rug in front of the fireplace holding hands and talking for hours. They talked about the rest of their journey, and about the family and friends they'd left behind.

After resting a few days, Christopher decided it was time to continue on their way.

They packed their things and Evalyn tossed a woolen blanket and pillow in the back seat so one of them could sleep while the other drove since they thought it best to avoid hotels.

Christopher added a couple of flashlights. Evalyn could see fine in the dark; but he needed help in that area. He packed the envelope with information about the safe house in Alaska, but left some of the cash in case they had to double back to the lodge. He didn't know what to expect from now on and he wanted to be prepared just in case the "Bureau"—which is what they called their pursuers for lack of any other name—picked up their trail again.

They left the safety of the lodge, crossed the border into Canada and pulled into the checkpoint. Christopher drove slowly, preparing to stop. A couple of the border officials appeared to be having an animated discussion. If necessary, he would show the licenses and passports Benson had given them.

Instead of pulling their car over, the officer waved them through the checkpoint without incident and turned to resume the conversation with his partner. Evalyn and Christopher breathed a sigh of relief.

Chapter 15

*J*amison was furious. He pounded his fist on the file on his desk and glared at Richards and Clarke, seated across from him.

"Let me get this straight." He repeated, sarcasm dripping from every word. "You lost two kids... kids who aren't even old enough to drink?

Richards looked uncomfortable; sweat beaded his brow. Clarke appeared cool.

"How did this happen!" Jamison roared.

"I had the investigation under control ...," Clarke offered.

"You've been dawdling for over a month now, so I took action!" Richards interjected.

"Action? You kidnapped two kids in order to interrogate them! You call that action?"

"Kidnapping?" Jamison was stunned. "Clarke, did you order that maneuver?"

"Of course not." Clarke tossed a disdainful glance in his boss's direction.

"And you have the gall to tell me they've just disappeared? How?" Jamison snarled at the two men. "You've got two months to take them into custody or I will find someone who will!"

"I've checked airports and train stations," Richards stammered. "There's no record of them leaving town. I think they're still around Omaha, just hiding out somewhere. We've just got to shake the right tree."

Clarke gave Richards the look he reserved for idiots. Did the cretin really believe these kids had stayed in their hometown with the CDC and the Bureau hunting them down?

Following a gut feeling, he ignored the large commercial flights. Instead he had focused his attention on the smaller airfields and his instincts had paid off. He'd discovered that several light aircraft took off shortly after the two teenagers disappeared—two Pipers and one Cessna. The Cessna had blocked tail numbers.

It was obvious that the kids were backed by someone clever, someone also in possession of a large bankroll.

With considerable effort, Clarke managed to acquire this information and track the flight. He looked away from Richards and studied the view from Jamison's corner office. He had a few more hunches but decided to play his hand close to his chest.

Based on this most recent fiasco, he was glad he hadn't shared additional information with the bureau. Next time—if there was a next time—he would handle things the right way—his way.

Christopher and Evalyn followed the directions Benson had given them and crossed over into Alaska.

Their scenic drive through Canada was uneventful, no one followed them, Christopher was certain. Mile after mile, on the Alaska-Canadian highway, they stared stare in awe at the breathtaking beauty surrounding them. Acres of evergreens were interspersed by magnificent White Birch forests. The wildlife was abundant. Overhead were flocks of birds. Occasionally they spotted Dall sheep perched precariously on the high cliffs, or glimpsed moose lumbering through the trees.

In Anchorage, they boarded another small private plane Benson had arranged for them. As the plane rose, the pilot, a grandmotherly sort, explained that in Alaska practically every adult had a pilot's license.

Below them were majestic snowcapped mountains, and miles and miles of forests. Christopher and Evalyn felt safe at the moment and more optimistic about their future, so this plane ride proved better than their last.

Although it was almost midnight, when the pilot dropped them down in a small, designated clearing in the middle of nowhere, the sun still sat at the horizon. Moments after the plane taxied off, a battered Jeep drove up. The driver rolled down the window, and leaned out.

"Benson Cunningworth sent me to pick up a couple—and I'm guessing it must be you folks," He hopped down with a broad smile.

Hi," he said, offering his hand. "I'm Jack Stonefield—welcome to the neighborhood." Jack appeared to be native Alaskan, in his early thirties. He had thick black hair that he wore in a braid down his back. Later, he referred to his tribe as "Unangan."

Christopher shook hands. Since both her hands were full with bags, Evalyn smiled in greeting.

Jack loaded their bags in back and took them on a bumpy ride through the bush. They gazed around in wonder at the beauty and abundant wildlife. Jack was a great guide, friendly and talkative. Several hours later, they pulled up in front a large two-story A-frame house built of logs and stone. There was a new Jeep similar to the one Benson drove parked in front.

"The keys are in the Jeep, and the phone is working, at least for now. There's a back-up radio and when the weather's particularly bad, my wife and I keep the channel open, just in case," he informed them. "The crew finished remodeling the basement yesterday," he continued, "Didn't think two weeks would be enough time, but Mr. Cunningworth's orders were to 'get it done,' and so it is." Christopher and Evalyn shared a meaningful look. They had so much to thank Benson for.

"Cunningworth hired me to take care of the grounds, keep the snow off the roof, and to handle any repairs that come up." He waved his hand toward a huge pile of firewood stacked neatly against the side of the house.

"It's warm enough now but in a few months it'll start to snow. At least the early kind of snow..."

Evalyn looked puzzled. "The early kind?"

Jack laughed good-naturedly. "Around here snow is called by at least a dozen different names, depending on things like its consistency and when it falls."

Evalyn glanced at Christopher. She wondered if he'd be able to tell the different types of snow apart by their smell. Time would tell.

"There's enough wood here to get you through the winter. And in case the power goes out—as it's been known to do— there's a generator in the garage."

Jack helped Christopher carry in their things. "We stocked all the basic household supplies we figured you'd need. My wife, Sarah stocked the kitchen according to Mr. Cunningworth's request." He added, "He specifically had us order two crates of ketchup." He shook, his head laughing. "That should cover a whole lot of french fries. Anyway, you should have everything you need for at least a couple of weeks. The nearest grocery store is about an hour's drive away."

Scribbling his number on a slip of paper, Jack said, "We're your nearest neighbors. We live about five miles north of here, off the main road. Call us if you need anything." He climbed into his battered Jeep, and leaned out the open window.

"Oh, yeah. One more thing. There's lots of bears around here, finishing off the last of the chokeberries, fattening up for the winter." *Bears?* Evalyn and Christopher passed a look between them.

Jack saw the look and laughed. "If you don't bother them, they usually won't bother you. But they don't like to be frightened.

You might think about getting a dog and putting a bell on its collar."

"Dealing with bears sounds like a cakewalk compared to what we've been through lately," Christopher muttered to Evalyn. With a quick wave, Jack backed down the driveway and turned left at the main road in the direction of his home.

Evalyn and Christopher explored their new house from top to bottom, checking out everything. It reminded them of the lodge, only smaller and cozier. The bottom floor consisted of a large room with comfortable furniture upholstered in shades of green.

Windows rose to the height of the loft, which opened to the floor below. There was a huge brick fireplace in the center of the room with one side opening into the kitchen. A small office had shelves of books. On the desk was a small computer. Christopher checked and found it operational, but it wasn't connected to the Internet. In the downstairs closet were two sealskin parkas, mukluks, and ski boots in their sizes. The hood of Evalyn's parka was trimmed in soft, white fur.

The kitchen was spacious with a small laundry room opening into the garage. The garage held two snow mobiles, snow shoes, and skis. Another door led to the basement downstairs. The basement had been converted into a room with mirrors and audio equipment, and new flooring. At one end of the room there were free standing barres as well as the wall mounted type. At the other end was a complete set of workout equipment and thick gray padded mats. Evalyn ran her hand admiringly over the barres.

"I was so afraid I'd not be able to practice, but he thought of everything," Evalyn said, her eyes bright. They both were delighted and grateful.

The upstairs had a large master suite furnished with light colored alder, decorated in soft cream and taupe. The two smaller bedrooms were furnished in warmer colors. All of the bedroom windows had thick draperies to keep out the sun during the days of endless summer.

"I call dibs on the master bedroom," Evalyn sang out, before running downstairs.

Christopher looked at the large, inviting bed dominating the center of the room and exhaled slowly. Every day he spent with Evalyn only enflamed his desire. He had spent most of his life with her and had always taken their physical closeness for granted—walking hand in hand when they were children, tickling one another until they were doubled over with laughter. Now he ached with wanting her. The smooth touch of her skin, the sounds of her soft sighs when he held her close in front of the fire, were driving him insane. Living with her was not going to be easy but it was a lot better than the alternative—living without her.

The days and weeks passed, and they settled into a comfortable routine. Indian summer faded into fall. They spent hours walking through the forests nearby, the white birch trees ablaze with leaves turned to molten gold.

As the hours of daylight lessened, they would watch television or play cards—although Evalyn often accused Christopher of cheating, which he vehemently denied.

Many evenings they would meditate quietly, tapping into the energy which they discovered increased easily when their efforts were combined. But mostly they thoroughly enjoyed each other's company and their lengthy discussions lasted well into the winter nights, which were getting longer.

"Imagine the possibilities, Evie!" Christopher exclaimed. "To have every question answered—every need met. If everyone could use their energy, think of what that would mean!"

His voice was hoarse, filled with emotion. "No poverty, no sickness...everyone could have any good thing they needed or wanted."

They toyed with this vision, imagining a fresh, exciting new world.

"I'm sure it's how humans were meant to be." She spoke softly, her voice mellifluous. "Glorious creatures of beauty and power."

They stepped outside, a thick fur throw wrapped around them, taking in the exquisite night sky, filled with brightly glittering stars. Their lives had intertwined from the moment they met.

The years together and experiences shared served to form a bond made from the best parts of each, strengthening and transforming them into something extraordinary and unique— like beams of water or drops of light.

They stood for a while, their breath frosting, watching the smoky pink and green lights twist and turn in the sky above, joining the stars in a spectacular night dance.

After a moment or two, Christopher broke the silence. "We've got to find others like ourselves—they're out there—I know it. People who sense that there's more to life and feel the urge to discover it."

"I'm sure you're right." Evalyn reached out and placed her small hand in his. She looked deeply into his eyes, allowing herself to drown in their blue depths.

"And, we'll teach what we've learned—to good folks like Benson."

They knew they wouldn't have escaped without Bensons' loyalty and devotion.

"I miss him," Evalyn murmured softly. "Do you think we'll ever see him again?" she asked, wistfully. Life without Benson and her mother left an unmistakable void in her heart.

Christopher exhaled deeply. "I honestly don't know."

She leaned against him. They didn't know what the future held, but tonight they held each other. He pulled her closer looking deeply into her eyes, finding everything he needed there.

Tenderly, passionately, their lips met. The air around them began to shimmer, expanding and surging until their light shot skyward, competing with the Aurora Borealis in the blackness of the Alaskan night.

About the Author

Marian Miller has a doctorate in psychology, and is a licensed marriage and family therapist. She has more than 25 years experience in the mental health field, many of those years spent working with children and adolescents. Vulnerable children in particular, have always held a special place in her heart. She has found her work with young people inspiring – particularly their resilience, courage, and hope for the future, captured in Light on Water.

Ms. Miller, her husband and children, live in the countryside near Portland, Oregon. Her passions are traveling, writing, and delving though the minds and hearts of others for hidden gems.

Debut novel: Light on Water
www.marianmillerbooks.com